I WAS ON THAT TRAIN

I WAS ON THAT TRAIN

Jeffrey Brett

ARTHUR H. STOCKWELL LTD
Torrs Park, Ilfracombe, Devon, EX34 8BA
Established 1898
www.ahstockwell.co.uk

British Library Cataloguing-in-Publication Data.
A catalogue record for this book is available
from the British Library.

For
Emily, Dawn and Jenny
For their interminable belief, support and encouragement.
Thank you
Love always.

ISBN 978-0-7223-4580-1
Printed in Great Britain by
Arthur H. Stockwell Ltd
Torrs Park   Ilfracombe
Devon EX34 8BA

LYN

We hope you enjoy this book.
Please return or renew it by the due date.
You can renew it at **www.norfolk.gov.uk/libraries**
or by using our free library app. Otherwise you can
phone **0344 800 8020** - please have your library
card and pin ready.
You can sign up for email reminders too.

CONTENTS

THE PERFECT MURDER

The Hackney coach driver was keen to arrive at the station entrance as he manoeuvred his vehicle in between other cabs that had already secured a parking spot. The historic facade of Victoria Station, London, was a welcome sight as he turned around to let his passengers know that they'd arrived. But what was he talking about *passengers*? He'd only picked up a single fare. It had been to say the least a rather unusual journey. A man, a gentleman so it would appear by his dress had hailed his cab outside the Grand Mansions, in Bayswater Road. A well-travelled man too going by the number of different station labels that adorned his large suitcase, his only item of luggage.

The journey had started out normally, as it always did, a little idle chit-chat that was the normal repertoire of a London cabbie, but somewhere into the short journey a third voice, a voice of scholarly distinction had joined in the conversation. That's when the driver despite checking his rear-view mirror and seeing only the man sitting alone in the back seat had decided to shut the interconnecting window mumbling something about needing to concentrate on his driving. Despite his humming to himself the voices had continued to haunt him from the back seat. As the man paid the fare and summoned the assistance of a porter for the suitcase, he looked back and thanked the driver. The taxi driver tutted to himself, he'd had a right nutter here, despite having the appearance of a toff. He pocketed the money and turned away from his parking bay, not even waiting to see if a return fare was waiting. He needed to be away from the man in case he changed his mind.

At the ticket office the trainee clerk raised an eyebrow when the gentleman asked for a single ticket to Brighton and a mysterious second voice interjected with 'Don't tell them I'm going too!'

The clerk raised himself higher on his stool to get a better view, but all he saw was the lone passenger and despite hearing a second voice he was definitely alone.

Doubt however still invited the question 'Are you travelling with a young child?'

'Oh no, sir, I assure you that I require just the one ticket, thank you!' replied the passenger.

The young clerk wasn't sure, but as the man picked up his suitcase and proceeded across to the platform barrier he heard the voice again. 'Steady on, Lord Fortney.'

He stood up again and looked around the station concourse not wanting to appear bewildered, but all he saw were other commuters going about their business. None appeared to be paying any attention to the smartly dressed gentleman as he arrived at the barrier. He must have been mistaken. It certainly was going to be a long shift and to make matters worse he spied the stationmaster looking enquiringly his way.

The guard clipped the ticket and bade the gentleman a good journey.

'The Brighton train leaves in ten minutes, sir, the station clock is accurate to the second. Plenty of time to kill. You find yourself a good seat now and there's a restaurant car near the back of the train once the train leaves Victoria.'

Heading down the platform a short distance behind the gentleman was a lady also from the Knightsbridge area, accompanied by her chauffeur. She berated the poor man as he struggled with her many bags.

'Do come along, Watkins, I could have done the porterage better had I arranged it myself!'

It was just as well that she was walking forwards as she missed Watkins' reply. He thought of her young niece Beatrice down in Brighton, questioning the girl's sanity as to why the girl had invited her aunt to stay.

Pulling open the coach door to the carriage compartment the

gentleman turned and saw the lady approaching. He politely offered her the compartment, but she refused his invitation on the grounds one never knew what intentions a man travelling alone could have, regardless of his appearance. Despite the rebuke the gentleman smiled anyway and nodded at Watkins. He entered the carriage dragging his suitcase behind him. He heard the lady tell her chauffeur that the next compartment appeared suitable to her taste.

A voice piped up, 'Cor, she's a rum 'un for sure!'

The gentleman agreed, taking his seat as he chuckled.

'Kindly ask the porter to have a reserved notice placed on the door, Watkins, it will prevent other miscreants from travelling with me.'

The beleaguered chauffeur refused to let the remark get the better of him. He looked at the porter who was nearby and instead raised his eyebrows, of course out of sight of his mistress. Quite often as was the case in hand, ignorance was best left to the unenlightened.

Watkins turned and walked away muttering under his breath, 'A whole bloody train full of people and she wants a compartment to herself, silly cow!'

'I heard that, Watkins.'

But the piercing whistle from the guard's carriage threw a shield of protection around the chauffeur as a gloved hand raised the door window into the closed position and promptly on 9.32 a.m. the train departed from Victoria.

Suddenly a voice boomed down the platform as Watkins was only feet away from the barrier.

'And don't forget, Watkins, to walk and feed the dog!'

The platform porters and barrier guard all laughed at the poor chauffeur.

'She's a right battleaxe you got there, mate!' one said.

Watkins nodded as a plume of steam wafted down from the roof of the train coaches and engulfed his mistress. It seemed the whole station erupted into laughter as the guard closed his carriage door with a wink of his eye. Watkins could be heard chuckling the loudest.

'So, Henry junior, do you fancy a tipple, old chap?'

'Have I ever refused, m'lord?'

The coach walls were not as thick as the designer had originally intended. The inference of a titled gentleman in the next compartment was overheard by the lady from Knightsbridge. She mused to herself that perhaps the journey was not destined to be as boring as she had initially thought. She wondered if she should introduce herself, but protocol dictated she'd best leave it a little while longer into the journey, it was never good to force yourself upon a man so soon.

Instead she placed her book down on the seat beside her and rested her head back to listen some more. There were distinct advantages of having the compartment to herself. As she cocked her ear to listen again, she surmised that the gentleman must have met somebody else on the train as there were definitely two persons in the compartment next door and the other voice certainly belonged to a younger person.

'Thought you wouldn't. This is going to be a messy business!'

'Not too messy, I hope, Lord Fortney, you know I'm a little squeamish.'

The Knightsbridge lady thought hard, did she know of a Lord Fortney? Her mind scanned the catalogue of her social acquaintances, but alas for the present no memory or image was forthcoming.

'Of course it all depends on whether Mother is home or not today,' continued Lord Fortney.

The younger man replied, contemplating his reply as he spoke. 'Umm, Tuesday is bridge night, Wednesday is the dogs and Thursday is her night off, that is unless Maud wins at bingo then it's down to the Duck and Dog. You know how the old girl likes to celebrate a win.'

'No, I heard Mother say the other evening that Maud's run of luck had apparently deserted her this week, so she should be home this evening.'

The Knightsbridge lady put a gloved hand to her mouth in astonishment. She could not believe what she was hearing, a titled man with a mother who frequented drinking establishments and gambling dens. Dashed rotten luck she thought and wasn't bridge on a Sunday traditionally!

'So who's going to do it?' the young man asked.

'We'll toss for it. Do you have a coin?'

There was a moment's lull in the conversation. With her ear still cocked she guessed that the coin had been flipped and the decision had been made.

'Unfortunately, old chap, it appears that you lost the toss so the deed is down to you!'

'What time do you think would be best?'

The lady couldn't believe the coolness of the young man. She apprehensively realised that this was probably not his first time. She was glad that she had not gone next door and introduced herself to the two men. She'd heard at the ladies' bridge club that unmentionable things happen to ladies on trains.

'Oh, definitely when she's asleep.'

'Too messy. Means you've got to dispose of the bedding as well as the body and she's heavy so it'd mean lugging her across the landing and down the stairs to the cellar.'

'Umm, I didn't consider that. Yes, the old girl has broadened her hips lately, too much port I suppose!' exclaimed Lord Fortney.

The Knightsbridge lady was aghast with shock. The plot being hatched in the next carriage was ghastly, where was Watkins when she needed him?

'Look, I've drawn a plan of the apartment, so we can choose where best to do it.'

'Why a plan? We lived there once, remember.'

'It's only because the old girl keeps changing things around all the time. It's an age thing, annoying and unpredictable. There's probably not enough to keep her occupied during the day so she moves the furniture about. She once told me that she does it to confuse the parrot.'

'Oh, I'm sorry, old chap, no offence intended.'

'None taken,' replied the younger man.

'I'd completely forgotten about the parrot!'

'So, of what consequence is the parrot?'

'Well the parrot will spill the beans should Scotland Yard turn up to investigate.'

'Do you know you're right? OK, the parrot goes too.'

The Knightsbridge lady pulled down the window to allow the

fresh air into her compartment. The air in her compartment had become thick with apprehension and dread. She was concerned that she might pass out.

'Right then, we do it in the kitchen tonight.'

'Can't, the parrot stays in the parlour, and what's with this *we*? I thought you lost the toss!'

'Well, I can't do the two of them at the same time, can I? If I do the old lady first the parrot will squeal and if I do the parrot before her, they'll both squeal.'

The lady from Knightsbridge inhaled a large intake of fresh oxygen, the plot had now turned to a double murder. She fought hard the feeling to faint, but she needed also to stay alert to hear the outcome of their conversation.

'OK then, I'll do the parrot and you do the old lady. Is it agreed?'

'That's settled then. How do we do it?'

'A knife's too messy, a gun's too noisy. How about we drug them?'

'What effect do you think the old lady's sleeping draught would have on the parrot? He might have a natural resistance to human medicine.'

'How should I know?' asked the young man.

'I thought Dr Doolittle was a friend of yours?'

'Don't be impertinent. I've only ever seen him backstage that once. I thought you had too?'

'Me? No. I was probably too busy looking about for your false leg.'

'Oh, my goodness,' gasped the Knightsbridge lady. 'One of them is a cripple!'

'Alright we forget the overdose of sleeping draught. Pity though because we could have implicated the doctor. How about a rope instead?'

'Do we have one?'

'We don't in the mansion apartment, but I'm sure Larry the doorman has one in his basement garage.'

'No. I couldn't use the rope. If we got caught the thought of swinging at the end of one would be too frightful to comprehend. It would seem like a premonition of things to come.'

'Well, what then?'

A sudden air of desperation had crept into the conversation as the seconds ticked by and the Knightsbridge lady waited, listening and wondering. It seemed that the two men in the next compartment were skilled assassins. She thought about going for the guard, but they might hear her leave and then who knows what might happen! The thought of her leaving the train quite suddenly flashed through her mind. She shuddered and decided to stay put until they reached the next station.

The younger man suddenly piped up which made the lady jump.

'I've got it, what about if we gas them both?'

'Now that's a good idea, it has some merit and leaves little evidence.'

'Definitely professional killers,' mused the lady.

'We could visit this evening and whilst she puts away the tea tray, I could release the gas tap to the lounge fire. It might take a little while, but eventually both would be overcome by the fumes.'

'What a grand idea. Not messy, definitely not noisy and will always be construed as accidental. The police like a neat, tidy investigation. The old girl's getting on into her dotage, and it's not uncommon for a lady of her age to be forgetful.'

'You'd have to check the meter. To see that it had sufficient monetary credit,' quoted the lord.

'I said this would be costly.'

'Small change compared with the money that we stand to inherit.'

In the next compartment the Knightsbridge lady couldn't believe what she was hearing. She raised the perfumed handkerchief to her mouth as she let drop a cry of incredulity. How unscrupulous could these two wretches be? They cared nothing for their poor mother and here they were busy plotting her murder tonight and also that of the parrot, an innocent bystander.

The two men overheard the cry from the other side of the compartment wall. They looked at one another, the younger chuckled menacingly.

'Of course,' he quickly added, 'if any other innocent bystanders get in the way, they might have to go too!'

The Knightsbridge lady bit down on her forefinger to stifle another cry. Goodness, now she too was in danger. She'd overheard their plot. She looked towards the compartment door waiting for one of them to enter. She wondered when she would be ungraciously thrown from the train, or failing that she'd probably be found dead in the lost property storeroom at Brighton Station. Oh, how undignified for her last moments alive.

She looked up at the emergency cord, but despite the danger that she was in, she resisted the urge to pull it, it would only mean they would get to her sooner. She was surprised to hear the conversation continue in the next compartment.

'We're settled then. Tonight just after eight, we do the deed and then leave by way of the fire escape.'

'Sounds perfect, but what about going in, won't Larry Perkins see us?'

'Umm. So many things to contemplate. Perhaps old Larry might have to be one of those innocent bystanders too. The list is getting longer.'

The Knightsbridge lady looked at the fingers of her gloved hand. That meant there could now be four victims, including herself.

'Goodness, the evening's activities are becoming involved. How on earth do we dispose of Perkins?'

'A bang to the back of the head. The area is always rife with vagabonds and villains, they're sure to get the blame.'

'Good thinking. Best we go straight to the club afterwards. Jenkins will give us a credible alibi as the hall clock never registers the right time and the old boy's eyesight is questionable at the best of times.'

'At last. The perfect murder. Shall we drink to our good fortune and that of our inheritance?'

'Bottoms up.'

As the train pulled into the station at Brighton the Knightsbridge lady could not constrain herself another moment and her forefinger was now astonishingly quite sore. She rushed over to the open window and shouted at the nearest railway official.

'Porter, get a policeman and be quick about it. It's a matter of life or death.'

The porter turned and ran in the direction of the station foyer. The other passengers alighting from the train together with those waiting to get on for the return journey all stood still, intrigued as to what all the commotion was about. As the gentleman made himself ready to depart the compartment he also wondered what was afoot. The lady in the next compartment had frantically asked for the police. He wondered what on earth could have happened to her. He loved trains and the journeys were always exciting, but today's might be that extra bit special.

A constable accompanied by the porter came running down the platform weaving between the throng of onlookers. The policeman had his whistle to hand should he need extra assistance.

'There,' pointed the Knightsbridge lady, 'there in the next compartment are two men. They've been planning the murder of their poor defenceless mother, the parrot and the doorman. Arrest them, officer. They might even murder me as I overheard the whole thing.'

The crowd on the platform laughed at the sight of the lady hanging out of the coach window, her large bosom making the circumstances more comical. One or two of the locals even thought it was a staged put-on by the Brighton South Eastern Railway Amateur Dramatic Society. The constable came to a halt between the two compartments of the coach.

'Are you quite sure, madam?' he enquired.

'Don't be impertinent, young man, otherwise I will speak to your superiors!'

The constable reluctantly stepped forward and opened the door to the compartment. He was immediately confronted by just the one male passenger, the gentleman. The policeman asked him to step down onto the platform. The man obliged and did as he was asked.

'I'm sorry to trouble you, sir, but the lady accuses you and your accomplice of plotting a murder on the journey from London to Brighton. How would you account for this accusation?'

The gentleman to the astonishment of the constable, the Knightsbridge lady, the porter and the other passengers, chuckled

15

to himself, before explaining. 'The lady's right, Constable, but if you permit me to explain, I'm sure all with be revealed.'

He stepped up into the carriage compartment and retrieved something from the carriage seat, then stepping back down onto the platform again with his right foot propped up on the carriage step he produced something that had the crowd in fits of laughter. Perched on the man's right knee was a fully clothed dummy of a young man.

Supporting the dummy from behind, he explained. 'Constable, my good lady, and the ladies and gentlemen of Brighton, let me introduce ourselves. I am Lord Archibald Fortney and this is—' But before he could give the dummy's name, to the delight of the crowd the dummy swivelled his head to look at the ventriloquist. 'And I'm Henry junior.'

Spontaneously the crowd roared with laughter and even the constable smirked, much to the annoyance of the lady. She looked across at the dummy in disgust. This amused the crowd all the more.

Lord Fortney explained to the constable that they had been rehearsing for a stage production that was going to be shown at the Brighton theatre that evening. The show, a comedy, included a murder scene in which Henry junior and Lord Fortney were appearing.

As the Knightsbridge lady stepped down from her compartment and onto the platform she looked at the gentleman and his dummy standing beside the constable and porter. 'What ridiculous goings-on and on a train at that? They should be arrested for disturbing the peace at least.'

With that she turned to leave wearing a look of disgust, but Lord Fortney called after her. 'Dear madam, we meant not to alarm you, please accept our apologies.'

But the lady was hearing none of the man's lame apology.

'I distinctly heard one of you exclaim on the train that I was a possible innocent bystander and that I would suffer a fate similar to that of your mother.' She held her hand up as the constable stepped forward to interject. 'And to make matters decisively worse you're not even a titled gentleman!'

Lord Fortney looked at the constable. 'I'm afraid Henry junior does tend to get carried away when he's rehearsing, officer.'

The constable chuckled.

Lord Fortney looked at the Knightsbridge lady. 'I use the title only as my stage name, ordinarily I'm just plain old Archibald Fortney.' He then delved into the lining of his coat pocket and produced two tickets. 'Would you do me the honour of accepting these tickets for tonight's show by way of an apology?'

Just then a voice appeared beside the Knightsbridge lady. 'Oh, how wonderful, Aunt Agatha, now we've something special to do this evening. We accept your kind invitation, sir.'

Before her aunt had time to refuse, Beatrice had taken charge of the tickets, thanked Lord Fortney and Henry junior. Beatrice thanked the policeman for his help then guided her aunt away from the platform before she got herself arrested, knowing how cantankerous her aunt could be in such situations.

But the Knightsbridge lady looked back determined to have the last word. She scoffed, 'To think I was threatened by a dummy. This show had better be damn good tonight, young man,' she exclaimed looking at Henry junior, 'as I already know the plot, who done it and who gets murdered!' With that she turned escorted by her niece and together they walked through the crowd.

Henry junior waited for the lady to turn into the foyer before he turned himself and looked at Lord Fortney. 'I knew we should have thrown her off the train!'

THE FLOWER FROM JERSEY

Heading towards the railway station down by the river I took one last affectionate look back at the place that had been my lodgings. I would miss it and hoped that one day I would return, but in what circumstances at the present I couldn't tell. It took about twenty minutes to walk through the hustle and bustle of the thoroughfares down to the riverside area in Norwich. I had always admired the grandeur of the fine stone buildings, castle and cathedrals that adorned this fine city. Of recent with the prospect of lower rents and rates the East Anglian province had seen an increase in commercial enterprise. Traders, bankers, farmers and landowners had prospered well, but pleasingly the age-old customs and traditions of this chunk of land that sticks out eastward of the British Isles never seemed to get swallowed up by the changes. It could take a good twenty years or more afore you're accepted as a local and folk hereabouts just don't like change. I would miss Norfolk.

They say that there's a pub for every church and a church for every pub, and believe me I reckon whoever had the onerous task of traipsing the streets to find out and document them all, made sure that they enjoyed every minute. As for me, well I can say that I've sampled many an ale in most of the public houses in the city and mighty fine establishments they are. At twenty-three years of age I still had the world at my feet as I was soon to discover.

As I approached the bridged corner of Prince of Wales Road I became aware of a line of ducks sweeping upriver from the Cow Tower over the Bishopgate Bridge heading my way. There was always something occurring that distracted me from my thoughts, but I would never complain as the distractions of this county had always fascinated me, even as a boy. I watched the ducks land safely aside the Nelson Hotel then crossed the junction towards the station.

For me personally Norwich had proved to be a grand place of different values, cultures and great opportunity. At the tender age of fifteen, in the year of Our Lord 1869, I had been fortunate to secure a junior role with the Theatre Royal in the prestigious capacity of stagehand. A position that had sapped all of my energies, but spending each day and every evening backstage was a magnificent apprenticeship for the career that I really wanted.

My luck changed the night that Charles Blondin appeared at the theatre. He performed before a packed house, tightrope walking from one side of the stage to the other. From the wings I watched in admiration of his skill. I had seen many plays and satirical shows, but this one man captivated the audience with his mystical presence. Mr Belton the theatre owner stepped up beside me as I had ready the curtain rope and asked if I was enjoying the show. I possibly answered too enthusiastically and should have held my emotions better in check, but I had genuinely never seen anything so breathtaking. Mr Belton told me that Charles Blondin had actually tightroped his way across the vast chasm of the Niagara Falls, wherever that was, but I imagined it to be wider than the estuary at Great Yarmouth, so it was huge. I let the rope slip through my fingers as Charles Blondin took a bow then passed by me heading towards the changing room.

I joined the small queue at the ticket office asking the clerk for a single fare ticket.

'You'll be off to London then, young sir?' he enquired, more inquisitively than a direct question. 'Folk here say the pavements are all paved with gold.' He handed me my ticket, as the people behind stilted their conversation and craned forward to listen. He then offered some advice, which I believed was for the benefit of the other passengers rather than me. It made him sound like an enlightened philosopher of the railway network. 'You be watching out for them there pickpockets though, only they might have got to the pavements afore you,' he said.

I heard the passengers behind muttering as I thanked him and turned, heading for the concourse.

A head of steam billowed majestically from the far end of the platform where the steam locomotive sat idly waiting for the carriages to fill before setting off. I looked up at the station clock to see the large hand come to rest on the hour. Ten in the morning seemed a respectable time to be heading away on a journey to the big city of London. I could smell the soot that infused the air beneath the glass roof canopy as I opened the door to my second-class carriage. Farewell, Norwich.

I chose to sit beside the window which had a small wooden table set between the seats, offering ample room for both passengers either side to read upon. I placed the books that I'd strung together with twine upon the table, then secured my bag above in the storage rack. I sat and watched from my window the theatre of station events as lovers wept and said goodbye to their sweetheart, friends and family members bade farewell to a traveller destined for adventure and well-heeled ladies and gentlemen walked arm in arm beyond the barrier to first class. Each was like an act from one of Mr Belton's plays, acted out so naturally. I continued to watch absorbed by the comings and goings of the station as porters hastily unloaded laden trolleys, the stationmaster offered advice and newspaper sellers walked up and down the platforms brandishing the early edition.

My daydream came to an abrupt halt as the stationmaster reached for his whistle, signalled to the driver and our guard, seconds before a head of steam billowed back along the platform as the train juddered forward and we headed towards our next stop at Wymondham. I untied the twine, wound it tight then put it inside my jacket pocket, but left the books untouched as I watched the terraced houses of Norwich dwindle into farmland and meadow. The door at the end of the carriage suddenly opened and a delightful young lady wearing a feathered hat entered, then walked between the seats until she reached mine.

She looked at me and asked, 'Do you mind if I sit here, sir?'

I outstretched my hand and invited her to take a seat. 'It would be my pleasure,' I said.

She gratefully smiled then withdrew the pin holding her hat in place before placing it upon the tabletop. She was quite beautiful a little older than myself and had a scoop of dark brown hair tied neatly with a bow just above the collar line. The white ruff of her blouse was pierced with a choker pin threaded neatly through the gathered neck, but what I found the most alluring was the blue pigmentation of her eyes. They were deeply rich and reminded me of the darkest summer's night when the stars infused the sky. I found myself staring and quickly looked away.

'I see you have a theatre programme amongst your books. Do you partake of the arts, or maybe you are an actor?' she enquired. I looked down at my collection of books and was amazed that she had seen the programme as only the corner was noticeable, although it was the corner depicting the small insignia of the theatre. 'Maybe one day,' I answered. 'At present I am only employed as a stagehand.' I rebuked myself for having made the answer sound despairingly ungrateful. I owed Mr Belton so much already.

She smiled and asked, 'Why maybe?'

'I know that I am not ready to set foot upon the stage, but I long for the day that it happens.'

She really did possess an enigmatic smile and I could envisage others being engaged by her smile alone. 'Everybody can act, believe me. Are we not just a cast of the human race who act out different roles each day? Do we not breathe, talk, walk down a street, meet people we know, lie beside a lover, grieve for a lost friend or play a game with children? Our whole life is spent acting.'

I listened intently, I'd never seen life as she had just described and in such a brief undertaking.

'If we attend a theatre, only then do we pay to watch a play, nothing less than what we experience every day.'

I sat thoughtfully back in my seat, I had never heard the role of a thespian as being so plainly described. I was twenty-three and for the past eight years I had released the curtain cord at the end of the show, perhaps I should have been the man taking the bow, but courage takes different forms and although Mr Belton had tried to encourage me to take that step up of faith, my knees had not remained solid enough to help me tread the boards.

'When you put it quite like that, I suppose we do all act somehow,' I replied.

Her deep-blue eyes sparkled mischievously as she whispered, 'Just don't go telling everybody, will you? Otherwise we might both find ourselves out of work, or sidelined.'

'Are you on the stage?' I asked enthusiastically, wondering if I had ever seen her somewhere before.

She smiled, but it was not a smile that I recognised. 'Yes, I am,' she replied. 'The train takes us to London today, where I have been most fortunate to have been cast in a play at the Haymarket Theatre. It is scheduled to begin next month. Would you come to see it?' she enquired.

I really didn't see how I could refuse and if only to have the opportunity to see her once again. A front row seat if possible.

As the train pulled away from the platform at Wymondham Station I shielded my eyes from the morning sun still rising in the east.

'It's like that sometimes on the stage,' she commented. 'You are under the spotlight and wonder just who exactly is watching you in the stalls.'

I moved across to the middle of the seat where the sun had not yet penetrated.

'And what would be the purpose of your journey to London, if you don't mind me asking?' she asked.

I proceeded to tell her that it was my ambition and intention to find work in a large London theatre, where a young man's prospects were supposed to be brighter and better, or so Mr Belton had informed me. I had learnt the ropes of my trade, so to speak, backstage and was a valuable member of the theatre, but the calling of grandiose dreams had agonisingly gnawed at my stomach recently and Mr Belton had realised that the Theatre Royal in Norwich would not offer me the opportunities that a London theatre could. It was at his suggestion that I travelled to London to test my destiny, reassuring me that a place would always be open for me back in Norwich should I ever want to return.

'Mr Belton,' she mused momentarily. 'Yes, I know of his

acquaintance. We once met at an evening banquet held at a place called Gunton Hall. Someone there asked him about a production that was running at the time at his theatre and he delivered a rather lengthy promotion of the show. I liked him and admired the way that he considered his audience, giving thought to his answer. He was very well received that night and even had a flair for selling tickets for the show. The night boosted his ticket sales and I admit to say it was a splendid show. What did you say was your name?' she asked suddenly.

I didn't think that I had, but obliged all the same. 'William Charles Chattaway.' I was about to enquire of hers, but she pondered for a minute before remembering a poignant memory from somewhere.

'Yes,' she started, 'I suppose you could say that it was after seeing the show at Mr Belton's theatre that I first thought about my own aspirations of being an actress. I became smitten with the whole experience, the thought of dressing nightly in beautiful costumes, hearing the appreciative applause of the audience and being part of the arts was as alluring as jewellery is to a thief.'

I still didn't know her name, but took the next pause to ask 'What is the name of the show that you have been cast in at the Haymarket Theatre?'

'*She Stoops To Conquer*,' she replied and smiled, only this time I got the impression that the smile was meant for someone else, although the seats around us had emptied at Wymondham. I remained mystified. 'A role fit for a prince to watch,' she continued. I saw the sudden look in her eye not realising what it meant, but instead, she finished the sentence: 'or perhaps a princess from a foreign land.' This time she laughed and I joined her. I knew nothing of the rumours of the royal court. News didn't travel as far away as Norwich.

'William Charles Chattaway,' she pondered over once again. 'The name has a certain theatrical ring to it, one that should adorn a billboard in a theatre foyer. You know, William, I predict that someday soon I will see and hear your name in theatrical circles.'

I didn't know what to say. She was truly enchanting and I think that whatever she had said would have attracted me to her. My own perception of myself saw my name recorded only on the backstage production helpers' listing and yet here was a beautiful young actress challenging my ambitions and already promoting me to a career that I believed was way beyond my reach. I was about to offer a reply, when she appealed that we stayed silent whilst she took the opportunity to go over her lines. Of course I agreed. She apologised and said that my being opposite her would invoke the spirit of the theatre and help her absorb what she needed to learn.

Although I chose a book from the pile before me I hardly read a word as the countryside travelled in reverse to my view. I tried hard not to look across, but it was a battle that I was losing as the miles from Norwich increased and the stations towards London lessened. She caught me watching her once as we travelled through a tunnel, but said nothing, just smiled. I closed my eyes and saw her deep-blue eyes float towards me in a vision of serenity as the wheels beneath the carriage clattered away.

When you want time to pass quickly it always drags in reverse and when you want it to pass slowly, the devil arrives and flicks it all the quicker with all of his cunning. All too soon the motion of the carriage wheels on the track below began to grind as the crossover points became more prominent. I noticed a heavy head of steam from the engine pass our window denoting we were slowing down and then without warning the first signs of Liverpool Street Station appeared. Our time together was almost at an end.

I placed the book that remained unread back on top of the pile, re-knotted the twine and put my arms through the sleeves of my jacket which lay beside me. As the train came to a halt with a gentle shudder I watched as she reached for her hat, replaced it neatly upon her head and engaged the pin once again. I photographed her in my mind, knowing that I would hold the image inside of me forever. As doors started to open along the length of the train, she stood and held out her lace-gloved hand. I applied the minimum of pressure as I shook her hand in mine.

'I enjoyed our journey together, William. You really are the most delightful travelling companion and I feel sure that our paths will cross again soon one day. Please do come and see my play.'

I said that I would and as she moved away from her seat I suddenly remembered that I didn't know her name. I asked.

'Well, William, originally it was Emilie Charlotte Le Breton, but more commonly nowadays I am called the Jersey Lily, or almost certainly to my friends.' She smiled once more then turned towards the door and was gone.

I watched as she walked past the carriage window. I whispered, 'Goodbye, my flower from Jersey, the pleasure was all mine.'

Having settled my meagre belongings in a room recommended to me by Mr Belton I then started to walk the streets of London visiting the many theatres looking for work. I was disappointed that none of the pavements were paved with gold, but remembered the Norwich ticket clerk's words about watching out for thieves, perhaps he had been right after all. It took a couple of days before I managed to find suitable employment, similar to my previous role.

It was a grand theatre auspiciously decorated of the like that I had not seen before and ironically it was called the Theatre Royal, only herewith of Drury Lane. The manager was a very impressionable man who went by the name of Augustus Harris. It was a very classic name and I wondered if his parents were of true Italian decent with origins that dated back to the times of the Romans.

Mr Harris however was a good man and the Theatre Royal was a very popular venue especially with the inhabitants of London. I engaged myself immediately and enjoyed working there, being well received by the other backstage hands and the cast. It was easy to make friends, although my thoughts of Norfolk were never far from my mind. It was around this time that a production of the Carl August Nicolas Rosa Opera Company appeared at the theatre. Carl Rosa being a very enigmatic and successful German musical impresario. The production played to packed houses every night and I had the pleasure of seeing every show backstage.

Then one night tragedy befell one of the extras of the cast during a showing of *Esmerelda* from the Parisian production of *The Hunchback of Notre Dame*. The extra, not a prominent figure, had portrayed a peasant, but on the night had accidentally stepped backwards down the stage steps beyond the curtain rather than going forward across the pavement outside of Notre Dame and subsequently suffered a fractured ankle. It was anticipated that he would be out of the production for three months.

That night I hardly slept a wink and early the next morning in a rush of bravado I knocked on the door of Augustus Harris's office where I put myself forward to replace the extra. Following a short discussion Mr Harris approached Mr Rosa who agreed, provided Mr Harris paid my wages. And so for the want of a pun, not at the poor unfortunate who broke his ankle, that's how I got my first footing on the rung of the acting ladder.

I relished every moment of being a lowly peasant and naturally I wore tatty clothes, very little make-up and had no lines to speak other than throw the crowd a prompted grunt every now and then. It seemed like money for old rope, but I never did complain. Stardom was for the gifted and I was still not confident enough to approach the front of the stage even in the crowd scenes, but as the weeks went by my fellow thespians encouraged me through the different scenes, offering helpful hints and where to stand, what actions to make, which facial expressions attracted the audience and how not to steal a scene especially from the main characters.

I was enthralled and enraptured with every minute of the production. When I was on the sidelines behind the curtain I would listen intently to every word of the other cast as they effortlessly played out their roles. When my part was not required I would make the costume assistants and make-up artists perform their tasks backstage where I could study, watch and listen to the show.

Acting was as Emilie had said an everyday occurrence that none of us actually realised. What she failed to tell me was just how exciting it was. When you entered the dressing room the butterflies would nestle in the pit of your stomach, but the moment you stepped out and onto the stage the butterflies flew away silently in a cloud of adrenalin that didn't go away until your head fell upon the pillow that night. Of course the final moments before slumber remained sacred to Emilie and had done for a long time now.

I suppose that we were halfway through the third month of *Esmerelda* when a buzz went around the dressing room prior to the night's evening show that there was a very special guest in the audience and that the show must be one of the best. Speculation and rumour as to who our mystery guest was remained rife amongst the cast, the dressers, make-up and the stagehands, but it was a secret that was not to be disclosed until the final curtain and only then would the theatre lights reveal our special member of the audience. Even Madame Parepa-Rosa the star of the show and wife to Carl Rosa did not know.

Needless to say everybody performed their part as if their life depended upon it, the show was a monumental success and when the curtain fell to announce the last few seconds of the final scene it was met with rapturous applause. Emilie had been right again, the accolade of the audience was something that money could never buy, you had to experience it to believe it.

And then it happened as I had never expected and I don't mean the revelation of our special guest who incidentally turned out to be the Prince of Wales, later Edward VII, but it was the guest seated at his immediate right. Of course there were others in his entourage, but my eyes fell upon the beautiful Emilie Charlotte Le Breton.

As the cast leant forward accepting the accolades of the audience another member of the cast reminded me to bow, I hadn't realised that I was still standing. Despite the tatty clothing and make-up Emilie recognised me and as my body righted itself again, I saw her wave and smile. It would have been easy to have mistaken both the gestures for recognition of somebody else, but when she tugged at the Prince's arm and pointed directly my way I knew then that if I was never exalted to the echelons of a front-of-stage performer with my name never appearing on a billboard, this would be my finest moment of stardom. I smiled back and bowed alone in response in her direction.

It would be a long time even after my head rested upon my pillow that night before I would fall asleep, every thought I had of the show that evening was of Emilie. I felt sure that she was pleased that I had at last stepped forward from behind the stage and onto the boards, but really it was all down to her and the short time we had spent together on that journey from Norwich to London. I did as promised and purchased a theatre ticket to see the production of *She Stoops to Conquer*, in which Emilie Charlotte Le Breton was the star. I could afford it nowadays even though I had reverted back to my role as a stagehand and yes I even managed to secure a front-row seat. Throughout that wonderful evening in the hidden shadows of the stalls I watched with complete adoration and a secret love the beautiful actress called Lillie Langtry, my flower from Jersey.

THE GHOSTWRITER

I paid for my one-way ticket to Cromer in Norfolk then walked through to the platform concourse where I became aware of several other late-night travellers milling about as they waited for their respective trains. I had always considered that railway stations had two very noticeable characteristics, they were always windy and cold, even in the height of summer the temperature beneath the lattice glass roof hardly ever seemed to rise and secondly they were extremely thought-provoking arenas.

As I stood before the timetable matrix checking for my train I rubbed my hands together trying to get my circulation to increase. However hard you tried you could never seem to find a warm corner to hide in. Others were walking around trying to do the same. The cold has an effect on us that immediately affects our head, I suppose because it's where we lose most of our body heat from, but don't you find that your mind wanders with the cold to places where it is more comfortable, where you'd rather be than here right now.

I found a seat near to a late-night fast-food stall where the escaping heat from the grill and the fluorescent lighting added some extra warmth to my chosen spot. I crossed my arms and my legs to prevent the chill air invading my clothing, I must have given the impression to other commuters passing by to use the station facilities that I was settling on the bench for the night. I exhaled and watched the pattern that my breath made before disappearing, then did it again, it was turning out to be colder than I thought. I recalled the places that I'd visited today and the people with whom I'd met. I realised that it had been a full day and sleep would be a welcome relief for my tired body.

I looked up at the roof. I had always admired Norwich Station, the wonderful architecture of the building with its large open areas of red and pale brick, interspersed with white-framed office windows where staff could watch the arrivals and departures, interrupt to make sudden public announcements and keep an eye on the general business of the station. Then there was and always is the station clock, generally a large round timepiece with a white enamelled backplate, italic black numbers and metal patterned hands. Very rarely did they have second hands, but I've always found them to be amazingly accurate, Swiss or German-manufactured I shouldn't wonder.

Norwich Station had a feel of being a family-orientated station where holidaymakers would arrive all excited, ready to meet the connecting train which would take them on to Great Yarmouth, Lowestoft, Cromer or Wells-next-the-Sea. To the side of the platforms there were still the remnants of a metal stockade where cattle and sheep had been herded before being transported to market. Even the advertising posters seemed from a bygone era depicting scenes from the beaches or the Broads, a national favourite of the area. Norwich had something magical about it, that artists and writers found inspiring, but I wondered if the local people took it all for granted. I checked the station clock, it was 11.23 p.m. I had seventeen minutes left before the train departed for Cromer.

I thought about getting a coffee from the fast-food stall, but suddenly the employee pulled down the shutter from inside and I heard the click of a padlock announcing business was over for the day. It was my own fault, I should not have skipped lunch or dinner and right on cue my stomach grumbled just to remind me. A girl nearby looked my way and smiled. Then from beneath the stone arch a young man appeared looking all the worse for having consumed too much alcohol. You always get one, don't you? especially on a late-night train, but as the girl moved away and manoeuvred herself to the other side of my bench, where I could offer her some protection, I noticed that he was a merry drunk, not aggressive.

We all watched as he selected a platform bench, promptly rested himself down then patted the bench slats before lying prostrate from end to end. Within seconds he was asleep, blissfully sleeping off his alcohol consumption. I very much doubted that he would be catching any connecting train this night. Relief showed on the faces of the passengers catching the 11.40 p.m. train to Cromer.

I stood up, smiled again at the young girl who seemed much happier then walked across to the platform barrier where I showed my ticket to the porter who clipped the corner before loudly announcing, 'Cromer train, platform six.' It struck me as odd that he actually needed to announce the imminent departure as our train was the only one in the station at the time, but that was a Norfolk oddity that you become accustomed to when you've been here a little while.

I politely thanked the porter anyway and proceeded down the platform to select a good carriage. As I passed the guard's carriage a voice from within caught my attention.

'Evening, sir. Nice night for a journey up to the coast, although there's a hint of a storm perhaps later.'

I said thank you and wished the guard a good journey too. I wasn't aware that a storm was due, I remember walking towards the station looking up at the skies above Norwich which were clear, starlit and with a full moon.

'Aye,' he continued, telling himself rather than me I suspected, 'Be a good night for old Ned to be out 'n' about too!'

Now I hadn't got the foggiest idea who old Ned could possibly be, so I just grinned and decided to select the first carriage that came to hand. It was clean, well lit and unoccupied which suited me just fine. However, as I turned to close the carriage door a hand rested upon my wrist.

'Not so fast, young 'un, I could be wanting this carriage too!'

I was confronted by a man who wanted to join me in the carriage. He was a big, powerfully built man, somewhere in his late fifties and had a mass of long unkempt hair that was matted. I wondered if he was a tramp. As I stood aside to let him enter he looked up at me, his face lined and weather-beaten and his eyes were sunken, dark and staring. He sported a mature beard that matched the texture of his wild hair. He decided to sit opposite me.

31

As I closed the carriage door I took a sniff of the night air, but instead an infusion of salty aromas invaded my inner senses, it was an unusual smell that had no clear definition. I studied the man as he settled himself. His clothes were rather unusual for the year, it was almost as though he had just come from a production at the local Theatre Royal. Then there was that smell again in the carriage, not an odour you'd associate with Norwich, but more like a walk along the quayside at Wells-next-the-Sea or at the end of Cromer pier.

'Are you from these parts about?' he enquired. He was definitely from this region and had a broad accent.

'No. I'm from Highgate in London,' I replied. 'I'm here on a sort of holiday.'

'Aye, they always are!' That was all that he said, as he turned away and peered through the mirrored image in the carriage glass. I had to admit that his manner made me feel a little uneasy and although he appeared to be looking through the window at the night outside the reflection meant that he could see everything that I was doing. It unnerved me somewhat. I needed a distraction so I took a small notebook from inside my coat pocket, then selected a pencil.

'Are you one of them there reporters?' he asked.

'Goodness no,' I replied. 'I am a writer, fiction mainly with a few reference guides thrown in. I'm up here in Norfolk to write a factual book on the myths and legends of East Anglian ghosts and spirits.' From my vantage point beside the carriage window I could still see the sleeping drunk on the platform bench. He was sprawled across the bench at an awkward angle, I guessed that when he did awake he'd suffer from some aches and pains too irrespective of the after-effects of the spirits that he consumed. I smiled to myself, he wasn't legend enough for my book.

'So it's ghosts you'll be after then?' my travelling companion asked.

'Well yes, that and other manifestations that are supposed to haunt this splendid county. I'm staying with an elderly aunt up on the north Norfolk coast. She's been trying to convince me that there are a number of haunts hereabout and some houses that are visited nightly by mysterious apparitions. You know the spectral faces in the windows of stately mansions, headless horsemen, wild-eyed black dogs and late-night ghosts that float about the countryside searching for lost loves.'

'So you'd be a cynic then, young man?' I deduced from his tone that he wasn't convinced by my explanation.

'No. Well, not entirely, but like any other person and especially as an author I need proof to pass on to my readers. If I'm to write about such myths and legends, then I need to convince myself first before I can expect to convince any reader.'

The man stared at me for a few moments, I got the impression that he was studying me. Yes, he was definitely studying me wondering whether I was worth conversing with any longer. I was convinced that he was definitely the thespian type, who enacted his role day and night, besides being deep and thoughtful. Actors always studied people and their habits, in case they ever needed to portray a similar character on the stage one day.

The train suddenly lurched forward to announce that we had commenced our journey. I gave the sleeping man a quick glance back glad that he was safe for the night. I doubt he would remember much come the morning. Another lost memory in a book full of forgotten stories. I chuckled to myself for he was probably a renowned travel writer with a string of books to his name and had been celebrating a career-breaking contract tonight. A nice thought, but probably very far from the truth.

As the train gathered speed, my carriage companion suddenly tapped the window. I looked up from my notes. 'There's many a man out there that can tell you a tale or two,' he said as he turned to face me directly. 'Aye, more than a few I reckon.'

I still had my pad open with my pencil poised at the ready. 'Have you come across any ghosts yourself?' I enquired.

'Me, lad? No, I only deals with the living. There's enough time being dead, without trying to talk with the buggers afore your time!'

'But you must have heard the stories, the tales etc. You're a local man and I'm sure you've had a friend or family member that's seen or heard something?'

He thought for a few seconds as he ran the fingers of his right hand through the mane of his beard. 'Well, now you mention it, young 'un, I did hear of a tale of recent. A right rum' affair it was too. If you're interested I'll tell you it, but only if you're interested mind. I aren't wasting no time on a story just to pass the time for you!'

I gave my assurance to the man that I was most certainly interested and I would avidly listen and I would also put aside any cynicism that I might have personally. I asked his permission that I could write notes as he related his tale. He agreed, then began.

'It was a night somewhat like tonight.'

Didn't all ghost stories start like this? But I remained tight lipped as I promised.

'There was a full moon, stars were out and one could follow the North Star should you need a guide home, but lurking out there on the horizon was a dark cloud hiding a raging storm.'

That was a coincidence, I thought, my travelling companion was the second person tonight to hint that a storm was looming. I looked out of the window momentarily, the night beyond appeared settled, a perfect autumn night, fresh, but definitely settled.

He continued: 'The fish were cagey that night, they were taking the fight to where they knew best, down into the depths and into the eye of the storm. Real clever buggers are them there fish. They knew that the fishing boats would follow regardless and that was just what happened. You see those fish knew their territory really well, much better than us old hands and they could feel the swell as the currents passed beneath. Often as a shoal they'd rise temptingly to the surface, tantalisingly long enough for the fishermen to spot the hint of silver as their scales glimmered in the moonlight, then down to the depths they would scurry. They were definitely playing a game that night with us. On deck the bosun yelled out to the Captain in the wheelhouse that a large shoal had been spotted starboard side towards the depths of Dogger Bank, thirty miles ashore of Flamborough Head. It was the shout that the Captain had been waiting for as he turned the wheel hard north-east to give chase.'

I didn't look up as I carried on writing in the notebook. I still had no concrete evidence that this tale had any merit, but the way the man told the story was certainly convincing enough to me.

'Aye, he'd convinced himself, did the old sea salt, that at last good fortune were for the taking. He gave orders to the crew to be ready and come about with the nets. But it was a strange night and the old sea dog should have noticed the signs. The fish knew, oh they knew alright. They knew the boat would give chase after them, but that the dark cloud approaching from the direction of Norway was waiting, lurking and getting ready to pounce. The crests of the waves were already now broadside of the deck as the bow dipped and dived, and port to starboard rolled menacingly. The crew looked at the captain in the wheelhouse for support, but he only had eyes beyond the bow as it rose then fell, reared high again then disappeared.

'The ship's bosun suddenly appeared at the door of the wheelhouse. "Dark clouds moving this way, Captain, from the east and bringing with it some war-of-the-gods lightning."

'The Captain looked out beyond his starboard side window and saw the looming monster as it suddenly flashed thunderously across the sky. "Get the deck lashed, Bosun, and be quick about it. Have the crew stow the nets, we won't be fishing this night until this storm passes overhead."

'The Captain's command quickly passed between the deckhands as they grabbed lines and ropes and began securing loose equipment. The remainder of the crew hauled as hard as they could at the heavily waterlogged nets that had not long been cast. The fish had indeed been crafty tonight as the initial catch had only netted a handful of lost stragglers. The angry cloud moved quickly across the sea towards the fishing boat as the crew watched in deathly awe, this was a storm like no other that they had ever seen. The sky seemed to embrace their fear as silence fell amongst the men on the boat. They waited for the impending doom that was heading their way. Their heads craned towards the wheelhouse for the Captain to come about and ride out the vicious waves.

'But it was the turn that caught them broadside as the high waves crashed down onto the deck, the fishing boat shuddering at the ferocity of the sea. The bosun ordered the crew below decks for safety as the Captain steered the boat south-westerly back towards the Wash or a safe harbour, anywhere this night would do.

'But the storm wasn't letting go, not now that it had got a hold of them, instead it continued to toss the fishing boat about like a cork on a windswept lake, as the Captain struggled to hold the wheel on a straight course. The North Star was elsewhere tonight and would be of no use for the journey home. In the distance the Captain could see the land lights along the north Norfolk coast as they winked back through the falling rain guiding the fishing boat closer and closer to land.

'Then all of a sudden a freak wave hit the port side of the boat followed by an almighty crack broadside from bow to stern. Screams echoed out into the night as the Captain felt the rudder line snap and the bow of the fishing boat rise skyward. The wheelhouse took on a deluge of water as the door crashed aside inviting the sea in. The Captain saw the bosun struggling as he pulled himself along the waterlogged deck before disappearing into the night as another wave swept through the boat.

'The waves seemed to then be relentless almost merciless as timbers cracked, glass shattered, metal twisted and water thrashed all about. Then the cries seemed to end as quickly as they had pierced the storm winds.'

My travelling companion suddenly stopped talking to make sure that I was still listening.

'I hope you're getting this all down, lad. It's a tale that needs a-telling to folks hereabouts!'

I reassured him that I was getting it all almost word for word. Then as if by coincidence, although I hadn't actually noticed having been so preoccupied with writing, I realised that it was raining outside and the wind too was getting up. The odour in the carriage seemed stronger too and I wondered if it was the man. He saw me sniff the air, then with a look of scorn he continued.

'An eerie silence suddenly fell upon the fishing boat as the waves consumed the stern first, before quickly engulfing the bow. As it sank to the depths of Davy Jones's locker the lights south of Blakeney all went out one by one, as though the people of the town admitted that there was nothing else that could be done for the boat or the crew. Even the storm had suddenly changed direction and headed northward towards the ravages of the Forties. A vast blackness descended upon the whole area as the stars reappeared, including the North Star.'

I looked up from my notebook. 'They all died?'

He nodded. 'It's tragic, the crew didn't stand a chance.'

I knew I had to tell the story. Then to convince myself that I had heard right, I asked, 'Didn't even one of them make it to shore?'

'Nay, lad. They all went down to pay their respects to Davy Jones, but the sea don't give up its dead that easily.'

'Were any of the crew recovered, you know, buried like?' I asked.

The man scoffed and I wondered why. 'That's the strange part of this tale lad. None were buried in sacred land as you might say, instead they're buried beneath the cliffs somewhere south of Blakeney Point along down to Weybourne.' He then paused, which made me look up at him. 'By the way, you're not writing anything, lad!'

I quickly scribbled down the last bit about the burial ritual then looked back up to ask more questions, but to my astonishment the carriage was empty except for me. I even closed my eyes for a moment or two before reopening them to ensure that I had not nodded off or that I had been daydreaming, railway journeys can sometimes have that effect upon you, but outside the rain was hammering down against the carriage windows and in the distance I could just make out the odd house light. I was awake and when I looked down my pad had recorded the tale of the lost ship and all of its crew.

When the train came to a halt at Cromer Station I virtually jumped from my carriage out onto the platform quickly scanning up and down, but there was no sign of my travelling companion only a few passengers further down the train who got off and headed straight towards the station entrance. I walked the length of the train, but the carriages were all empty. I even gave the ticket collector a description of the man, but he stated that nobody matching the man's appearance had passed through his barrier. He advised instead that I'd best be off home soon as the storm was almost at its height.

I walked through the town back to my aunt's house recalling the journey to Cromer and the story that I'd heard from the mysterious man. His sudden disappearance had me bewildered. I lowered my head to fight off the stinging droplets of rain, but as I walked past the church I was sure that I heard the sound of a man calling in the distance. It seemed a ridiculous notion on a night like tonight, but I heard it once more and again there was that familiar fishy odour, although admittedly we were near to the sea. I was convinced that I was letting my imagination run away with me. Although minutes later at the corner of Cliff Drive, just before I opened the gate to the front garden, I heard a voice say, 'Tell 'em it all, lad,' and then it disappeared. I'd turned around quickly expecting someone to be standing directly behind me but the street was empty.

Aunt Millicent was still up when I walked into the lounge and sat down opposite her absorbing some of the heat from the fire, which was invitingly spitting forth flames from the log back into the hearth.

'Have you had a good evening, dear?' she enquired. 'It's suddenly got up stormy, quite surprising really considering the lovely evening it was earlier.'

I hesitated to tell her about my journey from Norwich to Cromer and the mystery of my travelling companion, but I needed to tell someone. It was as if an inner voice was prompting me to relate it and so I told her, including the bit about the mysterious voice that I had heard between the station and her home.

When I'd finished she surprisingly stood up then left the room going through to the kitchen. 'Cup of cocoa?' she called out.

'Yes please,' I replied a little perplexed. Aunt Millicent had seemingly dismissed my tale out of hand, that was quite obvious. Perhaps she'd become accustomed to the ramblings of a semi-professional author.

Several minutes later she returned with a tray of two steaming mugs of cocoa and a plate of biscuits. Just what I needed and just to prove the point my stomach growled rather convincingly.

'That voice, the one that called out to you as you walked home is more commonly known in these parts as that of a ghostly man that wanders the countryside of Norfolk. Nobody really or rightly knows why or exactly who he was, but some of the locals have nicknamed him Ned. He particularly haunts hereabouts on wet and windy nights, just like the storm tonight!'

I listened to Aunt Millicent as she told me about one or two people that she knew who'd told her that they had seen or heard Ned over the years. I remembered my earlier conversation with the man on the train, about my being cynical, but the evidence was stacking up so any cynicism I had was lost with the storm. I sipped my coca and dunked another biscuit enjoying the company of my elderly aunt.

She caught me by surprise, I must have been daydreaming. 'So what do you think about the man on the train and the tale of the sunken fishing boat, David?' But before I could answer or give an opinion, she replaced her mug on the hearthstone. 'There was a fishing boat that sunk in a very bad storm around the turn of the century. The storm was recorded as being the like as never had been seen before. All the crew were drowned and their bodies were washed ashore several days later. Nobody is certain as to where exactly the fishing boat came from, whether they were from our shores or foreign waters, but nevertheless they all died that tragic night. It is rumoured that their bodies were buried beneath the pebbles on the beach or in the cliff cracks and on a wet and windy night you can hear the sounds of pebbles being disturbed or thrown about.'

'But what about the Captain, did he drown too?' I asked.

'Oh yes,' she replied emphatically. 'The Captain drowned along with his crew. They say that on a stormy night an unknown mariner roams the north Norfolk coastline calling out for the crew. Some local fishermen purport to have seen the mysterious mariner down north of the pier walking the beach late at night heading towards East Runton. Admittedly none of the fishermen have heard the names of the lost fishermen, but they know he calls out. When they've approached to see if they can help, he suddenly disappears.'

We stayed up very late that night till the rain had stopped lashing the window and the stars reappeared. I'd even looked out of the scullery door and sure enough there was the North Star. Everywhere was quiet, completely silent. It was time to go to bed as later that day I had a story to write.

Why the mysterious man on the train, possibly named Ned, had decided to pick me that night as his travelling companion I really cannot tell you, but if he did travel with me from Norwich to Cromer to actually prove to me that ghosts did exist in Norfolk, then believe you and me, he certainly made a good job of convincing me and without a shadow of doubt I can honestly say I've seen the evidence first-hand. Oh, and there's a last-minute inclusion that I might add to this story. Should you yourself ever have reason to be on that last train out of Norwich to Cromer on any given night of the week and especially if it's wet and windy weather, or a storm is imminent, I suggest you have a notebook and pen handy. Be nice to drunks too only they may well be hard up, but happy working travel writers.

A JOURNEY OF CONSCIENCE

As I turned into Drummond Street and walked along the pavement towards the grand edifice known locally as Euston Arch my attention was drawn to a young man walking in the same direction that I was but on the opposite pavement. He seemed agitated, furtively looking around as though he was looking out for somebody. Nothing unusual I suppose as we all tend to do this at some time in our life, only the man seemed extremely nervous about approaching the railway station.

There was nothing strikingly obvious about his actual appearance, a two-piece suit nothing special but smart enough, normal again for the era, but showing some signs of wear. It didn't however look like it had seen the light of day for some time. The man was clean-shaven with a moderately groomed hairstyle. As we walked towards the arch I estimated his age to be early twenties. It was so strange to see a young man in London as most were away at war. He checked behind again and I looked too. There definitely wasn't anyone paying him any real attention.

Having just come off duty and with a two-day leave of absence for personal reasons, namely to visit my ailing mother, I hadn't had the opportunity to change so I was still in my day clothes consisting of a black thin-striped suit, a trench coat and black trilby hat. If anybody had been taking an interest in me which I seriously doubted they could have reasonably mistaken me for a local spiv or spy. However, the police warrant card inside my jacket pocket said otherwise. I was proud of my profession and the job that I did. I'd worked

41

hard to reach the rank of detective sergeant.

I was careful to keep my pace going at an even stride as I approached the station entrance making sure the brim of my hat was lowered sufficiently to obscure my eyes, but still offer me a good eyeline to keep watch on the pedestrian opposite. I couldn't put my finger on what exactly was strange about him, it was just a hunch, but it was there and I couldn't shift it.

I watched him pass beneath the arch a short distance from the station, walking directly into the entrance increasing his step towards the ticket counter as he went. If I didn't know better I would say that he was nervous about something and certainly had a secret or two stashed up his sleeve, not a thing to be caught with during the war, that was for sure.

Waiting in the queue at the ticket office I purposefully allowed a middle-aged couple to join the queue before me, it placed them immediately behind the young man appearing all the more normal. I couldn't quite hear where he purchased a ticket to, but when he turned and headed in the direction of the train that I intended to catch I realised that I would see him on the train. The couple thanked me as they walked away from the counter and I stepped forward to purchase my single fare to Adlington, Cheshire.

'Nice part of the country, sir!' exclaimed the ticket clerk. 'I've an aunt and uncle from thereabouts.'

'Yes it is,' I replied, 'it'll be good to be back home again.' I discreetly produced my warrant card opening the fold to show the ticket clerk my identification. 'Where did that man in the suit, before the middle-aged couple purchase a ticket to?' I enquired.

'Why, same train as yourself, sir, only he's going on to Chorley the next station up from yours. I'd hurry along now, sir, as they'll be getting a head of steam up ready to leave soon.'

I thanked the ticket clerk and proceeded over to the platform barrier.

The stationmaster clipped my ticket. 'Nineteen eighteen on platform five, sir, you've got just two minutes left before the guard blows his whistle.'

It seemed a strange time for a train to be leaving, but that was the railways for you. Ironic too that the year was 1918 and the weather for September was still moderately warm despite the recent rain at the beginning of the week.

'There's a buffet car at the rear, but no alcohol I'm afraid, sir,' called out the stationmaster as I headed off down the platform. I waved my hand above my head in acknowledgement as he called across to the train guard, 'One coming Harry.'

I nodded at the guard as I passed his van, then jumped into the first coach near the rear of the train. Pulling the door shut behind me I heard the guard blow his whistle, seconds later the train shunted forward with a sudden lurch as all steam trains did as each of the carriage links caught up with the carriage ahead. It's funny how everybody knew it was expected and that it was going to happen yet it still caught us out. I smiled at myself, it was one of those quirky things in life that you never seem to forget and yet other events, possibly bearing more significance get lost in the annals of time. I held onto the handrails for support as I passed along the aisles between the seats. Using the interconnecting doors I passed through the carriages until I saw the back of the head of the young man again.

It hadn't taken me long to pass through from the rear coach to the fifth walking beyond his seat and to where I could select a position opposite, giving a perfect angle for observation. I'd noticed as I had passed by his table that he was engaged in reading a newspaper which he must have found on the train as he had not purchased one back at the station, but it was of no consequence as I settled in my seat. I saw him watching me as I removed my hat so I turned and looked out of the window as the old and missing buildings of London passed us by. We passed through a short tunnel which allowed me to see if he was still watching using the mirrored effect from the blacked-out window. The young man had his head down reading his newspaper.

An elderly man sat opposite him, I couldn't see his face clearly except for the dog-eared military cap that he wore to the side of his head, but it wasn't an unusual sight these days. As I'd passed their table moments earlier I had noticed the short scar above his right eye, again nothing unusual in the 1900s. They sat in silence as the younger man continued to read turning over the pages of the newspaper. It was just past Bletchley before the old soldier decided to engage the younger man in conversation.

'You've been reading that article over and over several times, young man. It must be of an interest to you?' he enquired.

The younger man looked up from the page. 'Not really, just reading about the war, that's all.' I noticed that his voice was weak and somewhat nervous.

The old soldier continued, 'Aye, be a bloody fine thing when it's all over with. Would have been a different kettle of fish if Kitchener hadn't croaked it in 1916.'

I watched the young man's expression and deduced that he was somewhat wary of the old soldier, but although guarded he politely replied, 'Where have you served during the war?' The question contained the overtones of doubt as I listened with fascination wondering where the two men's conversation would lead.

'Not this time round, young 'un. I served in the previous campaign, probably about the time you were born.'

'Where?' the young man asked, intrigued.

The old soldier started with an explanation. 'I was with Kitchener at Khartoum securing the Sudan from those bloody Mahdists. I was there when the Dervish capital fell alright.' He pondered for a moment, then went on, 'But it was a great price that was paid on both sides and I've seen enough of wars to haunt me to sleep on many a dark night, lad.'

As we entered another tunnel I turned and faced the window again where I watched the young man as he leant forward and crossed his arms across the page of the newspaper as though hiding the article that he'd been reading. I wondered what significance the article held that was so important. It wasn't long before I found out.

The old soldier had also noticed what the young man had done with the newspaper but instead he went on with his memories. 'Aye, 'twas a hard-fought battle that day and even when it was done the blood still continued to flow. Wars have a knack of doing that even when the generals say they're over. Don't you believe everything they tell you, lad.'

I wasn't sure exactly what the old soldier had implied, but the moment passed as I listened on. I wasn't sure if it was the rocking motion of the train as it gathered speed or whether the young man actually leant forward closer to the old soldier. I pricked up my ears too.

'What do you mean, after the battle?' he asked.

'As I said, lad, the blood always flows long after the final shot leaves the barrel. That's when the court martials start. As if there weren't enough bloodshed, the officers are never satisfied. Only this time it were three of them. 'Twas a bad affair too. War ain't no better sometimes than in peacetime. Kitchener himself presided over the court martial of three young officers, two of them buggers being condemned and shot by firing squad. The other, the lucky one he got two years' military time in one of their prison stockades.'

The young man sat back. I could clearly see the shock pencil across his face. The old soldier's tale had affected him and I wondered why. The young man's forehead was etched deep as he kept his thoughts to himself.

'Why, what exactly did they do that was so wrong to face the firing squad?'

Once again the question was asked by him demanding an explanation that the young man was seeking only for himself. He definitely had a secret that was gnawing away inside of him. That much was evident.

The old soldier looked around as if to see who else might be listening, but my eyes were fixed on the darkened window next to my seat. I couldn't determine whether the old man was enjoying relating his tale of woe or whether it was purely for the ears of the other passengers.

'Orders stated that allegedly they shot their prisoners!' It was the old soldier who leant forward this time. 'That story, that one there in the paper. It means something to you personally, young man, don't it?'

I watched and listened as the young man replied. This time there was a distinct hesitation in his voice. It wavered as he withdrew his arms away from the article in the paper. Spinning about the newspaper he pushed it across to the old soldier. Then in almost a hush, tinged with a resonance of sadness he admitted, 'I was there not too long ago.'

The old soldier quickly read the article, then looked up at the young man again. 'But the war ain't over, lad!'

This time I strained hard and only just heard the reply, 'I know.'

The old soldier enquired sympathetically, 'Are you wounded then, lad?'

The young man paused before answering. 'If only I was,' he replied. 'It's my soul that hurts the most and my body feels like it walks the walk of a dead man!'

The old soldier said nothing as he looked down at the newspaper again. Then suddenly he closed it, folded it and put the paper on the seat beside him. 'Are you in trouble, lad?' he asked.

The young man looked straight at the old veteran. 'The worst kind, sir, and it's that which ails me.'

As the train emerged from the tunnel back out into the natural light of the evening, I turned away from the window. I knew it, call it a professional hunch if you want, but I'd guessed as we had both approached Euston Arch that there was something peculiar about the young man. The worst kind could only mean desertion or murder. I wondered how the old soldier would react now, however what came next I have to admit took me totally by surprise. I eased back and listened as they continued their conversation, watching them more closely.

'Don't fret, lad, as I won't ask the reason. That's between a man, his conscience and the Almighty. We all have sins of war that only we know about. Those sins can eat away at our very existence and we have to live with them till our dying day. No man is ever innocent, lad, whatever his faith, religion or position.'

What the old soldier had said bore some truth to it and it made me wonder about my own sins. Oh yes, policemen do sometimes get it wrong. They can be construed as our sins. I wondered if I had done things differently, then maybe some of the victims might not have been victims. I pondered the journey of conscience that we take through life often never eases. I looked across at the young soldier.

He saw me watching, but continued, 'I've brought shame upon myself, my wife and daughter, my parents, family and friends. Some of them are still out there on the Hindenburg Line. Some are never coming home ever.'

The old soldier pointed to his forehead. 'You see this scar, lad? Well, some lucky bastard was fortunate enough to put a round across my temple during the battle, only it didn't have my name on it, but I'll tell you this, lad, it certainly had the poor bastard's name on it that was behind me though. As it sliced its way across my forehead it travelled on and hit him dead centre between the eyes. Poor blighter didn't see it coming, but maybe that's the best way to go if you gotta go!' He scratched the scar on his forehead, then continued, 'At the time I wasn't that far from the gates of Khartoum when it happened. The devil must have looked up at me and instead took a back seat that day only as my platoon advanced and charged through into the city. I didn't know it then of course, but I guess that as I lay unconscious outside those ancient walls the buzzards eagerly sat on the arch stonework waiting for a lull in the firing before they pounced only the stretcher-bearers found me breathing and twitching. It was enough to steal them of their next meal as I was carried back to the army field hospital.'

'At least you did something heroic and have something to prove for it!' the young soldier remarked.

'You think so, lad?' remarked the old veteran still rubbing his forehead. 'Some overworked field surgeon cleaned the wound, then without any available anaesthetic, he pulled together my wound and stitched as best he could, resulting in this 'ere scar. After about an hour of recovery some no-nonsense, diehard bastard of a sergeant comes into our field tent, takes one look at me, then orders me to rejoin my unit inside the city walls. Kitchener himself was going to shake my hand he said. Well, I tell you this, lad, at that moment I didn't care if Kitchener, the devil or the Lord Almighty himself were there and wanted to shake my bloody hand, once outside of that field tent I made tracks in the opposite direction, bloody long strides they were too. I ripped my corporal's stripes and regiment insignia from my uniform. Searching about I managed to come across the dead body of a war correspondent. I stole his arm insignia and running as fast as a bloody rabbit I made my way firstly to Atbara, then on to Port Sudan beside the Red Sea. If I came across any advancing British units I would take sketchy accounts from their officers before leaving them to their fate. Eventually by means of bribery, luck and proffering my soul to the devil, on more than one occasion I guess, I finally ditched my army uniform and jumped ship to Portsmouth as a deckhand.'

'Didn't anybody come looking for you?' asked the bewildered young soldier.

'No, lad. You see I was officially a dead man. Some of my mates who were beside me as we rushed the walls of Khartoum saw me go down in a spray of blood from my head wound and as I didn't get up they probably thought I'd died in the battle. There was so much carnage at that siege that I doubt anybody knew exactly who had died, been injured or lay dying that day. To the war effort I was just another casualty of war. I returned to our shores a free man, I took another identity, even a new life. You, lad, could do the same!'

I checked my watch as we didn't have too long before the train pulled into Adlington. Thoughts of my mother hankered at the back of my mind as I pondered the present circumstances and the flight of these two soldiers. I had a public duty to perform of that there was no doubt, but I also had a duty as a son. I decided that I would get the train stopped at the next station and hand them over to the local constabulary. The second surprising instalment to this story then took place. Again I wasn't prepared for what I heard.

'So what happened to you then, lad?' asked the old soldier.

The young man saw me looking his way. He ignored me. 'I was at the Battle of Epehy, part of the 100-day offensive in the war, it was sheer hell. We'd received scant reports along the line that over 260 men had been slaughtered and over 1,000 wounded in just one offensive. Some of them were friends, men that I had gone to school with. I saw them mown down as soon as we hit the field, it was like a turkey shoot. They were either immediately shot or blown to pieces in the mortar fire. Three of them, my age, just disappeared before my eyes as a mortar exploded in front of us. When I awoke from the concussion hours later, I realised that my friends had taken the full force of the blast thus protecting me. I came round in a foxhole hours after the battle had ceased. Everything was an eerie silence as I couldn't hear a thing, the blast had damaged my eardrums. I was completely disorientated as I wandered around aimlessly looking for my regiment. I felt a strange feeling of hopelessness and unnerving solitude as though the armies of friend and foe had deserted the battlefield. Reading that article in the paper was the first time I knew anything about the outcome of the battle.'

'But how did you get back to England, lad?'

The young soldier recounted as much as he could recall. By this time he knew I was listening, but he had no idea who I was.

'I remember thinking that I would have to walk during the night using the darkness for cover and rest up as best I could during the day. I hid amongst bushes, in disused barns and under bridges. I often heard the shuffling of feet on the march going overhead or passing me by, but I didn't dare look up or outside as I didn't know to which side they belonged. All the time my eardrums sounded as though the ocean was running through them, the sound just wouldn't stop, it nearly drove me insane. I walked for days and weeks until eventually I reached a small place beside the sea called Étaples where I managed to get aboard a French fishing boat. Despite the Germans patrolling along the beaches and harbours the French fishermen risked everything as they took me across to the Kent coast, where I swam the last couple of miles to our shoreline. I wanted them to come with me, but they all had families back at Étaples and wouldn't leave them. I know how they felt. I landed back with nowhere to shelter and had no money. A kind farmer found me asleep in his cow byre. He fed me and gave me this suit. I worked on his farm for about a week where I managed to earn a few shillings, enough to pay for my fare home. One day I will repay his kindness and return his son's suit, although he told me that his son was somewhere fighting in France, he said I'd get better use of the suit than his son. He was a realist. The farmer never asked why I was back in England, I think he guessed. The rest you know and here I am on the train heading back to my home in Chorley.'

The old soldier scratched the bristles on his chin, pondering as he thought. 'Technically, lad, you're still a soldier and technically you haven't deserted your regiment, they deserted you. The Lord Almighty was with you at the front and by some good fortune you've managed to make your way back to England unscathed.

You're not a deserter, lad, just one very lucky bugger!'

I looked out of the window at the evening beyond. I haven't been to war myself so I could never begin to understand the thoughts and feelings that haunt the men that do, the men that survive, that is. I'd heard my colleagues talking about the rage that haunts a soldier, but having never experienced it, I didn't know it for myself. I realised that the young soldier had been through a lot in the short space of time that he'd been in France.

In the reflection I watched the young soldier. I suspected that it was a wave of emotional fatigue, a sense of bewilderment, a monumental fear and an unexpected relief that finally swept across the young man's face as he shielded himself from prying eyes and suddenly started to cry. He wept openly into the palms of his hands for several minutes before regaining his composure. The old soldier proffered a handkerchief to him for his use.

'I expect you've travelled a long way to be back with your loved ones?' he enquired.

'Yes, I suppose I have, it seemed at times like the world had been spinning slowly in the other direction as I made my way back to Blighty,' he replied. 'I doubt my daughter will recognise me as I've been gone so long. I'll probably look like a stranger to her. I took their image with me wherever I went. In the foxhole when I wasn't sure whether I'd live or die theirs were the last faces that I saw.' The young soldier gazed into nowhere for a few moments then concluded, 'I wonder if my wife still looks the same.'

I watched as the old soldier picked up the newspaper, folded it again and secreted it into the depths of his coat pocket, he smiled. 'Old habit I suppose of when I was a war correspondent, lad.'

For the first time and I suspect not for a very long time since, the young soldier smiled.

'You know, lad, despite a few missing weeks over in France and you're in the clear for that in my book. You go find your doctor and get him to look at those injuries of yours and I feel sure he'll back up your story of being in an explosion. Oh, for sure the army being the bloody army might still want to give you a couple of weeks in the guardhouse cos they got to be seen to always have the stiff upper lip and all that crap, but you take my advice, first up you go home and you see that wife of yours and you get to know that little girl again. You spend some time with them, lad, before you report back at any bloody barracks.'

I don't know why he did it, instinct I suppose, but it was at this point that the old soldier looked round and winked at me. He didn't say anything to me, but it was as if he knew that I'd been listening ever since we'd started out on our journey.

'And don't you worry about what anybody thinks, lad. No man can pass judgement on another man's action especially in times of war. Too many consequences present themselves in a battle for any one man to comprehend in a lifetime. The Lord Almighty watches and he waits for those who come to sit beside him and he watches the progress of others that live on before they too join him as we all do in the end.'

'Thank you, sir,' said the young soldier.

'Now who are you to be calling an old war correspondent sir? I was on my way home too, lad. I live on the outskirts of Preston in Lancashire and it's been a very long time since I saw my wife and kids. It'll be them that won't recognise me!'

I looked out of the window at the night that was developing outside. This sure was a right old pickle that had presented itself. I'd been a policeman for twenty-eight years, a constable for twelve, a detective for five and a sergeant in investigations for eleven. In all that time I don't think I'd heard two stories with such distinct differences and almost the same ending, but each had a definite twist of fate. I pondered my options.

On the one hand I had an old soldier who definitely was a deserter, but who was returning home after almost sixteen years to face a family who had thought he was long dead. I weighed up the scales of justice as would a judge. Should I arrest him and let him face the army where justice would be served albeit so many years later or should I let him return home and face the music from his wife and children? The latter had its merits.

And then there was the case of the young soldier who had bravely fought in battle, received his wounds as a result, but as a consequence of his injuries couldn't differentiate between his own forces and that of the enemy. Somehow he had miraculously found his way back to the shores of England and like any husband and father his only thought was to see his wife and young baby daughter again.

The young soldier was not a deserter, this point I agreed with the old soldier on. He was just a man who loved his family. And as the old soldier had told him the army would in all probability arrest him when he turned up eventually at his barracks, but again like the old soldier, I thought his punishment, if any, would almost certainly be very short-lived. In my eyes the young man was a hero of the war as were all that went to fight. And last but not least, there was my mother. Now didn't she deserve to see a son in her last days of this lifetime?

It was strange and maybe right too, but I don't recall the rest of the conversation between the two soldiers as they carried on talking. It was as though a temporary deafness had affected me. Perhaps it was summary justice for having a suspicious nature, but then don't all police officers? I reached across and picked up my hat then headed for the carriage door without looking their way. Fate and destiny would decide where the lives of these two soldiers lie, mine was sitting beside my mother to hold her hand.

Then as the brakes were applied and we stopped I turned and took a last look at the tops of their heads as I exited the carriage. I stepped back as the train left the station and coffered my hat, silently saluting them both. I wished them well as their window passed by me. I saw the old soldier look and smile and then the train was gone.

As expected my dear mother departed this life as she had always wanted on a crisp Sunday morning as the church bells pealed high in the belfry. She always said it was the way it should be and that St Peter would hear the peal and know that she was on her way up to heaven. I know I will miss her.

It was several weeks later and with great rejoicing that the newspapers were full of stories of heroism and remorse of those who bravely gave their lives so that others could live, be happy and prosper long into the future. The Great War had finally come to an end, not as predicted initially after only a few months, but after five long, hard, arduous years. It would take the citizens of all the nations engaged in that awful conflict years to recover and probably some never would.

As I turned the page of the newspaper on my desk I remembered the train journey a short time ago and the two men who had unwittingly been my travelling companions. I can still see their faces quite vividly and I often wonder why it was that we should all have been on that train at the same time that day. But when I think of the story that they both had to tell on that journey, I'm glad that I did nothing that night except get off the train at Adlington. My conscience was then and still is clear. I hoped that the two men felt the same.

THANK YOU, MR WRAY

You would consider travelling on the railway to be one of the safest forms of modern transport as opposed to flying, sailing and travelling by road. By and large it is, and very rarely does anything happen unless by the intervention of human error. This is a story that encompasses such an event where error did play a part, but so did the spirit of human sacrifice.

I have deliberated a good number of years, but have finally decided to tell the story because I was involved, although not to blame, however I want you to judge the events, the people concerned and what you would have done in similar circumstances. A jury can be quick to condemn somebody and the process of deliberation is to go identify the facts as true, so that a verdict can be reached. Be careful at how you judge, because at the end of the day, we're all human.

I need to explain firstly that this is not a ghost story, but involves a ghost, or was it? How are we to know? Have you actually seen one in real form, or are they purely a form of our vivid imagination or a trick of the light? Secondly, well, it's my opinion and mine alone; and I think you should be the one to decide. And thirdly, working on the railways early in the morning as the night turns to day, then late at night when dusk gives way to the night, the light albeit natural or man-made, not forgetting the sky itself all have a part to play in the journey of a train driver, or the guard at the other end of the train, they're all factors that can play tricks with your mind.

My name is William Tubbs and I've been a train driver for the past thirty-eight years. I left school, or more to the point ran out of it on my last day and then I joined the railways, the Great Northern Railway Company to be precise. It was a boyhood dream that came true.

I would leave early in the morning, report for duty at the depot, then armed with tin and duster I'd polish the brass nameplates that adorned the sides or front of the engine, sweep the footplate removing dead cinders, brush away wet leaves from the huge metal wheels and clean the inspection windows for the driver and engineer. I've been a very fortunate man as it has been a career that has taken me places, given me immense joy and settled the restlessness that every young man feels until he retires.

I should also not forget to introduce my engineer Oliver Walter Long. On long journeys north he'd often remind me, when the conversation had hit a lull, that he was actually born at his mother's home in Hornsey just before midnight. And I've always reminded him that with initials such as his, there'd be no mistaking that fact. His mother was a devout Christian and had always wanted Oliver to be a man of the cloth, a vicar no less and maybe one day a bishop. Primarily because she thought he was a boy with a weak spirit and a gentle disposition. Mrs Long certainly didn't know her little Ollie as I called him. He was as strong as an ox, would tell the most raucous jokes and being a vicar was the furthest aspiration from his human existence. I doubt he'd ever ventured inside a church in his entire life other than when he was baptised. Ollie was however a good friend, a skilled engineer and we had worked together for over thirty-five years. More than most marriages.

So there you have us. A couple of boys from the turn of the century who became men of the railway and that's how it was in them there days. The good old days as old timers would say, men who'd hung up their hat and gloves for the last time. To me though, these days are just as grand and as interesting in my book. Quite rightly there should be those who may oppose my optimism but, let's look at the facts, other than for the regrettable death of George VI, our king, at Sandringham on 6th February and the official proclamation of our new Queen, Elizabeth II, formerly the Duchess of Edinburgh, the year was still a damn good one. I mean to say – come on – Len Hutton captained the

England Cricket Team, the first man to do so winning the Ashes despite his controversial leadership. Anyhow I liked the odd game when time permitted.

However, our story begins on the morning of Friday 28th November 1952. As Ollie climbed up into the cab and joined me on the engine footplate, the smog decided to come along too, wafting across the coal tender and down into the rear of the cab. It was eerie, strangely cold and could set the hairs on the back of your neck bristling. We had been experiencing these bad patches of fog for some time now without any sign of it letting up.

November had been unusually cold and the damp was affecting my old bones, giving me a touch of nagging arthritis. Thank goodness that we only had a short couple of runs today. I touched the opening of the furnace with the back of my hand.

'Hurry up, Ollie boy, an' get that fire stoked up,' I said, rubbing my hands together, 'we're gonna need it today, this is a real thick 'un!'

Ollie looked behind at the smog creeping down his coals. 'You can say that again,' he replied, 'took me twice as long to get here from just the other side of Hawthorn Road as it normally does. I'll stoke up then put the kettle on.'

The kettle was an old tin vessel which had sat on the furnace hotplate for many good years and would boil away merrily after only a couple of minutes providing us with piping hot water, just right for a good brew. Unlike modern trains, steam trains had many advantages and this was one of them.

Behind us we could just about see the first of our twenty-eight goods trucks that made up the train. This was our assignment today, transport them up to the Hitchin depot, where another crew would take over and transport them further northward. That destination beyond was not our concern as long as our goods arrived intact. As shovel loads of coal dropped into the fire I released the brake, engaged the throttle and sounded the whistle. In this smog I wanted to make sure the signal box knew of my departure. Ordinarily I would not have bothered as we passed over the crossover track, but today I listened out for the sound of approaching rail traffic. The air was still, infused with a silent foreboding and lay across the body of the train like a heavy old blanket. Normally a crossover posed no trouble, but going across blind was always a risk I would rather not take. I gave the whistle another tug.

Ignoring the smog I pricked up my ears and managed to catch the heavy wheels of the last truck as they disengaged the crossover points. I felt the relief drain from my shoulders and I'm sure Ollie felt the same as he placed a mug of steaming tea down beside me. Overhead waves of soot-laden smoke danced towards the back of the train making the smog a much thicker, darker dirty brown colour. I was relieved that today's was a goods train and not a passenger-carrying train, I think the combination would have killed some of our passengers.

We proceeded northward towards Welwyn for the next track crossover continually looking out for known landmarks, but none presented themselves to us. Occasionally we heard the bleat of a sheep herd or the deep bellow of cattle nearby, but they too remained invisible. I doubt either beast liked the climate or the uncertainty of the weather. Ordinarily I would not have been concerned, but I regretted the trail of smoke that we had to leave behind, but knew that there was nothing I could do about it.

As the black gaping hole of the tunnel mouth came into view I ticked off the distance in my mind. We'd just entered the tunnel at Digswell where the blanket of fog that had haunted us all the way from the depot at Wood Green received an abrupt smack in the face. Although the tunnel was dark and quite long it was good to be rid of that awful smell and unerring silence of the fog. We had travelled a quarter of the tunnel's length when Ollie suddenly screamed across at me to apply the brake. Without questioning his reasons I instinctively yanked hard on the brake lever. If Ollie had asked for an emergency stop that alone was good enough for me.

I peered hard through the inspection window. Further ahead and silhouetted across the track was a large black shape. The train wheels slid on the damp track, metal passing over metal as the weight of the goods trucks pushed the whole train forward. Although my lever was fully engaged, we were still going to hit the obstruction. I shouted for Ollie to prepare himself for an impact stop. We braced ourselves as best we could, but the cab offered little protection against such calamities.

Throughout my career I had only been involved in two other collisions and both fortunately were in the shunting yard, involving unladen trains. The speed of the impact on those occasions had been minimal, but the effect was still a cause for concern, today however, we were travelling a lot faster and I realised the impact would be more serious.

As with any collision the seconds seem longer than they are in reality, it's as if time stands still momentarily. Personal safety flashed through my brain as I let go of all levers and instead held onto the security of the handrail, hoping the impact would not snap my forearms and that the handrail would prevent me from being propelled forward against the bulkhead of the furnace. The train came to a thundering halt as the head of the engine engaged the obstruction. I felt the cab wheels lift right off the track before dropping again and fortunately re-engaging. I immediately looked behind to ensure that the force of the trucks behind were not coming through the coal truck. I did not relish being crushed.

Although slightly dazed I checked myself for injuries, but everything appeared to function as much as my arthritis would allow. My shoulder seemed to have caught most of the impact and I knew I'd suffer some bruising later. I was lucky, which was more than I could say for Ollie who was lying quite still on the footplate. I turned him over to discover a nasty gash to the side of his forehead. It wasn't particularly deep, but looked nasty all the same. I gently shook his shoulders to assess the level of his awareness. Moments later he uttered a moan, then started to come around.

Ollie described how he looked back at the coal truck to check on the same thing that I had, when the impact had thrown him forward and onto the handrail. He hadn't recalled anything else until he felt me shaking him. I took a bandage from the first-aid tin and handed it to him. He held it to his forehead as I descended the steps down onto the track. Walking forward of the engine I inspected the underside as I passed by. I was surprised to see that only one of the pistons was letting out steam from a small crack along its housing, amazing really considering the impact we had sustained. It was an easy repair back at the workshop.

And then there before me was the root of our problem, I was confronted by a large mound of sodden earth and tunnel bricks, the side wall of the tunnel had collapsed in and around the front wheels of the engine. For the present we were stuck fast and the train could neither go forward nor reverse back clear of the landslide.

Ollie leant around the side of the cab and asked the extent of the damage. Rather than shout I walked back to the cab steps and told him what had happened. We only had one shovel on board as the other was in the workshop for a new handle. We realised we would need more than the one to clear the obstruction. I looked at my watch, it was twenty-five to eleven. The time was somewhat irrelevant as I wasn't aware of any other trains due on the line, but you never know if schedules had been changed without our knowledge and a signal box down the line had thrown a green light for permission to proceed. I needed to speak to the guard.

Ollie was still nursing his head and recovering from his lost moments, so I told him to stay put for a while, whilst I went to check on Ernest our guard. It was not always necessary on a goods train to have a guard unless the goods in transit were of high value, but the depot manager had insisted that Ernest accompany the train today as the weather was so bad.

I walked as best I could to the rear of the train using the sleepers as guides as the rear trucks and coaches were beyond the safety of the bridge and lay back out in the fog. I saw no wheel faults or misalignment problems. We had been most fortunate.

The news however was not as good in the guard's van. Ernest had received no prior notice of our impending collision so had been thrown the length of the carriage. He was not in good shape and unconscious when I arrived. I made Ernest as comfortable as I could using some old postal sacks and straw bales. His breathing although laboured was still strong so I thought it was alright to leave him. I would come back to check on him again soon, but first I had to get help.

Both Ernest and Ollie had head injuries and then there were the railway authorities who had to be made aware of our circumstances and that of the tunnel. I returned as quickly as I could to the engine, but the wooden sleepers and gravel were very damp and this made conditions hard underfoot. When I reached Ollie he was busy mopping the injury with water from the kettle. I quickly told him about poor Ernest. It was obvious to us both that Ernest needed a doctor or to be at the hospital.

'We must protect the line first though,' said Ollie.

'I know. First out should be the warning flares at the head and rear of the train. I checked the metal signal lights in the guard's van, but they were all damaged in the crash. Then we must get some sort of notification to the signal box at Welwyn to prevent other trains travelling up this line.'

We decided who would do what and why. Ollie would take a handful of flares, go to the head of the train and place the flares every hundred paces along the track, then proceed to the Welwyn signal box, where they could arrange for help and he could get better medical attention. In the meantime I would stay with the train and return to the rear coach, check on Ernest and then place flares further back down the track to halt any oncoming trains following behind. I helped Ollie down from the engine and handed him the torch.

I heard him shuffling along the sleepers inside the tunnel as I leant out of the cab and called out, 'Ollie, don't be alarmed, I'm going to sound the whistle with intermittent blasts like they did back in the war. If I get it right it should sound similar to the distress signal, somebody at Welwyn might hear it and come see what the commotion is all about. It will help speed things along.'

Ollie agreed it was a good idea before putting his hands over his ears to prevent the echo in the tunnel from damaging his eardrums. I saw him walking along the tunnel wall protecting his ears as I tugged on the whistle cord. The blasts were deafeningly loud as they bounced about the tunnel. I wondered if the sound would be strong enough to penetrate the fog outside.

Taking a handful of flares I proceeded back along the track towards the fog once again. I had become accustomed to the dampness of the sleepers underfoot so I soon reached the guard's van. As I closed the door behind me I was suddenly surprised to see the figure of a man hunched over Ernest. He'd heard me enter and looked my way with a friendly smile.

'He's OK I assure you. You go and set the flares whilst I stay with him.'

Despite Ernest's injuries and the presence of the stranger, I knew my priority was the safety of other trains and passengers on the line. I offered the stranger my thanks then climbed back down onto the track. Somebody at least had heard the train's whistle. I was relieved that Ernest had somebody to care for him.

I set my flares and listened down the line for anything familiar to indicate another train, but I heard nothing only the sound of a horse neighing somewhere in a field nearby, although I couldn't see him. I thought the crash might have frightened him off. Satisfied that the flares would work I returned to see Ernest and the stranger.

I was happy to be out of the fog again as I pulled open the guard's door. I was surprised and somewhat astonished to see Ernest awake and propped up against a wall of wooden crates. He still appeared dazed, but otherwise had made a good recovery since the last time I had seen him. I looked around the guard's van, but we were the only two occupants. The stranger had disappeared.

'I'm so pleased you're OK, Ernest. Is there anything I can get for you?'

Ernest shook his head. 'No, thank you, William. The man made sure I was comfortable before he went for help.'

I was intrigued, but didn't want to push Ernest for an in-depth account as I considered that he was too dazed to give me one. Just who was the mysterious man who had appeared so soon after the crash, helped revive Ernest then disappeared again to go for help and to whom? Ernest mumbled on about being thrown headlong down the carriage and asked what had happened. I told him about the tunnel collapse and assured him that the flares had been set, normally a guard's duty. I also told him that Ollie had gone off to seek help.

Ernest started to shiver so I decided it was best to get him along to the engine where the furnace was still warm and would offer some warmth rather than the chilly atmosphere of the guard's van. We walked along the side of the train both relieved to be away from the fog. Resting Ernest against the bulkhead of the train I opened the furnace door. He rubbed his hands together accepting the warmth from the flames.

As the pallor of his face improved I asked Ernest about the stranger that I'd seen in the guard's van. He told me that the man had suddenly appeared leaning over him as he lay injured on the floor. Ernest couldn't recall how the man had got into the van as it required a key, but it wasn't a point we needed to dwell on now. He described the man as calm and softly spoken, but mostly he remembered the unusual effect of the man's hands as they swept across his head. He recalled it as being surrounded by a warm halo. I had no reason to doubt Ernest's explanation, but remained intrigued all the same.

The shouts and sound of men's voices echoed along the tunnel as Ollie and a band of men clambered out of the fog and over the collapse. As they got closer I could see the men were wearing green uniforms. I got the kettle ready again. Ollie climbed back up onto the footplate and was pleased to see Ernest was alive and well. I looked at them both, they looked like a couple of Sikhs shrouded in head bandages.

Ollie explained that after setting his flares he had as planned walked to the signal box at Welwyn where he'd found the signalman already on the telephone calling through to other boxes down the line to halt the train behind. The call was not a minute too late as the upward train had been stopped at Hatfield, the line was safe once again. I wondered how the signalman had been alerted to our dilemma, but I let it go. Ollie continued to tell us that a group of soldiers en route to Cambridge had been waiting at Welwyn for the train behind. The officer had told the signalman to call for the local fire brigade and together they would come along and dig us out.

The council had also been informed and were sending along a gang of men to shore up the tunnel, to prevent any further collapse. The stationmaster had called the control room at King's Cross and all trains scheduled to use the line had now been cancelled. I knew that there was nothing left for us to do, except wait for the line to be cleared. I poured the hot water into three metal mugs.

As we sat and sipped our tea I told Ollie about how I'd found Ernest injured and unconscious, about the mysterious man who had helped. And how Ernest had made a miraculous recovery before the man had left to get help. He put his mug beside him, then Ollie told us about the time between leaving the tunnel and his arrival at Welwyn. I listened in complete fascination oblivious to what was happening at the front of the train.

He'd set his flares a hundred paces apart and proceeded awkwardly towards the signal box at Welwyn as arranged. Ollie had thought the signalman had heard the distress signal of our train's whistle and that's why he was on the phone when he'd arrived, but it was not the case. Sure enough the signalman had heard a whistle, but he could not determine from which direction it had come, as the fog had distorted the sound. He wasn't sure which tunnel it was coming from as Welwyn has two tunnels, north and south. The signalman was on the phone to the stationmaster at Welwyn Station asking for some assistance when a stranger appeared at his signal box. He told the signalman that a crash had occurred in the south tunnel due to a collapse, involving a goods train and that the engineer and the guard had concussion injuries, but the driver was safe and sound. He said that it would take a large group of men to dig out the train. When the signalman had come off the phone again after speaking with the stationmaster, he'd turned to find the signal box empty. The stranger had disappeared moments before I'd arrived.

It wasn't until I asked Ollie to describe the man that had gone to the signal box that I made the connection, it was the same man that I'd seen in the guard's van. All three of us looked at one another, it was impossible, but there was no mistaking the description. It matched and all three of us agreed it was the same man. How he could be in two places at one time is something we just couldn't agree upon.

Working collectively under the command of the army officer, the soldiers and the firemen soon had the track clear of debris and the men from the council shored up the collapse safely until engineers could make good the necessary repairs. It was the railway company's policy that any injury whilst on duty to railway personnel meant that both Ernest and Ollie were transported to the local hospital for checks and observations as both had suffered head injuries, regardless of any objections they may have had. I advised them both before they left not to mention the mysterious man to anyone and that I would look into it myself. The railway company sent another fireman and guard to Welwyn where I picked them up at the station and taking it slowly we limped the train on to Cambridge where we delivered our goods train. It was housed in the sidings so that the repair to the cracked piston housing could be rectified.

The next day I had to visit the divisional offices of the Great Northern Railway to complete a report on the events of the crash. Ernest and Ollie were still in the hospital at Welwyn and it would be Monday at the latest before they were released so the pleasure of the report was all mine. As usual I walked across the forecourt towards the office block through thick fog and it seemed no clearer than the day before, I wondered when it would give up and we'd see the sunshine again. My report was short and concise, just the way I liked them. There was no need for glossy bits or fancy words. I sat opposite the divisional manager who read it as I sat patiently waiting for his response.

He took off his glasses, laid down my report and sat back comfortably into his chair.

'That's a remarkable account of the events, William,' he exclaimed. I was about to remark when he palmed his hand into the air to ask for my silence. 'It's not that I don't believe you, because I do. But all the same it is truly remarkable. Perhaps I should tell you a story and maybe it will help answer some of the questions that surround your crash of yesterday.'

I sat back ready to listen.

He told me about a train crash that occurred in the last century, on 9th June 1866 to be precise. It was the account of a tragic set of circumstances where human error was to be the contributory factor. It involved three trains, each a goods train and all heading in the direction of Welwyn Station. Two were heading north and the other heading south. All using the same line, but obviously at pre-scheduled times so that the southbound train would pass through when the northbound trains had crossed onto another line.

The first train hit mechanical problems and came to a halt in the north side tunnel a short distance beyond Welwyn Station.

The driver rightly refused the guard's suggestion to reverse the train using the gradient of the line, company regulations forbade such an action. The Company are not completely aware of all the circumstances obviously as it was such a long time ago, but the guard failed to set his warning detonators at the rear of the train. Consequently a short while later the second train, the train following, crashed headlong into the first train. The guard of the first train was critically injured as a result. Due to a communication error involving the use of the telegraph system the signalmen in their respective boxes south and north of Welwyn misinterpreted the signals that had been sent and thinking the tunnel clear of both northbound trains allowed the southbound third train into the tunnel.

It was one of the worst railway crashes ever recorded and the board of inquiry recorded it as due to a series of human errors. Regretfully the guard, a man named Mr Wray, died as a result of his injuries a couple of days later. It was never known why he never set the warning detonators.

Coincidence or sheer fluke I couldn't determine which, but I was stunned that two accidents had occurred on almost the same stretch of line only a few miles apart and either side of Welwyn. I had previously heard the older rail hands suggest that the line was cursed, but I didn't believe in such superstitious nonsense. I leant forward and asked the divisional manager why he thought that my report on yesterday's crash had been remarkable.

He got up from his seat and went across to a shelf at the side of his office. He selected a file and brought it back to the table. His fingers quickly shuffled amongst the batch of old papers before pulling out a dog-eared brown envelope. He opened it and produced a clipping from a newspaper dated 12th June 1866. It was a journalist's report on the three-train crash in the tunnel at Welwyn three days previously. I carefully spread out the paper as I wanted to look at the photographs that accompanied the story. The first was of the tunnel and the wreckage, another portrayed one of the signal boxes, it wasn't clear whether south or north box, but most importantly and last was a photograph of the guard, Mr Wray.

I sat there staring at the image that was looking back at me.

Mr Wray was definitely the man that I'd seen in the guard's van attending to Ernest and he was the man the signalman had spoken to about our crash. I looked up at the divisional manager dumbfounded.

'That's why it's so remarkable, William. It would seem that the ghost of Guard Wray saved the lives of Ernest, Oliver, you and countless others yesterday.'

I handed back the photograph, but told him that Ernest and Ollie would need to see it when they left hospital. He agreed. The file had been in his office for almost 100 years, it wasn't going anywhere.

As I left the offices I stepped outside, needing some fresh air. Surprisingly the fog had lifted and the air seemed a whole lot fresher, the day had taken on a different perspective suddenly. I looked back at the upstairs office from where I had just come and then at the rail station beyond. The railway had always been my life and so had the men that I had worked with. I had a great respect for most of them.

I raised my hat from my scalp and respectfully said, 'Thank you, Mr Wray.'

I wasn't there in 1866 and so I will not comment on any aspect of the crash or who did what and why. We all act instinctively throughout our lives and we have to be judged on what decisions we make, rightly or wrongly. You can be as sceptical as you like and like me have an opinion about the story that I've just told you. Feel free to judge accordingly, but remember sometimes you just have to be there.

I turned away from the office and headed over to the gates, I decided to catch a bus to Welwyn where I had a remarkable story to tell Ernest and Oliver.

2ND LIEUTENANT THOMAS FREDERICK MARSH

Standing before the glass divide of the ticket office, I looked up and momentarily caught sight of my reflection. The dark green of my cavalry uniform appeared much darker in the gloomy backdrop of the station foyer. Morten Sydenham was not a large railway station compared to others that you would find along the line, well not as you'd expect from Ashford or the metropolis terminal at St Pancras, London. However, I had always considered it a pleasing rural monument to steam travel that offered comfortable amenities that were similar to the larger stations. I paid for my ticket, thanked the ticket clerk who wished me a pleasant journey, then picking up my service bag I stepped away to find an empty platform bench. I noticed a young couple on the opposite platform, obviously awaiting the southbound train. I nodded at them and smiled. They looked happy as they waved back, it was good to see somebody so happy once again.

I chose a bench away from the station foyer and close to the signal box, where I could be alone. It might have appeared unsociable to others, but necessary and I needed the solitude, where I could maintain a good vantage point both mentally and physically. The evening had grown darker as the night clouds merged with one another blanketing the sky in a patchwork mesh of dark grey. The moon tried to help every now and then by jumping out from behind a cloud to offer a few moments of night light before disappearing again.

I wish I could have appreciated it all and you'd have considered that a man in my current circumstances would have, but there were things about me that were beating at my low esteem, keeping me from rejoicing and wondering why me, why was I the lucky one!

Had you been at the Battle of Omdurman only a couple of months ago and survived, you would have considered yourself both fortunate and extremely lucky, but it wasn't the case, the bullet wounds to my leg, which had seen me treated at first in the field hospital, then later transported back to England had taken me away from the immediate danger. But landing up in a warm, comfortable and safe ward on the second floor of Guy's Hospital had only deepened the anxiety I felt at leaving my men, and my regiment back at the Sudan. I knew that I was lucky to be alive if only I could feel it.

To the thousands of wives and mothers, fathers and brothers of those that lay dead on the battlefield in the Sudan, never coming home, never again able to talk with, hold, hug and kiss, I must have appeared ungraciously selfish and unworthy of my rank, uniform or human existence. As I sat on the railway bench feeling dreadfully sorry for myself, I would have willingly swapped places with their loved ones right now. Death had cheated me or maybe it was the other way around. I could see the young couple looking my way and the young lady raised her hand and waved. I waved back feeling very guilty.

Not more than an hour ago I had met with my fiancée in the town. She was a beautiful young girl from Kent, the garden of England as it was known. She was the kind of female companion any man would have wanted in this dreadful war, a woman who had written so many times throughout the overseas campaign encouraging me to be careful and return safe and sound. Our promises to one another, before my embarkation of marriage upon my return now seemingly lost this night, just like the moon.

The meeting had been a difficult experience made all the more intolerable by my moodiness. Quite inexcusable I realise now, however when I had informed my fiancée that I had wanted more time to think about our life together, the situation had worsened. You know how things go, a man will utter forth a sentence not rightly considering the impact it can have on a woman whose sole purpose is full of romance, but whose resolve is destroyed in a single moment. I had not meant it to sound so final, I just needed the time to adjust as part of my recovery, but an argument had ensued ending with her running towards her home and I walking off in the opposite direction, ending up here at the railway station. It seemed as good a place as any to be sitting. I knew the young couple were talking about me. I looked out for the southbound train, willing it along, so that they would get on board and leave me to my solitude.

A shadow suddenly eclipsed the platform light to my left, I looked up to see the stationmaster standing before me. Seeing that I was an officer he graciously saluted me. I returned his courtesy.

'Begging your pardon, sir, but I regret to say that the train will be a few minutes late due to a stray cow that wandered onto the track this side of Down Much Haddam. It will only take a short while to remove the dead beast then the 8.40 p.m. will be with us.'

I thanked the stationmaster, but didn't really care how late the train would be. I had no particular hurry to be anywhere as my actual destination had yet to be decided. Time was also irrelevant, in fact nothing seemed to matter just now. I felt a sharp twinge shoot down my leg as I watched the elderly station man walk back down the platform to inform others travelling on the same train as he passed them by.

The engineer's whistle reverberated loudly along the walls of the brick tunnel before the train emerged in a long tongue of steam which licked wildly at the parapet wall overhead. I watched it approach and saw the driver lean out of the cab window acknowledging the signalman in his white box.

'Sorry, Bert. That cow took some shifting. Farmer had to use a carthorse and tackle in the end. Do we have anything running up behind?'

'No you're safe. Only a mail and coal train, but nothing's due till after 10 p.m.'

As the carriages slowed then passed me by I quickly scanned the windows looking for an empty coach. With a sudden escape of steam from the engine the train finally came to a halt. I picked up my service bag and opened the carriage door nearest me ignoring the other passengers further down the platform. I pulled shut the door and pulled down the window blind. Tonight was not a night to admire my reflection.

With a whistle from the guard's carriage the train slowly left the station. It crept past the young couple opposite as they both waved our departure. A pang of deepest guilt decided to embody itself in my stomach. I realised that I hadn't eaten since lunchtime. My stomach growled as I waved back and then I was alone again. I felt the rocking of the coach wheels as they raced along the track beneath and decided to hoist up my legs onto the carriage seat opposite before folding my arms.

I must have dozed off, exactly for how long I'm not sure because I woke again with a start, I could have sworn that a sudden breeze had entered the compartment. I lifted the cap from above my eyes where to my surprise on the seat opposite me sat a young 2nd lieutenant wearing the insignia of the 17th Fusiliers.

'Good evening, sir. I hope you don't mind my joining you, but I saw you rested here all alone and took the liberty to enter. I'm not that familiar with civilians just yet and a friendly army face from overseas will definitely help serve sooth the nerves.'

Company on the journey was the last thing that I had wanted or expected this night, but from the expression and the pallor of the young lieutenant's face I felt that I could not rightly refuse.

'You're welcome, Lieutenant, and it will help pass the time,' I lied although he would not have guessed. 'Although I warn you that I may not be much of a conversationalist on this journey.' Of course I had lied, didn't all senior ranks at some time. Anyhow I'd also decided it was time to stop feeling sorry for myself. I removed a metal object from my side pocket and offered a swig from my hip flask.

'Thank you kindly, sir.'

He gulped the contents, coughing embarrassingly as though it were his first for a very long time.

'My apologies, sir,' after he'd recovered. 'It's a while since I've tasted alcohol and good stuff too.' He handed back the flask.

'I see that you are an officer of the 21st Cavalry. You must have been close to Omdurman and General Sir Horatio Herbert Kitchener?'

I huffed more than laughed, but it surprised me for the emotion was my first in what had seemed a very long time. I thought or more daydreamed of nothing for a few seconds, private thoughts, before answering. 'I was probably the one that caught the bullet that had his name on it!'

The Lieutenant chuckled. Certainly I would expect not out of any disrespect, but men at war face death or injury in every heartbeat and to have caught another man's fated bullet might well be seen as bloody unfortunate. 'I hope the General appreciated it, sir!'

'I think so, Lieutenant, he personally saw me onto the hospital carriage, before returning to the field tent. That however was the end of my overseas campaign in the Sudan. I was shipped back to dear old England and ended up in Guy's. I'm not actually sure if it was to recuperate after the surgeons had removed the bullet or to try to poison me. The food was bloody awful and no better than what the field canteen produced.'

We both chuckled, knowing how ridiculous I must have sounded.

'How about you, Lieutenant? How did you get back to England?'

The young lieutenant looked at the door to the carriage then across at me. He was suddenly very serious with his reply. 'The Prime Minister and the War Office have drawn up a set of secret intelligence reports and strategy initiatives that they believe will help bring the war to a quick conclusion. I am on my way to London to collect these documents and then travel back overseas again delivering them personally to General Kitchener.'

'That's a very important mission, Lieutenant, but how come you are travelling on this line to London and why you personally?'

The Lieutenant took a small card from a wallet hidden somewhere inside of his tunic jacket and handed it to me. It was quite a bland card with only his name and the title 'MI6 – OHMS'.

'The Prime Minister has an audience with the King to appraise him of the situation overseas. I am to take delivery of the documents at Whitehall tomorrow morning.'

He suddenly came and sat beside me, before continuing.

'To answer your question, sir. I was secret service before the war, I still remain as such, but being with the regiment helps with my cover. My journey has been fraught with danger on several occasions since receiving my orders and I have had to change my route on a couple of occasions. I had a contact offer me intelligence that an assassin belonging to Muhammad Ahmad is out to stop me getting back to the Sudan. I ended up in Folkestone instead of my intended Dover as I'm sure somebody was definitely hot on my heels. In an attempt to throw a cold trail onto the route I decided to leave the port and visit my sister and my two young nieces at Loxley Heath.'

'Good God, wouldn't that have put them in danger too?'

'I feel sure it did not compromise their safety, sir. They live five miles outside of Folkestone and it's not that easy to follow somebody to their village without being spotted. I know the countryside best and rather than spend it in London where the opportunities are more plentiful for a trained assassin to succeed in his quest, I considered the countryside to be safer. Besides it's been three years since I have seen my sister and we are a very close family.'

There was a moment's silence as I recalled the events of my own evening. The awkward meeting with my fiancée, the argument and our walking away from one another.

'You take a great risk, Lieutenant. Do you think that a skilled assassin is not that clever and without any mercy?'

'I love them dearly, sir. My sister's husband and my niece's father, a chemist, died of pneumonia, a couple of years ago. Quite ironic that he could produce a remedy that could have prevented his death, only he was too ill to speak and tell the medical staff treating him. The death left my sister and nieces heartbroken. This was the first time I had been back to these shores and I felt it my duty to see them.'

I did not pursue the issue of the assassin. 'I'm sorry for their loss, Lieutenant, and I hope that they enjoyed seeing you!'

'I feel sure they did, sir.'

'Are you married, Lieutenant?'

'No, sir. I am betrothed to a farmer's daughter. Beth is her name. I haven't seen her either for the past three years since I left England. She's a fine girl. Has a strong mind and determined spirit. It took me a long time to win over her affection, but it was worth it in the end. It might be a while before I see her again, but we correspond as much as the war permits.'

I found the young lieutenant engaging and as much as I had wanted to be alone on the journey I was pleased to have his company.

'Tell me about where you live and what you intend to do when you come home, Lieutenant?'

The young officer looked up at me and if I had not known better I would have said that there was a lost look beyond his retinas. This was something not uncommon amongst servicemen. The hell of war goes deep, much deeper than any of us actually realises and death is the only release.

To the public that remain behind and wait we are portrayed as heroes, men of valour and fortitude, especially by the sensational press, but it is not until you are forced to live and breathe beside the many souls of your fellow men that you realise not just your own strengths and weaknesses, but that none of you, regardless of status, religion or belief are any different from any other man, friend or foe.

When the cries and the whistles sound to climb from the safety of a foxhole, jump the savagery of the wire and rush headlong across a field of crossfire towards an unknown enemy, no amount of prayer or self-belief can prevent your knees from wanting to buckle, your stomach to retch, or your spirit to be elsewhere. The enemy feels no different, of that I am sure.

The certainty of our death, the finality of war's embrace albeit in heaven or hell will hold short of solace to either side. I would go further to argue that all wars start and finish because of two ancient manuscripts. The Holy Bible and the Koran. Men who have faith, irrespective of whichever denomination will offer prayer to those going into battle, prayer for the Almighty to give strength in battle and a safe return, but rest assured that those same men will walk among the critically injured and the dead giving prayer once again, only this time asking the Lord or Allah to accept them into everlasting peace.

The one and only thing which has any common ground in any conflict is that there are no real winners, as time and death catch up with us all at some preordained moment in our earthly existence. Either way Gabriel or Jibril will be there to greet us.

Wars are the playgrounds of gods. Again my thoughts returned to my fiancée Sarah, was I playing God?

The Lieutenant interrupted my thoughts. 'When I'm home, not in the office, I'm an ordinary blacksmith working the forge with my younger brother. It's a good cover for my secret work. My brother's out there, you know, the Sudan. He's in the infantry. I haven't heard from him in a while, but I wish him well and pray that he's safe. I still live with my parents at Upper Stoke Weald about two miles beyond the home of my sister. My father is the vicar at St Peter-le-Poer and my mother a teacher at the local primary school. None of them know about my secret life. I don't feel it right to involve them.'

The Lieutenant gave a short curt laugh at the last part of my question.

'When I come home, sir, I intend to see my fiancée, drag her up the church path as fast as I can and marry the girl. Father had already put up notice and read the banns, but the Wednesday of that week, a week before our wedding my office superior gave me my papers and hence I was called to my regiment. We didn't really get the chance to say goodbye. I hope that all that good living on the farm hasn't broadened her girth, otherwise it will be another delay whilst the wedding dress is altered.'

'What say you, Lieutenant? Perhaps you too may not fit your shirt tails!'

We smiled at one another in a moment of normality. Just then the train slowed and seconds later the carriage passed beneath the lattice iron roof of St Pancras. Indeed the journey had passed quicker than expected. I stood up, replaced my cap upon my head and straightened my jacket. My travelling companion remained seated.

'We're here. Are you not coming, Lieutenant?' I asked.

'I will be presently, sir, but I'll hang back a bit and make sure that I wasn't followed. I don't want to involve you in anything sinister.'

'Thank you.' I held out my hand to my travelling companion and fellow officer.

The Lieutenant shook my hand then smartly stood to attention and saluted me. I returned his courtesy.

'Before I leave please tell me your name and I will be sure to come visit you and your wife following your return to England.'

'Thomas Frederick Marsh, sir, and you'll always be welcome.'

'Thank you, Thomas, and Godspeed with your quest.'

I turned the handle of the door and allowed it to swing open as the train travelled the last few feet to the buffers.

Then as the train hit the buffer, we both stood firm.

'I know it's not my place to say it, sir, but life can be cut short at any time and we should take every opportunity we have of happiness. I wish you good fortune, sir, and know that one day we will meet again.'

I smiled and stepped down from the carriage. I turned and pushed shut the door to give the impression that I had been the only person in the compartment, but to my surprise the compartment was empty, Lieutenant Marsh had already left. He really was a slippery customer to be sure, no wonder he'd been chosen for the mission back to the Sudan.

I breathed in the air of London as I walked along the platform towards the platform barrier and once again thought of Sarah. I stopped walking, looked up at the station ceiling where the moon was shining through the roof lights and there I questioned what the hell I was doing in London. Sarah was not the enemy, nobody was, only my stupidity. I was running away from a situation that should have only one ending. Before I reached the barrier I turned one last time to see if I could see 2nd Lieutenant Thomas Marsh, but still there was no sight of him. I turned around and handed the ticket collector my ticket.

'Is the ticket office still open as I need to purchase a return ticket?'

The ticket collector smiled almost knowingly.

'The passenger train left an hour ago, sir, but if the Captain don't mind getting the goods train, that train will be leaving in fifteen minutes from platform six. Joseph hasn't shut up shop yet, so you get along over there and get a ticket home.'

I thanked the ticket collector then ran across to the ticket office, calling out as I ran for Joseph to hold with the shutter.

The guard on the goods train didn't enquire why an army officer should be travelling amidst boxes, crates and other victuals, rather than a comfy passenger train, he just accepted my ticket and said that he'd make available his chair at the end of the carriage where there was a window. It must be in our heritage that makes us such an understanding nation of peoples, where questions of the mind go unanswered.

As the goods train pulled into Morten Sydenham the hour hand was just approaching 6 a.m. and sunrise was on the horizon. The journey on the goods train had been slower coming back as goods were distributed or collected along the way. I thanked the guard, stretched my limbs and picked up my service bag. I had just started to walk back along the platform when the porter taking delivery of the early morning papers walked over to me.

'Begging the officer's pardon, I wondered if you'd be interested in an early edition.'

Reading was the thing furthest from my mind, as I just wanted to see and be with Sarah, but I thanked him anyway and slipped the paper into the side pocket of my bag. It was a short walk to Sarah's parents' house and as I walked I reasoned with myself as to what exactly I was going to say, what precisely could I offer as an excuse for my totally irrational behaviour the night before?

By the time I reached her front gate the debate in my mind was still raging, but my composure was steadfast. I couldn't say the same for my courage however. I looked at my watch realising that it was only 6.45 a.m. I had no wish to wake Sarah or her parents at this hour so I sat on the front garden bench seat listening to the early song of the birds.

I remembered the paper the station porter had given me. The front page was about General Kitchener's successful campaign to recapture the Sudan. Skilled illustrators had drawn cartoon images of what they believed was correct, but in reality they were far from the truth. I felt indifferent to the article, instead I turned the page to find something different.

I still cannot tell you why, not even to this day, I felt my eyes drawn to a small article, a news report in the bottom left-hand crease of the paper. I read the reporter's version of events twice in disbelief.

Sometime during the afternoon of yesterday the body of an army officer, believed to have been in the regiment of the 17th Fusiliers, was found amongst wooden crates in a warehouse in the storage depot at Folkestone Docks. Enquiries with the regiment's headquarters and identification found on the young man name him as 2nd Lieutenant Thomas Frederick Marsh. It would appear that Lieutenant Marsh had been stabbed in the back resulting in his death. The regiment had no idea why one of its officers should be in Folkestone and said that the matter was being investigated. No assailant had been apprehended or seen in the vicinity. The case remains a mystery.

I closed the paper more in shock than in horror. My thoughts returned to our journey to London and how much Thomas had wanted to see his sister and his two nieces. How he was waiting for the war to be over to be with Beth again. How Thomas Marsh had been my travelling companion when he was already dead. Now I'm a man of firm resolve and not given to fantasy or speculation, but I could not fathom the reasoning troubling my thoughts however hard I tried. Somehow though I knew that Thomas had been with me on that train for a reason. I looked skyward. It's ironic we do that, whatever our religious beliefs we all do it.

A sudden shrill cry of relief pierced the silence from an upstairs window as Sarah yelled my name and then she was gone. I heard the unlocking of the front door.

I looked up again as Sarah emerged beyond the open door and came running towards me. I silently thanked Thomas Frederick Marsh and I knew that destiny would one day see us meet again.

WE ALMOST MADE IT BIG

Like every good robbery it was planned with meticulous precision. Every aspect of the job had been surveyed, double-checked and rechecked. We knew the times, the schedules and even those smallest details that every criminal gang always seemed to miss or just never considered. We had watched the police too, when they came on shift, when they went off shift and we got to know the faces of the officers who worked the area. We had even rented a house to watch those that might be watching us too, you know the ones I mean the curtain twitchers, normally the old ladies.

So there you have it the prelims of our intended crime. Let me introduce the gang. First there was Henry the Hatchet, a quiet man who thought a lot. I had never asked if he actually owned a hatchet, but Henry got his name because he supplied the tools for any job. Henry was the man for meticulous detail and when the plan had been hatched Henry had telephoned the weather centre to check on the long-range forecast for that day, as I said a very thoughtful man. Now don't you go getting me wrong though just because our Henry might be quiet, he was a big man, broad as well as being tall, not normally given to having a funny side to his docile nature and neither was laughter high on his list of appealing characteristics so nobody dared question his reasoning, they simply accepted that Henry was always right.

Henry advised us that it was going to be good weather on the day of the robbery, cloudy with spells of sunshine, interspersed with the odd shower of summer rain, but the gentle breeze would blow it all away to settle before the evening. All in all we considered that Henry hadn't left much more to chance and had most of the weather fronts covered. He would have made a good weather forecaster on the Six O'Clock News had he not possessed a garage full of tools.

Then there was Jules the Jelly. The good solid member of the gang, but worryingly and still the medical profession didn't know why he had an unexplained wobble to him as he walked or knelt. His body always seemed to be on the move and especially his hands, which when you consider that his main role in the gang was the man who supplied and set the dynamite it was extremely worrying. Nobody really wanted to be standing alongside Jules at a job with his jitters, but he was reputed to be the best in the business so he got our vote.

And then we come to Bob the Blast, my best friend from our days at school. Some folks that we know say that Bob is just a very funny man, because everything he did in life always had a funny story attached to it. To me personally though Bob was a real blast, he never meant to be that funny, he just always found himself in the right place at the wrong time. Oh, don't get me wrong Bob's timing was impeccable, as were his explanations especially to the various associates of the law, it's just that whenever he tried to vindicate himself he only succeeded in making people fall about with laughter, even some judges before they passed sentence.

I'll give you an example. I remember there was one time when Bob had done a job at the jeweller's in the High Street. Not always the best place to be doing a job especially on your doorstep so to speak, however when the police had nabbed him for breaking and entering a butcher's shop, he'd tried to explain to the officers that it had all been a big mistake, he'd meant to do the jeweller's instead. Standing before the custody sergeant and arresting officers they almost split their sides laughing. Only, you see, the butcher's had been the jeweller's previously, until the owner retired. But as Bob told the judge and the jury, the shopfront looked like the jeweller's only it still had the same metal mesh security shutter just like all jewellery merchants have and that's what had confused him.

It wasn't until the butcher, a man from our northern shores gave his evidence and told the court that he'd seen no reason to change it when he'd bought the shop from the jeweller that the penny dropped for poor old Bob. The butcher further promoted that the shutter had served him well especially at Christmas time when he'd had a big batch of black Norfolk turkeys out back in the cold store. So there you go, as I said poor old Bob, right place, wrong time. Now had Bob not been doing a five-year stretch at Her Majesty's pleasure at Maidstone Prison for a burglary at the local recycling plant, another story for some other time maybe, he'd have known the jeweller had retired and sold the premises to the butcher. Some say that you could hear the laughter in the jury room as they deliberated the case.

I really liked my mate Bob and he was great fun to have around especially at family and Christmas parties. Before I forget, I suppose you're wondering why Bob's called Bob the Blast, well it's because he's the backup jelly man to Jules, just in case his jitters get too bad and we need a trigger man to flick the switch on the detonator.

And lastly there's me. My name's Frank the Fence, I'd like to think the brains of the outfit, but maybe it's best that I start off by telling you that at school my annual class report always said the same thing, that I excelled with my hands, but lacked the mental application that I needed to be a lawyer. Pity that because I could have represented myself on quite a few various occasions in the past. Good at sport, they said, but my top grades were in metalwork and woodwork. I'd always found the practical know-how of using a blowtorch very gratifying. My old dad was so proud of my achievements at school especially the fishing box I made him when I was fifteen. It's a pity I can't say the same of him now though.

Now with talents like mine you'd have expected me to have left school and joined a fencing manufacturer or forged a living as a blacksmith, but not with hands like mine, I found instead that I had a natural talent for wheeling and dealing as you might put it and I'd rather turn a batch of the green readies than work a lathe. Somebody would offer me some goods, which I'd buy, then applying some of that missing mental application I'd find somebody else that had a use for those goods, so they'd buy them from me. Good business sense I'd say and profitable at the end of the day. Teachers cannot always be right.

I can't really say in all sincerity that I'm overly keen on my being referred to as a fence or the whole dictionary implication behind it. I've only ever really considered myself to be just an honest business entrepreneur who delivers a service to the needy. In fact you could say I was a latter-day Robin Hood. It's a real pity that the authorities didn't see it the same way, but in my defence I'm not always party to prior knowledge as to the origin of stock and I cannot be held responsible if some of it turns out to be hot or illegal. My old mum used to tell me, 'Ignorance is blind and the man who loses his white stick is lost forever.' I've never really worked that one out, but then she was of Mandarin Chinese origin. I did ask Bob once if he knew its meaning, but his school reports were similar to mine, probably because we always sat beside one another in class.

So that's done with the introductions, let's get back to the job in hand. I had been sitting opposite my old dad last week one evening as he read the late edition of the *Evening Post*, when he'd suddenly flicked over to the next page to read his horoscope and there on my side of the paper was a full-page advert about an ancient artefact from China being exhibited at our local Castle Museum. I studied the picture in the advert, it represented an ancient warrior's shield and had a look about it that expressed it could be valuable. It had a rounded metallic appearance and a strange patterned facia encrusted with inset red rubies, or at least they looked like rubies and there were lots of them, most certainly enough for four men to share. I was reading the times of the exhibition when my mother entered the room with a tray of tea. She saw the advert.

'Ah, I know this fling, it velly old.' She put down the tray and took the paper from my father as she studied the shield more closely. 'Yes, it flom imperial emperors' time, Qin dynasty.'

I looked at my father and he looked at me in surprise, we didn't realise that she knew about such things, but then father didn't really know much of my mother's history as they'd met in a gambling den somewhere in darkest Soho. That did it for me though, it was all that I needed to hear only I'd read about the Qin dynasty in school. If that chink of armour was as old as the dynasty and the rubies were real then it must have been worth a mint.

I left them both in the room as I went into the hall where I quickly rang around and in less than half an hour Henry, Jules, Bob and me were sat in the snug of the local pub armed with four pints.

'Your call sounded urgent, Frank,' enquired Jules, 'what's up?'

I showed them the cut-out of the museum newspaper advert, I'd left the rest of the paper with my father. I watched them as they each studied the advert looking at the shield then at me. It was the mask of blank expressions etched on their faces that prompted me to think of my mother's old saying, perhaps this is what she'd meant.

'That's a Qin dynasty warrior's shield from around 221–206 BC,' I exclaimed, 'and it's probably worth a mint. Look at the rubies!'

Bob leant forward to get a closer look. 'They look as big as my dog's eyes. What do you reckon it's worth, Frank?'

I sat back on my stool and tried to look entrepreneurial, then gave the question my best shot. 'To be honest I'm not entirely sure, Bob, too many blood-reds to put an exact value on it and of course it all depends on the colour, the deeper the red the more their worth, but the whole thing's bound to be worth a fortune. My old mum says it's a Qin warrior's shield and I guess only somebody like Sotheby's would sell them and for millions.

'I'm in,' said Henry, raising his right hand.

'But you haven't heard the job yet,' I remarked, 'and put your hand down, Henry, you look like you need the loo or something.'

But to tell the truth we were all in. We sat there till closing time discussing the job, planning how it was to be executed, how much the shield could be worth and how I would fence it. A week later Bob and Jules visited the museum posing as tourists, snapping photographs all over the museum and especially the room containing the shield. Discreetly they recorded the locations of the closed-circuit cameras, stood beside security beams mentally noting the heights, they snapped the mosaic-patterned tiles on the floor, why exactly I don't know, but I think it was for Jules's wife who was interested in interior design and finally the construction of the door to the room. Most important though were their photographs of the mounted glass case that housed the Qin warrior's shield.

Henry and I did the footwork. We followed the officer around on his beat, we hopped in and out of shop doorways observing the number of patrol cars as they passed us by. We sat up the road from the police station and observed officers arriving for duty or clocking off on their way home again. We even did the same overtime as them as we waited patiently in our car until they went home. Henry said that the overtime probably meant they'd caught somebody in the right place at the wrong time. I hoped that Bob was at home with his feet up.

I rented the house opposite the museum for a three-month period informing the landlord that I was an insurance assessor trying to catch benefit frauds. When I'd originally phoned to make the appointment to view the house, he asked for cash up front over the phone, but for some inexplicable reason had changed his mind when we met stating that payment could either be made by cheque or banker's order if it suited me better. Naturally I paid him cash anyhow knowing that he wouldn't bother us again.

On the day we were due to do the job despite Henry's prior telephone call to the weather centre, we all decided that it was too bold and too blatant to do the job during daylight hours and so we took a vote and opted for a night-time raid instead. We decided it would be that night, Harry said there'd be a full moon. A good thing and a bad thing to any burglar.

We set and synchronised our watches for 9.20 p.m. The plan was that Jules would blow open the rear door of the museum as Bob threw a diversionary house brick through the glass-panelled doors at the front reception. This would give us an additional few extra minutes to escape. Like all good coppers they would bowl in through the obvious point of entry and

83

especially where there was a gaping great hole in the glass.

If we got our timing right we would catch the local police station on the customary duty changeover at ten o'clock when off-going patrols arrived back ten minutes prior to the hour and on-coming patrols wouldn't hit the streets again until ten minutes past the hour, finishing off their briefing cuppa and the duty sergeant's instructions. There were only ever two patrol cars on at night so once they were both on scene outside of the museum, we calculated that the route to the railway station would be clear.

Having created an opening in reception Harry would then enter the building, locate the fuse box and with the assistance of a useful screwdriver short-circuit the museum power. Bob and Jules around the back would go in via the rear door then make their way to the exhibition room where Jules would niftily open the security door applying his gifted talent.

Now you might ask what my job was in all of this daring raid. Well, as I've told you, I am commonly referred to as the brains of the outfit. Tonight was my moment to show the gang that I had the right reputation. At precisely 10.08 p.m. I went to the railway station where I used the public telephone box around the corner. I dialled 999 and informed the emergency police operator that a large group of youths were fighting in the ticket hall of the station. This would ultimately dispatch both cars, the only two night-time cars from the police station to the other side of the town. The railway station was at least six to seven minutes across town from the museum and this would give Bob sufficient time to smash the display cabinet and grab the Qin warrior's shield.

We would then all meet outside the railway station at 10.30 p.m. in time to get on the 10.40 to Doncaster. And what about the tickets I hear you ask? No problem as I had already purchased four one-way tickets before making the call from the box around the corner. This way the ticket clerk will only have seen one of us and my use of a false beard and moustache would prevent him giving the police any proper visual identification.

As planned the job proceeded like clockwork, almost down to the second. Jules added the jelly, Henry donated the museum a house brick and Bob relieved them of a warrior's shield, with

84

the local council providing a large black plastic waste-bin liner that Henry found in the fuse cupboard. It was nice to know that you get something back on the rates.

They told me later that as the three of them had emerged from around the street behind the museum in a stolen van and turned left into the High Street, two police cars had screeched to a halt outside the museum front reception doors, or to be precise what was left of them, and as predicted they all ran in through Henry's open door!

Dumping the van at the side of the railway station in a darkened corner we anticipated that it wouldn't be found until the next morning when the early morning train drivers arrived. By then we would be long gone.

As the station clock hand dropped onto twenty-five past the hour Henry, Jules and Bob walked beneath the brick arch and saw me waiting inside the station concourse by the empty flower stall. Following the plan Henry and Jules walked past me ignoring my presence and proceeded across to the late-night tea bar where under a seat by the corner table Jules found the concealed envelope containing the two train tickets that I had left there earlier. Henry had under his arm an artist's black canvas-carrying case. Inside was the Qin warrior's shield.

Bob ignored me also as he went into the gentlemen's washroom. He found his ticket lying on top of the stack of paper hand towels inside the dispenser unit. I checked my watch against the station clock. It was approaching 10.29 p.m. We'd made good time. It was time to get the train. The platform porter clipped my ticket as I watched the others walk down the platform and board the train.

As the guard blew his whistle and the train driver released the brake lever then engaged the throttle handle I felt the train move away from the platform. I peered out of the carriage window back down to the ticket hall and the station concourse. Not a policeman in sight, we'd done it, we'd pulled off the perfect crime. Nobody got hurt, only the pride of the museum curator, the police and the insurance company. In the process we had only damaged a few panes of glass, a couple of doors, a glass display cabinet and the museum's fuse board. There wasn't much left for the police to investigate. All in all so far it had been a good night's work.

Closing the door to my coach compartment I walked along the interconnecting corridor towards the back of the train where minutes later and unseen I walked into the compartment where Henry, Jules and Bob were seated. We congratulated and smiled at one another. Bob had the biggest smile on his face only for once it was a case of right place, right time! However, before we started to blow the fanfare trumpets of success we had still stage two of the plan to complete. As Henry pulled down the night blinds we sat back down again and went over the final details. We checked, set and synchronised our watches again. I then left the three of them as I proceeded along to the next section of the train.

Selecting a coach almost at the front of the train I found a seat that would suit my purpose just fine. On the opposite seat was a gentleman who was fast asleep and my ideal candidate to help initiate the next stage of our plan. Sitting down opposite him I checked my watch, 10.55 p.m., the time to act was now. I groaned rather loudly holding my stomach as if in considerable discomfort. As expected the gentleman woke with a start, then looked straight across at me and my predicament.

'Do you need help?' he enquired full of concern as I continued to writhe convincingly.

I just nodded which alarmed him all the more to think that I could not speak as the pain was so severe.

He stood up and informed me that he was going to get the guard, then with that he left the compartment. I smiled to myself, perfectly enacted just as planned.

In the coach near to the rear of the train the other three saw a worried man run past their compartment then minutes later reappear with the guard, both heading towards the front of the train. This was their cue. Harry opened the compartment door and followed the man and the guard keeping a coach length's distance between them, whilst Jules and Bob slipped out of the carriage compartment in the opposite direction, heading for the guard's carriage with the artist's bag.

I heard the guard open the door and step up beside me.

'Evening, sir, can I be of any assistance? This gentleman said you looked as though you'd been taken quite ill?'

I looked up at the guard and the gentleman with a smile which surprised them both. 'I would thank you both kindly and for your generous concern for my welfare, but I think the moment has luckily passed. I had a fish supper not too long ago and I believe a bad prawn to have been the culprit. I expect the blighter disagreed with being boiled just as my stomach disagreed with his arrival.'

Relieved the guard proffered a salute to acknowledge that all was well. It was a nice easy resolution to the problem and meant that he could return to his own supper of sandwiches and treacle tart. As the guard left and closed our compartment door the gentleman passenger sat down opposite me again. He didn't look very happy.

'I really am very grateful to you,' I said by way of an excuse for my earlier interruption of his sleep, 'but perhaps I will get a breath of fresh air at the corridor window, it will probably complete my recovery.' With that I left the compartment as the gentleman rested his head against the headrest once again, watching me with one eye still open and the other shut just in case I decided upon another bizarre farce.

I rejoined Henry, Bob and Jules again as we contemplated the success of the second phase of our daring plan. Bob proudly announced that the ancient Qin warrior's shield had been safely transferred into one of the postal bags in the guard's van and was headed for Doncaster under the watchful eye of the guard. Unsuspectingly he provided the perfect alibi, and he wouldn't be suspected as he unloaded the postal bag at Doncaster Station, should any quick-witted detective put two and two together back at the museum.

'Grand,' I said. 'Part two complete. We've just got the last part of the plan to see through at Doncaster sorting office then we're home and dry.' I asked Bob what it felt like to succeed and not get caught.

'Best job I've ever been on,' he told us, And the prospects of him being at my Christmas party were looking very favourable this year. 'At least I can have turkey with you and Doreen,

Frank, instead of eating with 300 other blokes!'

We all laughed and even that bad prawn felt better too.

To make our arrival at Doncaster Station all the more convincing we split us again and walked through the train selecting a different coach from which to disembark from the train. I spent the remainder of the journey, contemplating and wondering just whom I could trust to negotiate the sale of the shield with.

Normally I would use Bargain Bert from Bradford, but this was a piece of ancient history and way out of his league. Then there was Charitable Charlie from Cheltenham. Not always as charitable as you'd expect, but occasionally on a good day, he could offer a good price, but Charlie could be dodgy and he didn't always appreciate the finer things in life. Occasionally too some of his stuff would end up with the Sally Army on behalf of his old mum and her sister working for the William Booth brigade. The Qin dynasty warrior's shield wasn't exactly the right charitable piece to be ending up in the Citadel Bazaar.

As the night-time outside flashed by with Doncaster approaching fast I suddenly flicked my fingers together, I'd got it. Antique Alex from Aldershot. He was the ideal bloke albeit way down south. Alex wasn't exactly my cup of tea either as the bloke thought he was a real connoisseur of the arts and even his bloody antiques shop was named after Alexander the Great. But I was sure he thought he was related because he was real mustard about antiques and he knew a thing or two about fine art and he could probably fence the rubies for us.

At last the train pulled into Doncaster Station. I stepped down from the coach and onto the platform sucking in the night air. I ignored Henry, Bob and Jules as they headed towards the barrier and through to the exit beyond. Instead I chose a platform bench where I could watch the guard and the station porters unload the postal sacks from the train. Even if the police stopped any of us or maybe all of us now, there would be no way of connecting us with the stolen Qin dynasty exhibit. We simply didn't have it.

As I watched the mailbags being loaded onto the trolley I saw the red top of the post office van pull up to the side of the platform. Part three of our plan was about to be executed. I watched two porters push the laden trolley beyond the barrier and down the slope to where the van was waiting.

As the train departed from the station the guard saw me waiting near to the exit. He leant out of the window as the guard's van passed by and called out, 'Hope you feel better soon!'

I waved and muttered beneath my breath, 'I feel like a million dollars already.'

I quickly left the station and joined the others in a waiting taxicab. Henry gave the driver the name of a street near to the sorting office, where he could drop us off and then we were on our way to the last part of our plan.

The cab driver was a jovial sort of chap enquiring where we'd been for the evening. We told him Hull to watch the match, it was our good fortune that he said rugby was his game, he didn't really care much for football so he didn't enquire about the score. The sorting office was only ten minutes' drive away from the station, so we didn't have long before we'd arrive. I went over the final execution in my mind.

Jules would drop a small incendiary device into the large metal dustbins around the side of the sorting office. Henry would break in through a washroom window and trigger the fire alarm. With the building evacuated Henry would open the emergency door and allow access for myself, Bob and Jules. It wouldn't take us long to find the postal bag from the train, Bob had sprayed one of the corners red, it would stand out a mile from the others. I peeked down at my watch, not long now and we'd be there.

The cab driver gabbled on as they always do, talking about anything and everything just to pass the time and make another journey seem twice as long. I ignored his mutterings as we proceeded down through the High Street, observing the red postal vans as one by one they passed us on the opposite carriageway. I'd already counted four or five when another two came around the corner. Even the cab driver mentioned that it was strange. 'Don't normally turn out till early morning,' he said, 'and I bet sometimes they're carrying a fortune.'

I heard somebody chuckle inside the cab, but didn't take notice who. The route from the station to the sorting office was flashing mentally through my mind, the sorting office should be just around the next bend. We were almost there, we'd soon be rich men.

However, what confronted us as we turned the corner wiped the smiles and anticipation from our faces. Her Majesty's mail sorting office was ablaze from end to end. Blue flashing lights from fire engines and police cars pirouetted the walls of residential houses and other small factories nearby. Suddenly a policeman raised his hand and halted the taxi.

'Sorry, gentleman, I cannot let you go any further, orders of the fire brigade.'

Jules who was occupying the front seat leant across the cab driver and asked 'What happened?'

As the policeman spoke we all sat in silence watching our fortune go up in smoke. He told us that a local burglar had been seen entering the sorting office about twenty minutes ago, but had been spotted by a night worker who'd called the police. Apparently he was after postal orders for Christmas. A chase had ensued and other night workers had joined in until eventually he'd been cornered. When the first police officers arrived they were directed to the corner of the sorting office where the man was cornered only he wasn't going without a fight. The burglar threw a match into the 'Lost and Found' section which was full of old, dusty cardboard, paper and goodness knows what other parcels. The place was like a tinderbox. We didn't need to know the rest, it was evidently there in front of us.

The four of us sat there momentarily open-mouthed, silent, and totally dumbfounded. Our master plan, our big job, our valuable prize was there before us going up in smoke. We paid the taxi driver the fare then got out to watch our future leap skyward as the flames got higher and higher. I noticed the uniform of a postal night worker as he walked towards us on the opposite pavement, a cigarette in his hand. I crossed the road to stop him, as the taxi driver accelerated and tooted as he left us. I saw Bob wave goodbye.

'Is everything destroyed?' I reluctantly asked.

'More or less everything,' he said. 'They only managed to save the bags from the Doncaster arrival.'

Optimism suddenly beat a heavy fist upon the door of my heart. 'What? How?' I almost screamed.

The others looked my way.

'That copper over there stopped the van before it travelled down the road. The night supervisor has turned around any deliveries and headed them back to the railway station. They will catch the interconnecting train back to Hull, where they'll be re-sorted and the senders informed.'

With a heavy slam the door of my heart shut tight. I walked over to where Henry, Jules and Bob stood. They could see by the look on my face it was not good news. I explained about the returning train to Hull and that our prized booty was probably already being loaded onto the Hull night express. We saw the taxicab turn the corner back into the High Street and then he was gone, we would never make it back to the station in time even if we found another ride. I realised too that by the time we got back to Hull the next morning the sorting office would have found the Qin dynasty warrior's shield and handed it back over to the police. As we turned and slowly trudged our way back towards the high road, we said nothing. We knew we were still free men, but Lady Luck had finally deserted us this night. We had been so close for once.

It was a night that none of us would ever forgot. There were other nights of course, pints in the pub and more planned jobs. Bob did manage to make the Christmas party this year and we all had a great time, but sadly he won't be at next year's do. Maidstone Prison has his company once more. Poor old Bob, wrong place, right time and Christmas dinner with several hundred other blokes.

We all went to his trial, as was customary, and as the judge passed sentence and Bob was sent down he looked up at the three of us sitting in the gallery, he winked and then gave us the thumbs up. We knew what he meant because this sentence would pass very quickly and it wouldn't be long before we were all together again. I watched Bob descend the stone steps down from the dock and thought about that night back in November of last year when we almost made it big, if only for a few hours.

PIRATES ABOARD

To a young boy of twelve years of age the thought of going on a train journey, any train journey was in itself an adventure like no other. Every boy at some time during his childhood had lay awake at night watching as the moon had moved across the bedroom windowpane and imagined himself standing on the footplate of a steam train. The roar from the furnace as the engineer applied more coal was like keeping a restless dragon at bay, whilst the steam bubbling away in the boiler hissed like an angry snake eager to strike. So much power and yet so easily released by the gentle pull on the throttle handle. Tell me the name of the boy that didn't want to drive that train and I will tell you that he is a liar.

So when my parents told me that we were travelling to Scotland early the next morning by train I could not wait to go to bed that evening and begin my dream. I had never been to Scotland before, but I had heard that it was gigantic, huge in fact and a whole country by itself; and that's why the Roman emperor had built a wall across it to keep unwanted visitors away from their land, why he'd wanted to do that though I wasn't quite sure. The moon was absent from my bedroom tonight, but still the shadows danced playfully about as I gave the order to the fireman to get ready another shovel of coal.

King's Cross is like no other railway station that I know, comprising an imposing grand main building reaching skyward tipped at the corners with towers and spires, as ornately carved stone windows watch out across the Euston Road checking upon the arrival and departure of the many rail travellers. Then beside this grandiose structure sits a much simpler building, but of equal architectural beauty consisting of two great arched windows which look over a vast train shed. But if you could get closer you would see that the glass windows are patterned in a mosaic of thin-layered soot-laden steam from the many locomotives that adorn the hidden kingdom of George Turnbull assisted by the Cubitt brothers, Lewis and Thomas.

I had on many occasion before walked past the facade of the station and had always wanted to go inside, if only to admire its busy thoroughfare and see the trains, but my parents were such busy people and different priorities had always beckoned upon their working itinerary. But today however, was very different, today I could stand outside of the grand magnificence of this Victorian design and revel in the fact that I was actually going inside. I looked up at the compass dial clock that adorned the middle of the two arched windows noting that it had just ticked its way past 7.30 a.m. on a bright sunny June morning and from the inside I could hear the disquiet of the trains as steam hissed angrily from the belly of the engine, inviting passengers to board quickly so that their journey could begin. As we walked beneath the stone archway I didn't know what to look at first as there was so much to see and take in. It was like entering a walled city within a city.

I stood proudly beside my father as he paid the rail fares and collected three tickets from the clerk, then he handed me mine. He told me to keep it safe otherwise our adventure might be lost should it be mislaid. I looked at the long ticket reading every printed word, but it was the main element of the journey from King's Cross, London, to Dundee, Scotland, that I absorbed the most. The ticket-office clerk peered over the counter to look at me.

'And what an adventure there is before you, young master,' he declared. 'You'll enjoy it and be sure you pick a good seat.'

I thanked him and wondered how many times he'd said the same thing to all the other boys and girls that passed through the station, not that it really mattered because today this was my adventure.

Suddenly the shrill cry of a train whistle captured what

thoughts I had about the journey and instead I quickly reached down and eagerly grabbed hold of the handles of my bag then fell in step alongside my parents. At the gated wrought-iron barrier the stationmaster clipped the corner of my ticket and smiled.

'Ah,' he proclaimed in a seemingly expectant manner, 'we've been waiting for you to join us, young master.'

I looked at him somewhat puzzled.

'Many's the time we at the station have seen you walk past, but never come in to join us, but we knew there would be a day that you would. I am sure that you will find this journey to be very special and who knows you might even find a friend on board.'

I wondered who he could be referring to, as the journey to Scotland only involved the three of us and we weren't due to meet anybody known to us along the route. I put my clipped ticket in my blazer pocket for safekeeping.

As we walked down the platform beneath the latticed roof overhead, my mother who was beside me placed a hand on my arm. 'You see, Matthew, it is just as we told you, that this holiday would be an adventure that you would never forget.'

My father looked across and nodded approvingly and as usual I knew that they would be right. Father was a barrister-at-law and this holiday was our first in over five years and excitingly it was to be spent at my mother's ancestral home in Dundee.

About a week ago my mother had tried to explain her ancestral past to me, but even she had admitted that there were some important letters of correspondence that had been mislaid over the years and other vital documents which had been lost or destroyed, all of which could have provided the proof we needed to be sure that the inheritance was rightly ours. I was aware that both Mother and Father thought the quest almost impossible, but for the immediate present as Matthew Byrne the only son of Mary and James Byrne, I was the last in our ancestral line so as far as I was concerned the inheritance was more than safe. I am glad also that I didn't have a sister to lay claim on any fortune either as I had no interest in girls whatsoever. I was only twelve remember.

We arrived at the carriage door where Father opened it for Mother and secured our bags inside. He asked if I would like to walk down to the end of the platform and take a look at the engine with him. Mother secretly knew that it was he who really wanted to see the locomotive. She good-naturedly patted his shoulder and told him to take me, but not to be too long. I noticed the affectionate smile that he gave her, which pleased me to see him relaxed again and away from the stresses of his work. I know Mother noticed too that the lines on his face had disappeared as she smiled back at him before we both stepped back down onto the platform.

'Come on, Matthew,' he said. 'I've been waiting for weeks to see this locomotive engine, it's rather a special train.'

We stepped away increasing our pace both eager to be beside the magnificent beast as it disgorged huge volumes of steam and soot.

And magnificent it was. The enormity of its engine was as enthralling as I had imagined. I stood beside the huge metal wheels feeling rather small, then we walked to the front of the engine where I turned and took in the full splendour of the whole train. It snaked its way back along the platform for a good couple of hundred feet at least. I had never seen anything so wonderful. As we traced our way back alongside the engine I counted the number of wheels, marvelling at the size of the piston cylinders that sat above the big-end bearing. In all I counted six large and four small wheels beneath the main body of the train, with an additional ten more beneath the crew cab and coal truck.

The engineer suddenly leant out and saw Father and myself inspecting his train, he kindly invited us up onto the footplate for a closer inspection. Father thanked him then hoisted me onto the first tread of the metal steps. I could not believe that I was actually standing in the engineer's cab of the *Flying Scotsman*. The most famous steam train of the era. I knew that my school friends would never believe me. I wanted so much to live out my dream and scoop a shovelful of coal into the furnace, but the engineer said that it was such dirty work and my mother would not have thanked him for it, but I wouldn't have minded. Instead I had to be content in watching as he tossed shovel after shovel into the furnace reeling away as the intense heat seared my cheeks. This was much better than my dreams. Regrettably for us both Father said that we had better rejoin Mother as he gratefully shook hands with the engineer. I did the same ignoring the patch of soot that crested my palm. It was real coal soot from the *Flying Scotsman*, it would be a pity to wash it off later that night.

Father sat next to Mother as I stood looking out of the compartment window waiting for the train to move telling her about our visit to the locomotive's cab and how the engineer had shook our hands at the end. She tried to wipe my hand clean, but I refused and to help justify the moment Father held up his own palm which was dirtier than my own. She smiled at us both then desisted asking again. I think secretly she was pleased he had enjoyed the visit as much as I had. This was all so exciting and we were in first class too.

I watched as the other passengers arrived, some running down the platform as the stationmaster waved his flag and reached for his piped whistle. I heard the guard shout out then with a blast on the engine whistle the train started to move away. I waved at the stationmaster who acknowledged as we went by.

'Bon voyage, young master,' he said and then he disappeared in a cloud of smoke.

Mother interpreted for me.

I waved too at the signalman in his large white-painted wooden box, watching as he pulled down hard on the long brass levers feeling the carriage jump the crossover points heading us north out of the station towards the small suburb of Hornsey and beyond.

Then as I closed the window a wisp of white smoke dashed inside our compartment filling it with segments of soot. I tried to catch it between my hands, but it disappeared as quickly as it had appeared. I thought of the engineer racking up more coal into the mouth of the dragon as we increased in speed. I would have given anything to have been back on the footplate again. Finally I sat down and with my nose pressed against the window I watched the world pass us by. I tried to count the number of terraced houses on my side of the train, but there were far too many to record so instead I observed the different contours of the rooftops as they cascaded up and down and the array of chimneys that stood tall like soldiers guarding the residents below. A flock of gulls perched along a brick wall at the end of a garden suddenly took flight as we steamed on ahead, emerging the other side of the smoke cloud like hooded monks in white cloaks. I took it all in not realising that the adventure had actually begun.

We passed beneath the footbridge at Hornsey Station where the engine smoke cut itself in half resembling a forked tongue and I imagined the people crossing the bridge becoming engulfed as it travelled on through the station leaving them coughing loudly in its wake. We had left the outskirts of London and the rolling hills of the countryside started to merge into one another resembling an artist's painted landscape as the continuous green of trees, shrubs and fields became laboriously boring, I yearned for something new to engage my time, not realising just how long the journey was ahead.

I tried to read a book that Father had borrowed from his practice waiting room, but in the absence of any pictures the chapters failed to interest me. I flicked my wrist over and looked at my watch a present from last Christmas, it was only five past eight. Then in the distance I saw the long facade of Alexandra Palace with its tall radio mast. I wondered who had to climb to the top to keep it clean. As I fumbled in my pocket I remembered my ticket, I took it out to make sure nothing had changed. It wasn't until I turned it over that I realised the flip side had on it a printed image of the *Flying Scotsman*. The train was speeding along a track somewhere in Scotland I imagined as there were mountains in the background, much different to the hills beyond our window and beneath the palace grounds.

Just then an enquiring voice with a distinct lilt announced in my direction from somewhere opposite our seat. 'I've got one of those too!'

I looked up to see a boy similar to my age standing at the end of my seat. He proceeded to open the front cover of a hardback book and produce from within a train ticket similar to my own, only a slightly different colour.

'I hope we don't have to give them over at the end of the journey as I want to keep mine as a souvenir,' he said.

'Me too,' I exclaimed. I stood up to introduce myself. 'Hello, I'm Matthew Byrne and we're going to Dundee in Scotland on holiday. What's your name?' My new-found friend stretched out his hand and announced, 'Pleased to meet you, Matthew Byrne, my name is Lloyd Stevenson.'

'Wow,' I proclaimed, 'surely not one of the Stephenson family of the famous *Rocket*?' I gasped.

Our conversation had made Father look up from his book. He winked at me and I wondered if as a boy he'd had a conversation similar to ours about famous inventions with boys his own age. It had been a seemingly long time since I had seen him do that to me and I liked it. I wished that he wasn't always at work and instead spent more time at home with Mother and myself as he seemed to be so happy when he was. I know my mother had been worried too of late, especially when she had been speaking with Grandma. I had overheard the conversation. Adults don't realise sometimes the effect a family crisis can have on a young impressionable boy of twelve. I winked back.

'Goodness no,' he declared, 'nothing as exciting. My father is Robert Louis Balfour Stevenson, but he's only a novelist, poet and sometimes a travel writer. My father is married to my mother, Fanny Osborne, and I'm twelve years of age.'

I liked him.

'Me too,' I said again.

'Whereabouts in Scotland are you heading?' he asked.

I liked the way he spoke although sometimes it was a hard to catch a particular sound, but I soon caught on and made sense of what he was saying.

'Dundee. It's our ancestral home, on my mother's side,' I professed.

I saw Mother look up and smile, obviously pleased that our conversation recently regarding my heritage had seemingly been captured by me.

'And one day,' I announced, 'I am going to be the lord of all the estates!'

I didn't know exactly what a lord was or what duties it

entailed in such a position and my mother didn't think it an appropriate time to interrupt the conversation between two young boys to put me straight. She would tell me later that I was to inherit the estate only, not the title.

Lloyd Stevenson was captivated. 'Was your relative a laird or somebody rich and powerful?' he asked enthusiastically.

Then as all boys do Lloyd and I leant forward to continue our conversation in almost a hushed whisper, what we had to say wasn't for outsiders to hear. Boys of our age had lived long enough already to have secrets and I had one to relate that I felt worthy of and that he should be a party to. I started to tell of my most famous ancestor.

I proudly announced, 'I am the great-great-great-grandson of Captain William Kidd the famous buccaneer.'

Lloyd's eyes opened wide. 'Do you mean Captain Kidd, the pirate?'

'I do indeed.' Trying to sound more important and seeing that I had his fullest attention I continued, 'My ancestor Captain Kidd was born in Dundee, Scotland, in the year 1645. He was the son of John Kidd, a mariner himself but who was lost at sea.'

I couldn't remember the exact year Mother had said, but it didn't really matter as Lloyd sat beside me open-mouthed.

'Captain Kidd had wanted to follow his father on the high seas so he signed up as a mariner, but his adventures found him mixed up with an unscrupulous captain and a crew just as bad. Privateers of the high seas they were known as.' I quickly looked up to see if either of my parents were listening, but fortunately both were busy reading newspapers, so I continued. 'It wasn't long before William Kidd and some other members of the crew got into an argument with the ship's captain about being badly treated. A mutiny ensued and the captain was set adrift with the crew taking over the ship. They renamed the ship the *Blessed William* and made William Kidd their captain. The legend was born. However as they were already known as pirates, they stayed pirates and continued to sail the open seas seizing their fortune wherever they could prosper. It's recorded somewhere that a time around 1689 Captain Kidd and his crew attacked a French island called Mariegalante where they plundered, killed and looted the islanders of their treasure, said to be worth over £2,000 in currency, a king's ransom for its day.'

'Cor,' exclaimed Lloyd, 'real pirate's treasure. They must have had a lot hidden somewhere?'

I suppose they must have had, but I didn't rightly know, but I wasn't ready to confess as such, instead I told Lloyd that many of the ship's maps, possibly treasure maps had been lost down the centuries and that there was probably just one single map that had marked on it a special spot where the treasure was more than likely buried. It made the story sound much better and it was as convincing as every schoolboy wanted to hear. Even adults believed all pirates left behind treasure as their legacy. Lloyd's eyes grew large and wide, but all the same he needed an ending to my tale.

'So then what happened to Captain Kidd and the crew?' he eagerly asked.

I kept my own emotions in check as I wanted to keep the suspense going for a little while longer. 'Nothing much,' I said dispassionately. 'They were all captured by the British and returned to England for trial. Some of the pirate crew however went to prison, but the remainder including Captain William Kidd were found guilty of more serious crimes so they were hanged at Wapping in England in 1701.'

He had an ending to the story.

'Cor,' said Lloyd, 'a real-life ancestor that was hanged. It's like having Bonnie Prince Charlie in my wee family, but what about the treasure and the map?' he asked. 'Did they manage to hide it somewhere secret that only you know about?'

Again I didn't have an answer to his question, but I didn't want to let myself or Lloyd down so I improvised as much as a twelve-year-old boy could at that age. I told him that as far as our family knew prior to the capture of Captain Kidd and the other pirates they were supposed to have buried the treasure on an unknown island somewhere in the Caribbean. The location of the treasure was reputed to have been charted on a map that had been lost at sea during the battle with the English man-o'-

war. However, so the tale goes that whilst in prison and talking with another unrelated prisoner, one of the pirates that escaped the hangman's noose said that a map had been found aboard the *Blessed William* by the captain of the English ship, but to this day nobody knows whether he and his crew sailed to the Caribbean island and retrieved the pirate treasure. It remains a mystery the same as many other mysteries.

I was surprised, but the ending seemed to satisfy Lloyd as many adventures were sometimes best left with a cliffhanger of suspense. He told me that the story was tremendously exciting and that I should accompany him to the next carriage, where I needed to speak with his stepfather. I didn't know why, but I asked my mother if it was alright to do so and Father said that no ill could come of my telling what he considered to be just a myth, so they both agreed that I could accept Lloyd's invitation.

We walked through to the next carriage where Lloyd introduced me to his mother and stepfather. He told them that I was his friend, which I found very pleasing. I shook hands with Mr Stevenson, who upon hearing why Lloyd had invited me to meet him asked me to sit down with them. I then spent the next hour telling Robert Louis Stevenson the story of the infamous Captain Kidd and the buried treasure. He listened intently, encouragingly asking questions along the way, some of which I answered easily and some that still remained a mystery to me.

Not once did he dispute any of the facts and when I had finally concluded my tale, which he said was a wonderful account, he congratulated me on how well I had recited the story, similarly likening me to his own ability to tell a good story. I'm sure that I blushed, although I wholeheartedly accepted his praise. Mr Stevenson then honoured me by narrating one of his own stories, which at the end I found captivating and thrilling. It had been about a prince called Florizel and related the adventures from a book titled *The Lantern Bearers*.

I had to leave Lloyd and his family whilst I rejoined my parents for the scheduled stop at York Station where we took a short luncheon before continuing on our journey. It was a welcome break, although I was keen to see Lloyd again and especially as Mr Stevenson had promised to tell me some more about his work, more notably regarding his exploits and travels around the world, of the many magical cities of Europe and those of the new world in America, some of which was still uncharted.

I listened fervently to his adventures that gave me an insight to what travelling across an ocean on board a ship, travelling by train beside a desert or riding a horse up and into the mountains could actually mean. I might have told him just a story about a pirate, who was a real person from my past, but Lloyd had been so wrong about his stepfather, he was not just a novelist, poet and travel writer, he was one of the most fascinating men that I would ever have the good fortune to meet in my entire life.

The journey which had at first seemed a tiring passage through the many counties of England suddenly concluded all too quickly as the locomotive gently nudged against the buffers at Edinburgh Station. It left little time for Lloyd and myself to exchange addresses before we parted to go our separate ways. I promised to write and tell of my exploits and whether the time spent at our ancestors' home revealed any of the secrets that we had not previously known about. Lloyd and his parents were travelling onward to Colinton, a small place just outside of Edinburgh where I understood Mr Stevenson had spent a great deal of his childhood, as we took direction towards Dundee.

Just before we said goodbye Mr Stevenson gave me a small brown parcel, telling me that it would serve me well in the years to come, if only to write down my thoughts. Later that evening I opened the package and found a black leather notepad which contained on the inside cover a handwritten inscription: *'May your life be full of memorable moments, and your travels be magical. There are so many adventures to behold, enough to fill a head and a heart for a lifetime. We have a common interest, my young friend. I hope you find the treasure one day, Matthew. Yours, Robert Louis Stevenson, 1881.'*

Our holiday in Dundee was a mixture of sunshine, mist and rain, but nevertheless a thoroughly enjoyable time and Father appreciated the much-needed rest away from his office. Mother told me one evening when we were alone that she just appreciated having us both together and all to herself. Dundee would always have a special place in my heart for as long as I lived and that holiday was one of our best. When the weather kept us indoors we found the time to research the family lineage in a hope to fill in the missing blanks about Captain William Kidd and his family, but the mystery, the myth and maybe the legend rests in peace as we didn't turn up anything remarkably startling or new. Even Father helped and Grandma said the holiday had changed him for the better.

Parish records from the local church provided details of William Kidd's private life, but no treasure map or the like. William Kidd did marry a lady called Sarah Oort and from their marriage they produced two daughters, Elizabeth and Sarah, who both married. However, after the execution of Captain William Kidd at Wapping, Sarah remarried, although there is no mention made of the latter husband in her will of 1732. So I suppose my claim upon the Kidd legacy will be subject to further enquiries when I grow older. And until such a time if a treasure map still exists and there is treasure to be found, perhaps I might invite along a friend of the same age as he is the only other person to know the true story. But for now I alone know Captain Kidd was a real pirate and whatever his past, he is an ancestor of mine and the mysterious tale of lost treasure will live on.

And as we promised to one another Lloyd Stevenson and I kept in touch through letters of correspondence down the years. We both did well academically at school and college although Lloyd travelled further afield than I ever did during those years, living for a time in Hyères, Southern France, then crossing an ocean to the island of Upolu in Samoa. It is however, with the deepest of regret that I should have to inform you that the man with the wonderful imagination and ability to write from the heart, Mr Robert Louis Stevenson died, on the island aged only forty-three on 3rd December 1894. For a time the correspondence from Lloyd lapsed and this was quite understandable in the circumstances.

I myself was fortunate to reach an even higher level of education before I joined my father's firm as a solicitor at law and I have over the years managed to fill a number of the empty pages of my little black leather-bound notebook from my limited travels, but more so with my personal and some intimate thoughts. Mr Stevenson was certainly correct in what he said that day on the platform at Edinburgh Station about making a note of everything worth recording for we do forget many precious memories in a lifetime, memories that were good as opposed to the bad events, which annoyingly we could remember. We should all have a little black book to help bring back the good times especially as the number of years increase and our ability to remember lessens. The writing down of one's life as a memory can have distinct advantages.

Lloyd would write and tell me about where he was in the world, the people that he had met and mostly what were his ambitions, but most importantly and almost certainly to me was that he would tell me about any new publications by his father, prior to his untimely death. It was this news that I looked forward to with great expectation. I would eagerly await the publications in an English bookshop or library, where I could purchase a copy, but my prized possession is the novel *Treasure Island*. You may well ask why this one? Well, I believe that it was the enthusiasm of two young twelve-year-old boys on the *Flying Scotsman* train from London to Edinburgh that encouraged Mr Stevenson to write this famous age-enduring story.

Of course I cannot take all the credit because I understand that the weather at Colinton, Scotland, during the June of 1881 was an undeniably wet time and had restricted a young boy from the outside adventure that he sorely sought. Lloyd had written later in one of his letters soon after their return to London, that one afternoon at Colinton he had been with his father in the parlour whereupon Lloyd had taken a fancy to painting a picture of a map. The map had included an island which named places and objects associated with piracy. Mr Stevenson had taken an avid interest in his stepson's painting and from there the idea had become a written manuscript and in the May of 1883 the novel aptly named *Treasure Island* had reached the bookshelves of shops and public libraries. I believe

I was one of the first persons to make a purchase.

Most fortunately too I have a very special copy signed by the author himself which Lloyd sent to me in the summer of 1883. Inside the front cover is written *'To the great-great-great-grandson of Captain William Kidd. With grateful thanks, RLS.'*

I am extremely lucky to have a wonderful wife and son of my own, much to the delight of my mother, who has a story about a pirate relative that she wants to tell him one day, but only when he is older and maybe the pilgrimage for the treasure will be his, who knows. But for now I make sure that he studies and reads as much as possible, only knowledge is the wealth of our society and it costs very little to possess. One day too I will give him my copy of *Treasure Island*, but only when he is of an age to appreciate it. You never know it might just help with his quest and who knows maybe he might be fortunate also to take a train journey, meet a boy of his own age who will turn out to be the most valuable of friends. The stationmaster was right that day at King's Cross as I did meet a friend on a train.

I WAS AN ENGINEER FOR A DAY

I was eight years of age. Not seven any more, but a whole eight going on towards nine, well in twelve months I would be. Do you remember when you were that age? I expect the question itself has evoked some memory in you. I know it works with me. Do you remember when school finished on a Friday afternoon and that on a Saturday morning you'd eagerly await the chink of the metal lid on the front door letter box and through it would drop the newspaper? Inside would be a copy of *The Beano*, *The Dandy*, or maybe *The Hotspur*. All boys' stuff, though occasionally we'd let the girls read them too.

That time of our life was great. No cares, very few worries and definitely no video games, iPads, mobile telephones or PlayStations. Instead we would spend all day outdoors in the sunshine, the rain, the snow and even the fog. Nothing other than school time would prevent us from being outside where the fun was endless.

Outside was play and paradise from the time we were allowed to excuse the table from breakfast till the last rays of daylight robbed us of a good game. Games such as run-outs, marbles on sewer inspection covers and football wherever there was a patch of grass or tarmac. As I said pure heaven.

And school, arguably the best days of your life, regardless of whatever your teacher could grab and throw at you, normally the chalk rubber where the backing was actually made of wood, read on Esther Rantzen. And do you remember the days we were allowed to wear a uniform, when you'd proudly turn up in your Cub uniform for the Queen's birthday and saints' days, namely

George, Andrew, David and Patrick. Throughout the spring we'd take part in Bob-a-Job Week, pure child labour, but oh so much fun, then a week before the 5th of November we would pull together all our old clothes including Granny's cast-offs and dress up a rough version of a guy, or failing this dress up your youngest brother. The money hard-earned on a street corner of the local high street, spent as quickly on bangers and sweets. Go on be truthful, tell me you don't remember all the fun we had when we were eight.

And being eight I should think that most boys of that age wanted to drive a steam train. I know my name was top of the dream list and it remained that way ever since, even though I'm now closer to retirement age. I won't divulge my exact age or the headlong plunge towards the dotage years as they will remain my secret if you don't mind. But here and now though I should tell you that my dream came true, partly because of my granddad, my mother's father who had been a train driver for more years than I had been around, or that of my mother to be precise and I didn't have enough fingers to count that lot up, maths not being my strongest subject as annual school reports would record. Just what joy did those teachers get from writing the same thing every year about you? Could do better, would do better if he paid more attention and attending lessons would see him do a whole lot better. I would have liked to see some of their reports when they were at school.

So soon after the arrival of *The Dandy*, which was unashamedly stashed away somewhere discreet where my younger brother wouldn't find it and with breakfast consumed at the double, followed by a quick lick 'n' a promise in the bathroom, my hair brushed smartly then ruffled to give it that worn look, I'd don my jean jacket and was out of the front door and on my way over to Granny and Granddad's house before the milk float came down the road. The air about would still be thick with soot from the last evening's coal fires, but it smelt good, thick and strong, just like Granddad said it should be.

Waiting in the scullery he'd hand over to me a tin caddy which had been specially picked out for me, I never asked from where he'd got it. Inside Granny would have stored a jam sandwich, apple and some raisins. Granddad would check his own caddy then peck Granny on the cheek.

'You take good care of our young Harold,' remarked Granny, winking at Granddad.

'I will,' he replied as we exited the back door.

The railway yard was a place of pure magic. Miles of carriages and coaches, or so it seemed, the tall whitewashed structure of the water tower and the shunting sheds where the engines lived. A magician must have designed the railways. As we stepped over timber sleepers and disused lines we approached the shunting shed, where upon arriving Granddad pulled aside the huge metal windowed doors. I looked across at the revolving turntable, it looked like a giant clock face.

Inside the shed must have been where the magician lived because it was like entering Aladdin's cave. I looked around for the magic words to see where they'd been engraved around the edges of the door frame. I admit I was a little disappointed that there were none. At first I couldn't take it all in, there was just so much to see and smell. It really was the most wonderful sight I had ever witnessed. Lined up silently side by side, gleaming and inviting were half a dozen steam trains. They were absolutely magnificent, mind-bogglingly wonderful and everything that I imagined they'd be.

It took me a few seconds to comprehend the grandeur of the place, there was just so much for a young boy of eight to absorb. Granddad smiled, ruffled my hair and reality suddenly, annoyingly presented itself again as we walked down the gangway. Don't you find that annoying too, when we experience those magic moments of childhood or even the odd adulthood momentary lapse of sensibility where we feel the safest, lose ourselves completely in the fantasy of a daydream, that they are suddenly stolen from us, grabbed away by an unrelated force and reality returns instead? We are left wondering what would have been next, we are left compromising instead only the compromise leaves you half empty because you know in yourself it just didn't end that way. Not in your magic world.

We climbed aboard a King-class locomotive belonging to the

Great Western Railway. Granddad placed our caddies beneath the driver's stool then told me to fill the kettle from the wash tap. I climbed down and walked over to the wash tap. My first job on the railway, boy I walked proud that day.

Just then another driver appeared from the locker room. He came across to where I was standing.

'Hello, young man, you've got to be young Harold, Albert said he'd be bringing you this Saturday. You'd best accompany me to the locker room, I've got something in there you will need for your journey. Leave the kettle a minute or two, old Albert can wait a few more minutes for his tea!'

I followed the driver into the locker room and emerged minutes later wearing a pair of old gauntlets, perhaps a few sizes too big, but I didn't care and a real leather cap, now I really looked the part. I was almost a real railwayman. I retrieved the kettle and climbed back up the steps to the footplate. Granddad looked my way and approved of my uniform.

'Put the kettle on the hotplate, Harold, and come look over here as I'd best give you a quick run over the controls only once we're on our way there'll be little time to show you much then.'

I listened intently and double-checked my controls, the ones at least that I would be allowed to touch once out on the track. The other driver from the locker room saw me cleaning the throttle handle and waved over to me. I acknowledged back then like a true engineer spat on the brass handle again applying more elbow grease until it shone bright. The driver laughed.

He called across to our train, 'You'd best watch out Albert, young Harold here will be retiring you off early.'

I watched as the pressure gauge needle rose through the temperature calibrations until it flickered about the black arrowed pointer. Granddad tapped the gauge glass.

'We're almost ready, Harold,' he said, 'the fire's hot enough and we've a good head of steam.'

Joe our engineer suddenly walked through the shed door and headed over our way. He introduced himself to me then opened the metal door of the fire. I had to move back quickly to avoid being burnt, the heat was immense, much hotter than I had expected. Joe scooped a large shovel load of coal from the truck behind then tossed it into the fire. The coals hissed back, spat and crackled as they disappeared into the tongue of the dragon. Now I know how St George felt when he defeated the dragon.

As another of the shed engineers pulled aside the huge doors again Granddad tested the whistle as the engine fired into life.

'OK, Harold, give it a short, sharp blast, let Kenneth know we're coming back his way.'

I did as I was instructed, the shrill of the whistle becoming louder as the steam infused the aperture sounding more than my Granddad's. I saw Joe wink my way. Cor that felt good and Kenneth waved us back until we passed beyond the shunting shed doors. We slowly edged our way onto the platform dial of the turntable. I called out goodbye to Kenneth, but the noise of the locomotive drowned me out, instead he just waved back before pulling together the shed doors again.

As Joe turned the spindle arm the huge King locomotive commenced its 360-degree turn until we finally faced the other way. He engaged the turntable brake, then jumped back up on board. I was instructed to pull the whistle chain again and then we were off.

The immense power surged through me as I felt the wheels turn as the cranked big-end bearings slipped back and forth along the connecting rods depressing and releasing the pistons as they drove us forward. As I sat on Granddad's knee he placed his hand around mine and together we engaged the throttle handle for more speed. I watched through the inspection glass as the train gained momentum as we dropped with the gradient of the track.

As we approached I saw a group of boys playing football in the local park as the train steamed on by. They saw me standing on the footplate of the train so I waved at them as some of them were in my class at school. Suddenly one of them pointed at me, recognised me and called out my name in disbelief, then they all waved and ran alongside beyond the safety of the fence. I couldn't hear what they were saying, but I could see the envy in their faces. It was a defining moment for an eight-year-old hero of the age of steam. It was one of those daydream moments that I would allow myself to drift into in my older years.

On that first journey I never questioned why we didn't collect any passenger coaches as we passed through the stations. An elderly couple on the platform gawped in amazement as the locomotive passed them by with a boy driving a steam train, it was inconceivable. I'm sure the stationmaster just humoured them when they reported my escapade to him minutes later, but by then we had almost disappeared down the line. Our scheduled journey today however was to deliver the locomotive to another shunting shed ten miles down track. Whatever the journey had been that day, all that mattered to me as a young boy of eight, was that I was an engineer for a day.

We delivered the King locomotive as scheduled passing cattle, farms, horses, sheep and a level crossing before we arrived. We left behind a trail of steam that snaked its way back along the track before disappearing into the trees beside the line. Every bit of that journey was as exhilarating as I remembered it.

You'd be right to think that an experience of that magnitude had sown the seed of adventure and my life had been set in stone and that I'd follow my beloved granddad as an employee of the Great Western Railway. Don't think I hadn't contemplated it, that day lives inside me alongside the many others that I have experienced over the years, but my personal ambitions reached out for other places to be, other people to meet and an inner excitement that driving trains could not completely fulfil. Now don't get me wrong that was not a snub at my granddad, but merely as times change so do other things in the world, including trains.

The age of steam regrettably disappeared from commercial railways in 1968. I know because I was there. It was a sad departure of an era that had reached the hearts of many, including my own. During my time as a boy and the early years of my teens I was the envy of the boys in the park on many occasions as we passed them by on a Saturday morning. I eventually grew into the gauntlets, but unfortunately I couldn't say the same for the cap, so instead it has pride of place in my bedroom. It still does.

I followed my path of destiny, I have visited many cities in the world and I have met the most interesting people who were its residents and also some of its visitors. All in all I've had the most exciting of times and they have I can truthfully say satisfied most of my boyhood dreams, the dreams of when I was an eight-year-old. My ninth birthday came and went, but life hardly ever managed to touch upon the exhilaration that I had felt in the year that preceded it. That year when I was eight years old had a profound effect on my life and so did the steam trains.

I studied hard and through the inherent knowledge of my granddad and Joe, and the countless other special men in and around the train yards on a Saturday morning I learnt everything I could about trains, new and old. And then early in my twenties I qualified as a mechanical and civil engineer, designing everything that was connected with this wonderful mode of travel. My expertise took me to the different corners of the world where I helped build that country's railway infrastructure. I am proud to be associated with trains just like I was when I was eight.

But like everything else time ticks by second by second watching progress move forward at an alarming rate and just like me, it followed me to the four corners of the world and bounced back from the satellites that orbit our planet. We now use iPads and mobile telephones, we entertain ourselves with PlayStations and video games. I use a computer for my many designs and our office fax machine sends blueprints and data to an engineer's meeting somewhere in Japan. Progress however is impatient and if you look around you, tell me truthfully how many eight-year-old children do you see playing run-outs, flicking glass marbles across a drain cover or kicking a ball in the street or when do you actually see children playing over the park or as a train passes by and would they take the time to watch? I doubt it very much.

I miss the thrill of that piercing steam whistle as it echoed across the yard, the trail of white smoke as it snaked back along the line, the deep red colour of the coaches and the racing green of the locomotives. Most of all though I miss my granddad and it seemed that when it was time for the steam train to reach that last buffer plate and for the furnace fire to die away, so did my granddad. In honour of his long years of service to the railway the Great Western company named a shed after him. It's still called Albert Yard and I still go there occasionally. The locker room is still there and so is the wash tap. I remember my granddad as if it were only yesterday. I'm so proud of him and I know my mother is too.

And as I come to the end of my story, there's just one more episode that I must tell you about before I go. By chance I had to get up in the loft the other day for my wife and do you know what I came across? A box that I remember my own father had built for me when I was a young boy. When I opened it I found a batch of old comics inside, a grand mix of *Beanos*, *Dandy*s and *Hotspur*s.

That afternoon I sat alone in the loft and silently read through them all, until it was time to come down for tea. I never did find what it was that my wife had sent me up there to find, but I'm sure she'd send me back up there again another day. When I eventually came back down I gave them to my grandson to read, but told him to share them with his sister for they might well be boys' stuff, but little girls need adventures too. Times have definitely changed and so have children's games. Yes, when I was eight it was definitely the best year of my life.

THE STAPLEHURST ANGEL

As I followed the last of the passengers disembarking from the Calais-to-Dover ferry boat I reluctantly wobbled my way down the buoyant gangplank and onto the sidewalk. The crossing had been rough in places and my stomach still felt tender. I looked across the cobbled thoroughfare at the railway station beyond, then slipped my right hand through the leather handle of my suitcase again, the weight sufficiently heavy to distribute between both hands every couple of minutes.

My past year in France in a Montmartre nursing home had been a luxury that I could unfortunately no longer afford. Paris the wonderful city of romance, laughter and all-night dancing was colourfully vibrant, exciting and ruled the heart every day making you forget the senses of our reality. But the city is expensive and eventually my list of options had exhausted my purse and limited savings. Madam Moreau had begged me to stay on promising to increase my allowance should I agree, but the reality was that I had to return to England.

I looked down at the small chrome watch clipped onto my breast pocket. The time was already 12.55 p.m., only fifteen minutes to purchase a ticket and find a suitable seat. I changed hands once more relieving the pressure from the numbed fingers of my right hand and increased my stride with a purposeful intent on reaching the station entrance before changing hands again.

The busy road before the station facade was difficult to negotiate and I could hear the porters' whistles inside indicating the departure of other trains. I hesitantly stepped off the kerb to negotiate the oncoming vehicles, but a kindly gentleman suddenly took hold of my arm and relieved me of my suitcase. He told me to follow him across the road. It all happened so quickly that I didn't have time to ask who he was, but seeing as we were heading in the right direction I resisted the urge to challenge him or his motives.

We had safely manoeuvred our way between the traffic and finally stood underneath the entrance to the station. My mystery man handed back my case, politely bade me good afternoon, then as he smiled he turned to leave.

I grabbed hold of his sleeve to thank him and asked, 'How did you know I wanted the railway station?'

He pointed at the luggage label on my suitcase. 'GWR is all too familiar in these parts,' he exclaimed and with that he disappeared between the throng of well-wishers that had gathered near to the flower stall. I watched the back of his head vanish thinking how extraordinary some people can be and almost especially in England. They appear in your lives only momentarily and then are gone the next, as if they were ghosts just passing through.

I lugged my suitcase across to the ticket counter, purchased a single one-way ticket for the 1.15 departure from platform two. I lifted up my suitcase again then raced across to the barrier as I knew that the time was almost upon me and the train would be departing very soon.

The porter at the barrier gate looked up at the station clock. 'No need to rush, Miss, the train will wait and besides you've still six minutes left.'

I checked my watch and could have sworn that at the ticket office it had registered 1.12 p.m. I wondered if the ferry boat crossing had dulled my senses. The porter called across a colleague who kindly relieved me of my case and showed me to a second-class carriage.

He placed my case inside the corridor door and bade me a good journey, then seeing the arrival of another female passenger struggling through the barrier he approached and took charge of her luggage.

I breathed a sigh of relief, I had finally made it. I left my case where it was as I infused my lungs with the sooty odour of the station taking stock of the day. My early departure from the

Gard du Nord, the crossing over the Channel and the rush to disembark and get to the station had left me feeling drained. I had missed breakfast and the small parcel of pastry savouries that the kitchen staff had prepared for me I had given to a family with two small children on the boat.

A minute later the train lurched forward and the interconnecting couplings clanked heavily as the train headed away from Dover Station. I picked up my case and started walking through the carriage to locate a suitable compartment. I saw the young family who had accepted my breakfast in a compartment to themselves, but I resisted joining them as the children were boisterously flitting from one seat to another. I didn't blame them as it seemed that we had all been cooped up together since early this morning. The mother smiled as I moved on past.

The middle of the train appeared quite full and it wasn't until I had reached the first carriage directly behind the engine that I located a suitable compartment. I didn't object to being in the front carriage as I believed the buffeting motion of the train was all the more steady at the front than middle or end sections. As I entered the compartment a male passenger stood up, took my heavy suitcase and stowed it on the overhead storage shelf as I chose the vacant seat next to the window. I thanked him as he sat down again.

It was mid-June and the warm intensity of the early afternoon sunshine penetrated through the carriage window, it reminded me of the comfortable summer room at the rear of Aunt Julia's house in Lower Somerset. It had been a couple of years since I'd last seen her, I made a mental note to get in touch and arrange a visit before the autumn. I laid my head back against the headrest and absorbed the rays of the sun on my face feeling the cordial heat invigorate my tired eyes and lull me into an unconscious state of peaceful slumber.

I know that I was still dreaming because the people in it were not known to me and I had never in my life visited the temples of Istanbul, but I was abruptly transported back to reality by a violent rocking motion and my suitcase landing beside my feet, fortunately missing both limbs on the downward descent. I heard glass shattering and metal groaning as it twisted out of shape.

At first I couldn't see the man who occupied our carriage, but through the dust and steam from the engine I saw that he was lying prostrate on the carriage floor. He was holding his head although I couldn't see any immediate signs of an injury. I was suddenly aware of a warm trickle down the crease of my nose and as I pulled away my finger I saw that it was bloody. I traced the trickle to my forehead where a small cut had broken the skin, probably by flying glass. I realised that the window beside me was missing, completely gone.

The steam from the engine continued to pour into the open void of our carriage as I helped the gentleman to his seat, he seemed alright, just slightly dazed, but his speech was clear and coherent and his recovery was swift. He said that he should check on the driver and engineer as they would have suffered the full force of the crash. In the meantime the cries of a young girl in the corridor outside drew my attention several compartments back.

Opening the compartment door I found that the rear of the coach was twisted like an accordion as I climbed and crawled my way towards the sound of the girl. Twisted metal, broken glass and shattered timber panelling made progress slow, but through the haze I could see the girl curled up on the floor. When I was almost upon her a lifeless limb of a man suddenly dropped and slapped my shoulder. It made me jump and I was thankful that I didn't scream. I had seen a number of cadavers in the French nursing home at Montmartre so I quickly rested the arm out of sight where the young girl could not see it then crawled through to sit beside her. I drew her in to me as she sobbed mumbling that she wanted her mother, only I couldn't see her mother anywhere hereabouts. I aged the girl as about seven.

She finally stopped crying and I asked her name, she told me that it was Madeleine and that she had been on the train with her mummy. I comforted her whilst I checked that she had no injuries, telling her that we would go look for her mother very soon. The girl was slightly shocked, quite understandable in the present circumstances, but otherwise unharmed. I wondered how she had become separated from her mother, but crashes involving large trains or ships often resulted in people being tossed about like rag dolls. Impact had probably been the reason for her mother's disappearance. I took hold of Madeleine's hand as we started to wriggle our way to safety. I avoided the dead man on the seat as I didn't want to alarm her any more than she was already.

Jumping down onto the softness of the nearby grass verge I heard a woman call out Madeleine's name and looked up to see a woman descending from the top of the verge. Madeleine was quickly reunited with her mother who told me that the impact had thrown her clear of the wreckage as the compartment door burst open and was ripped off its hinges. She had been thrown out clear of the train and landed on the grass verge a couple of coaches back. The coach containing Madeleine had careered onward until it had come to a halt halfway up the verge. I left them cuddling one another and was glad it had been a happy outcome. I thought of the young family I'd seen earlier on the boat and on the train a number of carriages back.

I made my way towards the rear of the train, but saw the mother, the young boy and the girl together with their father already sitting on top of the grass verge, so I abandoned my quest to help them, they seemed fine.

Just then a man's voice quietly called out to me and asked for my assistance. I turned and saw a middle-aged bearded gentleman beckoning me to join him in what had been the first-class carriage. It was severely damaged as were the others behind. The man was sitting in a kneeling position in a small pocket of space between upturned carriage seats. I could hear the moan of another person as I climbed up and into the carriage compartment.

The kneeling gentleman had removed his own jacket, folded it double and placed it beneath another man's head, who appeared to be in a rather serious amount of discomfort. I noticed that beside the bearded man was an ornately engraved silver hip flask, the kind that only a gentlemen would possess for when he fancied a swift tipple. I imagined the contents were almost certainly rum, brandy or whisky. A luxurious extravagance for the times, unless you were in Paris and most definitely only ever seen by the privileged classes of this country. The bearded man looked up at me and saw the glass cut on my head, which had stopped bleeding.

He picked up the flask and offered it to me. 'You look like you could with a drink.' He unscrewed the top for me. 'It's brandy and will help with your injury.'

I gratefully received the flask, nodded and drank a mouthful, feeling the silky fluid sink down my gullet producing a warm sensation as it headed towards my stomach. I thanked him and handed back the flask.

'I recognise you from the boat,' I said. 'You were with two ladies. Are they both OK?' I enquired.

The man grinned and pointed to a point beyond the grass bank. I looked and saw his two female companions who were huddled together, no doubt unable to take in the full enormity of the event. He waved at them and they both returned the gesture. I'd noticed an angst look when I had mentioned that I'd seen him on the boat with the two ladies, but it was only there fleetingly and his smile reassured me that he was friendly as he offered the flask again. I declined.

'I saw you also on board the boat. You wear the distinguished and honourable uniform of a nursing Nightingale.'

I surmised his reference to mean Florence Nightingale.

'I thought you could help me with this poor soul.' He sympathetically patted the injured man on the arm. 'I saw you attend also to the mother and child. Are they safe and uninjured?' he asked.

I told him that they were both safe and happy to be reunited with one another, he seemed relieved.

'That's good. The child will recover, children always do. It is the mind of the adult which will bear the haunting of this tragedy, I fear.'

He gave the injured man a sip from the hip flask, as I undid his outer clothing to check on the extent of his injuries, but as I undid the neck buttons of his shirt I saw his eyes look directly at me, then at the bearded man, then close for the last time. I lifted the dead man's head up removed the folded jacket and gave it back to the man kneeling beside me. We covered the man's face then crawled back out of the space.

'We should look for others who might need help,' he said. And so we started to walk back along the track stopping at open doors to carriages, helping where help was needed.

I thought about telling him that there might be others dead, but although he had a kindly face I could see that he was also wise and appeared well versed with society and its misgivings.

I watched the bearded man as he moved about the damaged carriages, soothing the less injured, caring for the more serious and proffering his flask to the needy. There was a gentleness about him that was not unlike my own father's. I listened as his words comforted all who reached out for his benevolence, smiling again as he moved on to somebody else. I had a strange feeling that he had been in similar circumstances prior to today. I saw him remove his jacket when there was no cloth to hand and he preserved the dignity of an old lady. He saw me watching.

'Death has no date that we know about and precisely when it will come who knows? Others here do not need to see her passing or a premonition of their own.' He whispered as he placed an encouraging hand upon my shoulder.

I was surprised to see how many times he offered the small silver flask and I wondered just how much fluid the container held. He worked tirelessly amongst the injured until others from the local villages nearby arrived to give assistance. If I didn't know better I would have said that the man had a special talent with words as he seemed to know precisely what to say and in what circumstances. The distressed were clearly comforted by just hearing his voice, of that I was sure. Some even smiled rejecting the uncertainty of the situation. I thought my nursing training had prepared me for most eventualities in life, but it had hardly been a grounding for the collision of two trains.

When he eventually took a breather outside and allowed others to take over I went and sat beside him. I wanted to know who he was and from where he came. On the train and I don't know how or from whence he had found it, but he'd offered people water, once even from a hat that he'd found. If I had not seen him on the boat over from Calais with his female companions I would have said that he was an angel working under the directive of the Lord on earth.

I was about to ask when a policeman called for my assistance. The bearded man helped me up then walked towards the front of the train as I entered the carriage to where the policeman was waiting. Once or twice we saw one another as we continued to tend for the people who needed our help. We smiled at one another, but I never got the opportunity to ask the questions that I wanted answers to. Eventually the course of the rescue changed as it always does and all that remain are the rescuers, the rescued are somewhere else having their wounds treated. I looked around for my bearded angel, but I never found him. I just know that I could not have coped that day without his help.

I was given a plaster for the cut to my head and I was taken by bus to a nearby school, where we were fed and given a bed for the night, before being transported the next morning to a nearby railway station where I continued on my journey home to Lancashire. Yes, I actually caught another train home. They say that lightning never strikes twice so I was determined to prove them right. I did start at the back of the train and walk forward through the coaches, but I never found my bearded man again.

In the following week I applied for a nursing position at the local hospital as a ward nurse, caring for patients other than the elderly and ladies who could afford the indulgence of nursing-home luxury. The march of progress was moving on rapidly throughout the country and all over in large hospitals, surgeries and cottage medical centres nursing and medical practices changed with the times. Since that terrible day on the train I had a burning desire to know as much as possible and reflected upon my time in Paris as being like a snail shedding a used shell without a place to hide. I was fortunate that my studies and efforts on the medical ward hadn't gone unnoticed and after only a year I was promoted to senior ward nurse, then after a further two years to that of nursing sister. It was strange, perhaps a little spooky maybe, but made me feel good, but I often felt that gentle hand on my shoulder in times of crisis, giving me the courage to do something new or rise above a challenge.

You would consider my story over with now as I had achieved most of what I had set out to do, but there is a final chapter to this extraordinary event in my life, which I need to tell you about as it happened on a day like any other as I was returning to the hospital. I had made a home visit to a rather poorly patient who had only been discharged the day before and needed his dressings changed. As I walked past the park my attention was drawn towards a man sitting on a bench beside the watering fountain. I was immediately concerned because he seemed to be hunched over and I wondered if he was in pain. I walked across and sat down beside him.

'Hello,' I enquired, 'may I be of any help?'

The man righted himself and a smile pursed across his thin lips. I felt my eyes open wide in astonishment and then delight, it was my bearded angel from the train crash. He touched my arm and I could have sworn that I felt an energy radiate where he'd touched.

'You've achieved success, young lady, but certainly no more than you deserve. I never did get the chance to thank you on that tragic day. A day that will regrettably live inside of us all for eternity.' There was a sadness in his eyes that seemed to haunt him.

I held his hand. 'It should have been me that thanked you, kind sir, you did so much to help others without any reward. I looked and expected to see your story in all the newspapers, but alas real heroes very often go unnoticed.'

He sighed and took a deep breath to steady his thoughts. 'I only sat here for a moment as I had a giddiness of my body.' It was a strange way to say that he was unsteady on his feet, but I remembered his soft eloquent use of words. He then quoted me a verse and I'm sure it was said only to allay any concerns that I showed concerning his health.

'I am as light as a feather, I am as happy as an angel, I am as merry as a schoolboy. I am as giddy as a drunken man (he smiled at this point and winked). A merry Christmas to everybody. A happy New Year to all the world!'

I clapped and acknowledged his responsive use of verse. 'I have often thought of you and perhaps if I can be so bold to suggest that I have felt you by my side especially when I'm at work nursing the injured and the sick. May I please know your name?'

'I will give you mine willingly, as long as you consent to tell me yours? For my sins I am Charles Dickens, the author, and I am delighted to at last make your acquaintance.' He sounded like an actor rather than a writer, but it explained his well-chosen use of words.

'And I am pleased to meet you too, Charles Dickens, I am Sarah Atherton from Lancashire.'

He suddenly took hold of my hand and gently kissed it, as only gentlemen do.

I reluctantly checked my chrome watch and realised that I had been away from my ward far too long. I stood up, apologised and explained that I had to return to work, but before I left I asked if Charles would agree to meet with me after my shift at a local tea shop where we could talk for much longer. He readily agreed and said that it would be his honour to do so. I was about to leave when he produced a small book from within his cloak and pressed it into my hand. It was a beautifully bound red leather edition entitled *A Christmas Carol*.

I was very disappointed that Charles failed to show up for our early evening meeting at the tea shop, but I never thought ill of him. I feel sure that would have had a very good reason and my only concern was that he might have had another dizzy spell, so instead I prayed for his good health and that one day soon we might meet once again. As I left the tea shop I held the book tightly inside of my tunic all the way back to my flat and later that night when I lay in bed before turning out my light as with many nights that followed I would read a chapter of *A Christmas Carol*.

It is with great regret that I have to close this amazing story by telling you that I never saw Charles Dickens ever again as I read that he sadly passed away a short time after our meeting at his home in Rochester, Kent. I think of him often and of that day in the train where he performed so many acts of kindness, he will live with me forever. The little bound red book I cherish as though it was my most precious possession. Equally as precious was the day that I sat next to this extraordinary man in the park opposite the hospital for only a few minutes, enough to learn his name. I still believe in angels as I did the day of the train crash and I'm sure that the Lord has made Charles Dickens one for sure now.

But before we say goodbye to one another I would just like to say something else, there's one other thing that never leaves my side even when I am on duty on the ward and although the nursing matron has no knowledge of its presence, it is a small silver hip flask. It is always full of brandy for those that might need the odd tipple to sooth their nerves, allay their fears or just enjoy the luxury of being a gentleman again before the inevitable. And lastly the only other thing that has always puzzled me and for which an answer has eluded me is that my nurse's chrome pocket watch has never given the wrong time, not once for the past five years and yet that day in Dover I feel sure that if the station clock had not afforded me those seemingly extra couple of minutes and held back the train for me I might never have caught that fateful train and met the most amazing man, the Staplehurst Angel.

THE POET AND THE COMEDIAN

I was glad to be walking down the pier towards the town for the last time. The afternoon sun overhead was losing some of its warmth and evening was approaching. As usual the perpetual noise of the seagulls droned annoyingly as they swooped beneath and above the wooden promenade. I saw an angler take a swipe at one who was trying for his bait, but the seabird was as always too sprightly to be caught.

The only enjoyable time that I particularly found attractive about the end of the pier was when I could sit in deep serenity, watch the clouds pass overhead and follow the skyline down to the horizon where it would rest upon the murky green of the sea. I'd stay for hours just watching the line of anglers cast and reel in their fishing lines. Some would encourage the start of a conversation, but in general I preferred my own company, just observing them as they hauled in lumps of loose seaweed, burst beach balls and ships' flotsam. I admired their tolerance, hankering for the same level of patience that they all seemed to have, it represented the lifestyle that I could only dream about. Stress always seemed in abundance for me of late.

I waved goodbye to the tea ladies in the small tea room at the beginning of the pier, raising my free wrist to view the time, where I hoped that they would appreciate the urgency of my journey, but instead they mistook my gesture as time for a cuppa.

'Time for a char, Joe?' Mavis bellowed.

I smiled and changed direction heading over to the door.

Whoever owned the tea room was an astute businessman in my opinion as the position of the tea room either captured you on the way up the pier or on the return journey back into town, or perhaps there and back if you were approaching your dotage years. The breeze at the end of the pier would market a visit as well where a warm refreshment would invigorate chilled bones.

As I opened the door I knew that I didn't really have the time, but the ladies had become members of my regular audience at the summer season show, so I needed to pay my respects and return some loyalty before I left. 'Just the one please, Mavis, as I've a train to catch,' I requested, hearing the sneaky giggles from behind the preparation counter. They were a funny bunch of ladies and somehow managed to find humour in almost every scenario, whether it was hilarious or not. I for one would miss Mavis and her ladies. I resisted telling them that yesterday's show was my last of the season, it would prevent having to give a lengthy explanation and I'm sure that when I returned next year they would greet me back again as if I'd never left.

I entered the Northumberland Street entrance to the railway station at Morecambe and promptly walked across to the newspaper stall where I intended purchasing a bag of boiled sweets for the journey.

'Evening, Joe, wanna paper as well?' enquired Len the stall owner.

I politely declined his offer as I had seen enough reviews of late, some good, more often bad and a few indifferent, to last me through this season. Morecambe had had the best of my talent this year and I felt like a spent force. I said my farewells to Len and Daniel, the young lad who delivered the late edition to the seafront businesses, then left to purchase my ticket.

As I stood on the southbound platform – there were only two of them and you fathomed it, the other went north – I watched the aerial acrobatics of the seagulls as they glided over the building rooftops and down onto the railway tracks foraging for scraps left by earlier commuters, they were definitely persistent little buggers that was for sure. The evening sun struggled to stay any longer on the western horizon leaving in its wake a hue of brilliant red which blanketed the evening sky. If this was my last reminder of Morecambe it was one to savour, the sky was magnificent.

The train arrived on time as did a number of passengers, no doubt extending their final few moments in Morecambe to the very last. I opened the carriage door and stepped inside noticing that the compartment already had a passenger, a gentleman a little older than myself, I fancied.

He looked my way and nodded acknowledging my arrival. 'Grand evening,' he said, as I shut the carriage door.

I had to agree, it most certainly was.

The train departed to the tune of a porter's whistle, a loud hiss of steam and a judder of the carriage wheels. Train travel had hardly changed over the last century and had remained inexplicably enigmatic to many schoolboys. It was simply everything that was good about being British. I felt the surge of power as the locomotive engaged the track pulling us along the seafront and away from the station. The steam train was most definitely the hallmark of our industrial revolution, the days of my father's father. I looked out at the pier as it symmetrically changed shape through the fiery orange cast across the carriage window before the evening shadows stole the show and we were suddenly plunged into the dim light of the approaching night.

'It makes you feel like a hermit, doesn't it? when the sun finally disappears and night-time kidnaps the last rays of the day. It is amazingly beautiful for the last few minutes though, its beauty never ceases to inspire me,' said the gentleman opposite.

I looked away from the reflection in the window to face my compartment companion. He was casually dressed, although his clothes were smart and fashionable, nicely presented with sharp lines and elegant bearing. I had already deduced from our few spoken words that he had a good command of conversation and appeared well educated. Studying my fellow man had long been a particular hobby of mine. My agent would often tell me that an education would have served me better and given me a much broader scope to my act. Me personally, I didn't see anything wrong with the act. It was broad and bawdy at the same time, a compatible union which seemed to work well for me, but even so I could see his point.

I liked to imitate the local dialect wherever I was performing.

It seemed only right that I should engage closely with the patrons, it made them feel that they were part of the act and they would accept and appreciate my humour all the quicker. Copying them was one of the tools of my trade so to speak. Let me give you an example.

A colonel visits a detachment of his troops as they are doing a gas mask drill. As the Sergeant gives the order for the soldiers to don their masks, the Colonel walks along the line inspecting each man. He comes across a man that he knows is of broad northern origin. Avidly watching his donning procedure, the Colonel enquires of the soldier, 'Where's your anti-mist?'

The soldier pulls forward the mouthpiece of the mask and replies, 'I'm not rightly sure, sir, but the last time I saw her, she were oop in Oldham wiv my Uncle Bert.'

Perhaps a poor example to demonstrate the use of different dialects, but humour me, it's been a very long day, first there was settling affairs at my digs and then there was the matinee show which turned out to be exactingly hard work. The stalls were nearly all occupied with old-age pensioners, most of whom refuse to use any form of hearing aid so the act was punctuated with remarks like 'Aye' and 'What'd he say?' besides the ones who'd only come in to get out of the autumnal weather and discouragingly you could hear their snores from the rear stalls. So it was a poor example, but I thought it would give you an idea of just what a comedian can be up against. It's never an easy life.

I replied, 'I don't usually see this time of the day.'

'That is unfortunate,' he replied. 'Are you never available at night?'

'You could say that,' I moaned.

'That is such a pity, some might say that it is possibly the best time of the day, although I have always considered that nothing compares to the first light of day. It generally means that we have not been spirited away in the night and the freshness of a new day will bring with it new ideas, hopes and dreams.'

'Blimey, I've got a right one here.' I scoffed sarcastically.

'Now there's something that I could certainly do with.'

'Hopes and dreams?' he enquired, ignoring my derisive manner.

'No. New ideas,' I replied.

'You sound very downhearted, my good man. Has Lady Luck deserted your shores?' he enquired.

I huffed louder than I meant. 'Deserted them? I think she's emigrated for good! If I knew where she'd gone I'd follow her and marry her.'

The man smiled at me although I could see there was concern in his eyes. I think his politeness was more out of pity for me, not that he could possibly have any idea of my present dilemma. We were silent for the next few minutes as the train passed through a tunnel and the air pressure popped our ears. I looked at my reflection in the carriage window, I had stepped down onto the next rung of self-pity almost borderline depression some psychiatrists would call it, and the loss of the evening sun had not helped provide me with any sort of remedy to change my mood. I didn't like the look of the face that bounced back to haunt me.

'I could help if you would allow me?' the man suddenly suggested.

How could this stranger help? It wasn't as if he knew me and everybody gets down in the dumps from time to time.

'Are you a shrink?' I asked.

He laughed loudly at my suggestion. 'Goodness, no. I am but a humble writer, a poet.' He then proffered me his right hand. 'My name is William Samuel Alexander.'

I shook his hand, pleased that he wasn't a madcap quack. 'I don't suppose you've heard of me, I'm plain old Joe Johnson, comedian by profession, if I dare call myself that.'

He didn't say whether or not he had heard of me. 'I am pleased to make your acquaintance, Joe, and believe me nobody is ever just plain. Most certainly not a comedian. I would say that yours is one of the oldest professions around.'

'How come?' I asked. Now he had my attention.

He settled himself comfortably into the seat then went on to explain that comedians had been around throughout the centuries as the more commonly known court jesters who fell about, presented the audience with tricks and told jokes. It was their task to make the king and queen and their court laugh, to entertain the masters of a large household and keep at bay the bloodthirsty crowds at a public execution. The jester had to be a man of versatility and skill to perform before such people. His trade required a vast array of dexterity of confidence, intelligence, knowledge and wherever possible impudence.

'Well, I've none of that lot,' I confessed.

As I expected, there was that smile again. I wondered if anything fazed him.

'That is not the case, my dear Joe, you possess them all and maybe more.' I was about to protest, but he raised a hand as if demanding the privilege to explain. 'Like the jester, you have to be confident, Joe, to stand up before your fellow man and tell him of something that he already knows, but does not readily acknowledge, until you remind him of it. You have to be intelligent, quick-thinking and quick-witted. Wherever your travels take you, you acquire knowledge, a knowledge that you use in your act. I am sure you do. You probably know more about a man's wife than he does, chivalrously speaking of course! And maybe lastly you are impudent, you have mastered that skill possibly above all others to be a comedian. Do you not deride the audience with some of your tales or jokes? I expect one or two of the audience are unsuspecting participants, but they laugh all the same and I would go so far as to say that they laugh the loudest. Comedy is the challenge that drives you, Joe. We all know that without these traits jesters of centuries past would have languished in the dungeons, as opposed to the court had their audience not found them entertaining. We should all be proud of our profession, Joe. I am of mine.'

'That's OK for you to say,' I interjected. 'I'll bet that what you say or what you write lives in the memories of children right through to the day they meet the Almighty. Poetry is a thing of rhyme and beauty. Comedy is for the moment. It's said there and then, and forgotten in the next second, gone in the blink of an eye.'

William was undefeated and seemed to have all the answers, regardless of whatever I threw back at him. 'Alas, Joe, tell me how does my poetry makes a child laugh, an adult cry or a mother-in-law concede to using profanities that she despises? You have the knack to do all this and more. My expression of words may well be written, may well be beautiful, but people pay more attention to what you have to say than they do to me.'

I felt like I was losing the argument. The black of night outside offered me no solace as I struggled to reply, a rarity in a comedian. William was a complete stranger to me, but I had to admit there was something compelling about his manner, his conversation and his philosophy of life. Although I seemed to be playing devil's advocate, I felt that I needed his injection of belief to make me believe in myself again. I even smiled as I sighed, 'My stage act's been drying up of late, William!' It might have sounded like a cry for help and I hadn't intended for it to be phrased quite like it had left my lips, but there it was, it had been said and I couldn't retract it.

'Joe,' William said quietly, 'poets spend hours writing maybe only a few lines, seeing if they rhyme, if they have meaning, exploring the depth of the intention, searching for that magic formula that will make their work remembered for centuries. I spend my life travelling on trains, sailing on ships, walking fells and hills, over locks and around lakes, across fields or meadows full of daisies, looking for that all-singing, all-dancing inspiration, but still I might only write one line at the end of the day, whereas you can say just one line and have an audience remember you forever. Inspiration is all around us, we just have to find it and use it effectively.'

What I did next I knew wasn't really fair, but I needed proof. 'Show me, William, prove to me that you can actually help.'

William as expected didn't appear fazed by my sudden demand. Instead he opened the leather satchel that sat beside him, withdrew a notepad then proceeded to put pen to paper.

'Give me a few minutes, Joe, and I will hopefully give you your proof.'

I watched quietly as he thought, scribbled, chewed the end of his pen, then scribbled again. Finally he put aside his pen. He handed me the notepad and I read the page.

Alone upon a stage
Fame hath no friend
Go break a leg
Beneath the weary spotlight
Make an audience laugh
Funny lines here or there
The lonely comedian
A jester, like a lion in a cage.

I looked up. It had taken William no more than a few minutes to produce the poem. It didn't rhyme, but the depth of its meaning was profound, it was how I felt inside, a man trapped in a cage. The man was a shrink and maybe a mind reader, whether he admitted it or not. I handed back the notepad.

'That's good, really good, but I need jokes, something funny for my audience, William!'

He didn't reply as he turned over the page on his notepad and started to write once again, his fingers working like an artist's paintbrush flowing across a canvas. After several minutes he handed me back his notepad.

'Here, read this, Joe. It is only a spur-of-the-moment thought, but perhaps demonstrates how easily you could write your own material using the right application of your mind.'

I read his scribblings.

A zebra out walking one day crossed before a pride of lions on the Serengeti who were sitting beneath the shade of the trees.

One of the lions asked the zebra, 'Have you had lunch?'

Not perturbed by the presence of the lions the zebra thanked the lion, but said that he'd just eaten.

The lion said that the pride had all missed breakfast that morning.

The zebra continued on walking past, but told the lion that they should always eat at Seven and Eleven.

The lion said he had never heard of the place.

The zebra told him it was new, on the corner of Main Street.

Now the moral of this tale is you should always eat sensibly, don't miss meals and always trust a zebra crossing.

I found myself laughing, it was ridiculously funny and I had to admit good. I knew that I could use it in my act. I handed back the notepad.

'That's amazing, William. Would you mind if I use it in my next show?'

William seemed pleased as his smile broadened across his cheeks. 'Why, I'd be privileged you considered it good enough. It was only produced quickly to demonstrate that you too have the ability, Joe. Give me an example now, why don't you tell me a couple of your jokes?'

I straightened my tie just like I did in my act, then licked the tip of my finger and pointed at William, again part of the act. I pondered for a second or two then began. I recited a couple of jokes that I'd used on many occasions:

A man was walking along a deserted beach when his foot hit something in the sand. Brushing aside the sand he found an ancient lamp. He rubbed it three times for luck when suddenly out popped a genie. The genie was so happy to be out of the lamp that he granted the man three wishes, but warned the man that anything he wished for, his ex-wife would get double. The man agreed.

'For my first wish I'd like a big house.'

There was a puff of magic smoke and the man had a big house. At the same time his ex-wife had a house twice as big as his.

'For my second wish I'd like a million pounds.'

Another puff of magic smoke and the man had before him a million pounds. The wife was delighted that before her was a pile numbering two million pounds.

'Now remember,' warned the genie, 'the ex-wife gets double.'

So the man had a long think then clicking his fingers he said his third wish. 'I'd like you to scare me half to death!'

William laughed surprisingly louder than he had meant, he apologised. I just smiled, then continued with my next joke.

Sadly the husband was following the pall-bearers out of the church after the service for his late departed wife when suddenly one of the pall-bearers slipped on the stone steps and the edge of the coffin fell against a brick wall.

A faint murmur was heard from inside the coffin so the pall-bearers quickly opened the casket and to everybody's surprise the wife was found to be alive. The husband promptly fainted.

The wife lived for another ten years, but sadly she passed away and again the husband set in motion the arrangements. Again as befitting the service the husband followed the coffin from the church but as the pall-bearers reached the stone steps the congregation heard him cry out, 'Watch out for the steps and mind that bloody wall.'

It made William laugh again much to my pleasure. I hadn't heard anybody laugh like this in a long while. William was very complimentary and told me that I had real gift for telling jokes. He said that only a very funny man would make him laugh. It was good to hear and the jokes had even sounded funny to me. That was a strange thing to admit, but perhaps there was something quite magical about William that I didn't know about. He asked me to relate another joke before we arrived at Blackpool. I willingly obliged.

Two boys are playing football outside in the yard when they accidentally smash the window. Their mother calls the glazier to repair it. When he arrives she warns him that they have a pet parrot in the kitchen and that he is to be aware that he swears all the time.

So the glazier set about his works and sure enough the parrot starts using profanities towards him. He ignores the bird, but in doing so the profanities become more vulgar and so the glazier warns the parrot.

A few minutes later the parrot starts swearing again only this time it's really offensive and so profane are the profanities that the glazier grabs the parrot and puts him in the freezer.

The glazier finishes the repair, packs away his tools then remembers the parrot. He opens the door of the freezer only to be confronted by the parrot who he is surprised is still alive. The parrot hops out and up onto his perch. He looks at the repairman who raises a cautionary finger at the bird.

The parrot declares, 'OK, I promise no swearing, but just what the hell did the turkey do?'

We were both still laughing when the station announcement echoed down the platform at Blackpool Station announcing the arrival of the train. I got up from my seat and retrieved the suitcase from the overhead net mesh.

I held out my hand. 'This is my stop, I'm afraid, William.'

William shook my hand warmly and as expected recited a parting shot. 'You know, Joe, you're a damn fine comedian and I'm sure that your shows are very funny. You should use those jokes every time, they will bring the house down. Life's too short to be letting trivial things get in the way of happiness.'

I thanked him for his kind words, then from inside of my coat lining I produced two complimentary tickets. 'Please bring along a friend, William. I'm here for the next few months till Christmas, then off to pantomime in Norfolk. You'd do me a real honour if you'd accept.'

I handed them over and William accepted the gift. It was my way of saying thank you for finding inspiration that I thought I had lost.

As I walked along the platform towards the barrier I watched as the train left the station observing the faces of the passengers as they went by. I looked for our carriage and for William, but before I knew it the end of the train had flashed past and then it was gone. I was disappointed that I hadn't had the opportunity to wave. I watched until the train lights faded beyond sight.

That next night I eagerly walked into the dressing room of the theatre. I felt somewhat different about myself, there was a sense of belonging now, a real aura of confidence that had been missing of late. I felt younger and a need to be up on the stage before my audience. As I sat at the make-up table I could hear the clapping of the audience as the dancers appeared on stage.

The theatre sounded like a full house was in. Just then there was a knock at the door and a stagehand handed me a small package. The address label had been neatly written and was addressed simply to 'Joe Johnson, Comedian'.

I ripped open the parcel and found inside a beautifully bound edition of poetry by William Samuel Alexander. I quickly flicked the book over to the back cover and looked for a foreword or anything else that would appraise me of the author, but there was nothing except the publisher's information on the inside first page. It told me that the edition had been published by a London company in 1956. As I flicked over another page I found the short handwritten inscription, it read:

'Go break a leg, Joe. William.'

If William ever did use the tickets and bring along a friend I never knew. Stage acts very rarely see the members of the audience, blinded by the spotlight and beyond the orchestra pit it's normally night-time black. I had hoped that he did make it and that he liked what he saw and what he heard. I made sure that I gave it my all in every act and the winter season show in Blackpool was well received by audiences, with additional bookings for other venues diarised around the country.

And I have a special book of poetry that travels with me everywhere now and I often wonder if William's on another train somewhere, looking for that inspiration. I travelled on one in the early autumn of last year and found mine, thanks to a poet, named William.

THE QUEST FOR THE CODE

I slipped past the barrier guard and ran frantically down the platform waving my train ticket above my head to show that I had one, the guard resisted the urge to run after me, instead he just threw his hands into the air then turned away in disgust muttering something about the youth of today, but I really did need to catch this train and I wasn't youthful any longer as my twenty-third birthday was only a month away.

Grabbing hold of the carriage door handle I flicked it open and virtually launched myself into the compartment, my rucksack landing beside a gentleman that had already settled himself nicely by the look of it into his seat. He obliged by grabbing hold of my forearm and pulled me in, then reached out for the swinging door to shut it. Foolishly I sat opposite to where he'd been sat. That was an embarrassing introduction if ever there was one.

The man sat down again and adjusted his shirt so that it sat comfortably. 'Good morning, Fräulein, you must need this train rather a lot!' he announced. From his accent I deduced that he was a German national.

Feeling ridiculously foolish I probed my fingers through my hair in an attempt to smooth some order to my appearance, goodness knows what I looked like.

'Thank you. I really was very grateful for your help.'

He smiled and I noticed an almost boyish charm about him. My German was a little older than me, had shoulder-length dark-brown wavy hair, dark eyes to match and his facial features were angular, most definitely European. He was quite handsome. His pronunciation of the English language was good, but as with most Europeans it was gilded beautifully with a hint of his own dialect. It added to his charm.

I returned his smile. 'I'm sorry that my rucksack almost hit you.' It sounded like a feeble introduction for a chat-up line, but he was aware of my embarrassment and politely informed me that there was no need to apologise. I sensed that he was still bemused by our impromptu meeting. He handed back my rucksack.

'That's a well-travelled rucksack?' he admired.

To me it was just a rucksack and I didn't really put much store on how much I'd used it or for what purpose, I guessed that he was being polite.

'It serves me fine for getting my books back and forth to university,' I replied.

'Ah, so you attend university. That is very good,' he remarked. 'My own rucksack is like a second skin to me, I could never be without it.'

I looked up and saw a rather dog-eared bag lying in the storage net above him. It certainly was well worn and had no doubt been to many places from the look of it.

He chuckled and continued, 'I'm always getting mine thrown back at me, so it's nothing new to have yours land beside me.'

It was a strange thing to say and I wondered why somebody would throw his rucksack at him. He reminded me of a latter-day Indiana Jones. I looked back up at the storage net expecting to see his khaki fedora hat there. There wasn't one, despite his dress of faded khaki shirt with the familiar chest pockets, faded light-blue jeans and well-used brown leather jacket. You could easily have mistaken him for the character immortalised in the George Lucas films. I wondered if there was an angry girlfriend or frustrated wife waiting for him somewhere whilst he was away on his escapades.

I admit that I was every inch the archetypical student type, rather than a well-heeled administrative worker. The only letters that I carried about in my rucksack were from my girlfriends back home and my mum. I suppose too that my dirty tanned walking boots might have helped with his assumption of me.

'So where do you study?' he enquired, in true German style, no flowering up the edges, just direct questioning.

'I'm in my final year at Edinburgh University, Scotland.' It seemed a ridiculous thing to tell him that it was in Scotland as we were on the same train heading towards the Scottish capital. I added a bit more. 'It's why I needed to catch this train. My professor says that she will disown me if I'm late for another of her lectures.'

'It is good you study and important that you attend every lecture. Much more important that you understand them though.'

That was a strange thing to say and I wasn't too sure of his emphasis, but I let it pass.

'What are you studying?' he asked.

'History, the Classics and archaeology,' I answered. All good Indiana stuff and what had interested me from a very early age.

'That is very interesting, all good subjects and with good prospects,' he declared.

I wondered how he knew.

As the train rushed northwards our conversation was interspersed with periodic lulls as he read his book and I riffled through the various items I had secreted in my rucksack. I tried reading a novel that my mother had given me saying that it would help while away the evenings back in my digs, poor love she really didn't have any idea about how exciting our evenings were and they definitely didn't include reading novels. I discreetly checked that I had my feminine essentials, finally selecting a large reference book on ancient Persian history.

The train flashed through the smaller northern towns without stopping and I took no notice as to our progress. That was how travel was these days, passengers were only ever interested in when they had arrived at their destination and train travel had seemingly lost all of its romantic appeal. It was purely just a means to an end and mine was Edinburgh Waverley Station. I looked up once surprised to see that the German was looking across at me. We politely smiled at one another before I buried my head back in my book. I heard the stationmaster announce our departure from Doncaster.

'That's a very fascinating book you're reading,' he said, 'packed heavily with facts and perhaps the odd reference of fiction, but who knows!'

I looked up and placed my finger at the point that I'd reached. 'Sure is,' I replied. He wasn't wrong, I'd been ploughing through the content for the past two weeks.

'You are indeed a scholar,' he announced unexpectedly, 'with an understanding of ancient history so it would seem. Do you know of the book's author?' he enquired.

I had to admit that I couldn't remember the name of the author, but he said it was no problem and asked if he could look at the book. I placed a scrap of paper between the pages as a bookmark then handed it across to him.

He ran his fingers admiringly over the gold impression of the author's name, then flicked open the inside cover. '*The Biblical Code*,' he announced. He seemed as though he was confirming its origin rather than telling me the book's title. 'The author is Shmuel.'

Of course it was, now I remembered.

Shmuel had been the topic of several of our lectures and I knew the content of the book was very important to the Hebrews.

'It is good that you are reading this book,' he promoted. 'It's been a while since I have needed to refer to it.'

I was surprised that somebody would need to refer to such an ancient book. It was obvious that he had a copy too somewhere.

'What do you know about this book?' he asked. There he went again, direct and to the point.

'Our professor lectured us recently on the biblical code. I remember her telling us that the name Shmuel is ancient Hebrew and means the name of God. The book itself contains biblical text known as the Torah Code, but I have to confess that I don't know what that is yet. It's why I was reading it hoping to understand it.'

'First I need your name?' he asked abruptly. I say asked, but it almost seemed a demand.

I told him it was Lucy, Lucy Lawrence. I don't know why I actually agreed to give it and especially as he was a complete stranger that just happened to be travelling in my compartment, but although I couldn't explain it myself, and reason with the initial argument bandying about in my mind, I had. Although he was abrupt sometimes, possibly a European trait, there was also a trust in his eyes that made it seem right. The young men I knew at university didn't have that same look about them. I recall my father telling me before I left for university not to trust any of them. I knew exactly what he really meant, but I loved him all the more for trying to protect me.

Without any prompting I offered some more personal information. 'When I'm at home I live in a small village two miles outside of a town called Ashford in Kent with my parents. It's their home. I don't have a boyfriend.' Goodness knows what possessed me to tell him that, it just slipped out for some reason.

He grinned. I wasn't sure if he was pleased that I didn't have one, or whether he was only being polite. His being handsome most definitely didn't help.

He made no reference to what I had just told him, but continued quite unexpectedly to tell me something of his country's history. 'I expect that you've had lectures in the past about the history of my lands, especially that of this century. It is not a history we Germans hold with pride, but all the same there is no disputing our origins and regardless we are proud to be German whatever.'

As I listened I could see that his eyes portrayed a sadness in his eyes as he talked, but his head was held proudly straight with pride that he was a German national.

He closed the book of biblical text, his finger holding the place where he needed to save. 'Have you heard of the burning books of Berlin, Lucy?' he asked.

'Yes, I have.' I didn't mean it to sound so enthusiastic, but at last I could redeem myself and show him that I wasn't some dumb student who rushed late for a train and threw her luggage at other passengers. 'It was on the night of 10th May 1933 when the university students from Berlin raided shops, libraries, schools and the shelves and bookcases of private houses, they gathered all the books they could taking them to the central square. There they built a huge bonfire and set fire to the lot. Many valuable works by many famous and known authors were lost that night including Albert Einstein, Karl Marx, Ernest Hemingway, Sigmund Freud and Helen Keller, to name only a few. Anything that had been written that did not meet with the approval of the

'German' ideology was destroyed. Somehow the book of the biblical code by Shmuel survived.'

'That is very good, Lucy. First I will give you an explanation regarding the code so that you know and when you come to it in the book, you will understand. The Torah Code is the hidden code of selected equidistant letter sequences when every fiftieth letter of the Book of Genesis starting with the first *taw*, the Hebrew word Torah is spelt out. They are the words and phrases from the 3,300-year-old Hebrew Bible and demonstrate foreknowledge and prophesies. It is purported to hold within the text the very secrets of the Bible. Secrets that many men have desired to have for themselves throughout the ages. Many have sought its knowledge and some say power, but it would seem that only when the time is right do the secrets reveal themselves and only to those that are worthy, as chosen by God himself. Evil men may seek, but evil begets an evil that prevails until they meet their doom.'

I was totally fascinated and my inner yearning to know more must have pencilled itself across my face.

He continued. 'Lucy, do you know of the significance of Hitler's date of death?'

'He died on the night of 30th April and 1st May 1945 in his bunker in Berlin. His death was recorded as suicide, although it can never be confirmed. Isn't that night according to German folklore known as Walpurgis Night or the night of the witches?'

'You listen well to your professor, Lucy. Yes, that night our witches do meet on the Brocken, the highest peak of the Harz Mountains amongst a range of wooded hills.' He opened the book again at the saved page that he'd saved. 'The book of Shmuel was thankfully saved that dreadful night by a scholar that recognised it. He knew of its valuable significance and how important it was to mankind. It is not known how the book transferred hands, but Hitler himself heard of the book and despite its Jewish inference he regarded the book as an important find. Hitler had German scholars working round the clock trying to unravel the code's hidden secrets. He wanted its power, but as I said the book does not give up its treasures lightly. Hitler met his fate as it was written.'

'What happened to the book after the war and who possessed it?' I asked.

'The book does not belong to any man, Lucy, but to mankind. I'm not sure who took the book from the bunker, but somehow it found its way into the Harz Mountains. I was fortunate to have found it when I went up there four weeks ago.'

'Are you a warlock then or did you go looking for the witches?' I asked mischievously.

My suggestion made him chuckle. 'Neither, I happened to be potholing with my cousin Eric. We were following up another trail in my research, but instead the book presented itself to us. It was well hidden in the rock, but it was as though it wanted to be found. I've no idea why I should be the one to find it, maybe a date is approaching which is of significance. A date whereby the book will reveal to us one of its secrets. For the past few weeks I have travelled to the holy city of Jerusalem and there with the learned scribes we have spent long hours trying to unlock the cypher. We did not succeed.'

To say that I was hooked by the mystery was an understatement. He was a real-life Indiana Jones, but I needed to know his true identity. It was my turn now to be somewhat blunt. 'Who are you and what do you do?'

'But of course, Lucy. Forgive me, it is rude of me not to have introduced myself. Let me present myself, I am Ralph Lehmann and despite what others may say about me I am an archaeologist. My quests and my search for the truth take me all over the world where I work to unravel the secrets of our past. It is because of this book by Shmuel that I find myself here on the train travelling to Edinburgh. The quest takes me to the university which you attend as another man similar to myself told me a week ago that there is a professor there that has an understanding of these matters. She has a reputation for possessing a wealth of knowledge about Hebrew history. I'm hoping that she can decipher the code and reveal to me why the book presented itself to me and me alone.'

This was better than I had imagined. 'You've a date with Professor Hinching?' I asked.

'Yes, the very same lady, Lucy, and word has it that she has an excellent set of students this year. Perhaps they might be involved and help us unlock the secret.' It was Ralph's turn to be mischievous.

It was mid-afternoon before the train pulled into Edinburgh Waverley Station. Ordinarily I would have gone straight to my digs and together we would have chilled out during the evening cooking something simple like lasagne washed down with cheap wine before our return to university the next morning, however today was a whole lot different and had a purpose that was both beguiling and absorbing to the mind.

Ralph Lehmann agreed to my accompanying him to the university only, as he said, introductions would be made all the easier with Professor Hinching. The Professor had received Ralph's letter the week before, but of course I was not to know this. She was however expecting the renowned German archaeologist so when I knocked and opened the door to her study she rose from her chair to greet him, a little surprised to see me there. She however did pass me a smile and I guessed that she was pleased to see me back in Edinburgh early, at least I would attending her first lecture the next day. It was Ralph who explained my presence in her study. He told the Professor about our train journey north and the interesting conversation we'd engaged upon concerning Shmuel's book.

'You teach your students well, Professor,' he said, offering his hand. 'Lucy seems to have a good grasp of her subject.'

Wow, Brownie points for me and told in the presence of my mentor. This new term had already got off to a good start. I liked Ralph Lehmann all the more.

'Thank you, Mr Lehmann, I would agree normally with that sentiment, however I don't want the compliment to invigorate Lucy's ego beyond my expectations of her this term.' The Professor looked directly at me and I knew it had a meaning. 'Besides, she still has a 100,000-word dissertation to finish before graduation.'

I'd been shot back down to earth as quick as I'd climbed Everest. I smiled at them both as I stood back behind one of the chairs before the Professor's desk. It was Professor Hinching's way of paying me a compliment, but telling me to keep a level head on my shoulders. Previous and past one-to-one debriefs at the end of term had always ended with her reining in my ego. She was the best professor that I knew though and recorded criticisms were always kept to a minimum, but the more important compliments were said in private.

I realised that I wanted to grasp the world and all its mysteries with both hands sooner rather than later, especially as I was already nearly twenty-three and I was concerned that time would march on quicker than I could catch it up. My mentor however, always the inevitable angel of calm told me that it had taken centuries for history and events to evolve and taking one step at a time would not make any of them disappear overnight.

I was surprised, but delighted when Professor Hinching said that I could stay, provided Mr Lehmann had no objections. Ralph agreed as I took my seat beside him stating that an extra mind might be an advantage to explore the endless possibilities, dismiss the irrelevant facts and help formulate the answers that we needed. He looked at me and winked. Indiana Jones had come through for me as I smiled back.

Professor Hinching opened the discussion telling us both that during the autumn recess, she had been looking into the known facts and events surrounding the discovery of the Dead Sea scrolls. Now for those amongst us that do not know and need to be enlightened, the Dead Sea scrolls are an ancient set of scrolls, written mostly in ancient Hebrew, but with some Arabic and Greek included. They are reported to be dated around 408–318 BC and are said to be the product of a 2,000-year-old puzzle. The scrolls were discovered in the Qumran caves at Khirbet Qumran in the Judaean Desert, about two kilometres inland from the north-west bank of the Dead Sea, hence how they derive their name. The scrolls were found purely by chance by three Bedouin shepherds, Muhammed Edh-Dhib and his cousins Jum'a Muhammed and Khalil Musa. The story goes that Muhammed whilst tending to his flock had accidentally fallen through the roof of the cave and found the scrolls safely preserved in a number of glass jars. The scrolls were found to have been produced from papyrus, parchment and bronze.

The distinct lack of a formidable education or knowledge

surrounding such writings presented a problem for the Bedouin shepherds as they did not know what was written on the scrolls or what they represented and they were unsure where they had come from. In an effort to show seniority the Bedouin elders had stretched the scrolls between their tent posts until they decided what best to do with them. Eventually though one of the cousins took the Dead Sea scrolls to Bethlehem. Records show that two other scrolls were found in 1979 at Ketef Hinnon, south-west of the Old City of Jerusalem. These are said to contain the priestly blessings from the Book of Numbers, the oldest surviving text of the Hebrew Bible. The two small silver scrolls are said to be dated around 600 BC.

As she flicked through the middle of my book she made reference to a chapter. 'We know that Paul, the Apostle, had written to the Romans telling them about Christianity and that the Romans had devised, like many other races, their own code.'

Ralph nodded his approval, agreeing.

Professor Hinching continued. 'The foundation of the constitution of the Roman peoples through the periods of the kingdom, republic and empire were formed as a result of the twelve tables somewhere around 449 BC by the Emperor Justinian I. The twelve tables represented the laws of the people by which they could all be governed. They remained in effect until the 14th century by what is commonly known as the Byzantine period.'

Ralph interrupted the Professor at this point knowing exactly where her explanation was leading. 'And in Germany, Roman law practices remained in place into the 18th century under the basis of the Holy Roman Empire. Many of the practices still exist in today's Germany.'

'Precisely, Ralph. You know only too well of Hitler's obsession with anything biblical, the Ark of the Covenant, the Spear of Destiny and the Holy Grail?' She expressed her regret for touching on an era which most Germans wished to forget, but the reference had an important bearing on Ralph's presence at the university.

He told her that such misgivings had been the bad tidings of men throughout the centuries and thanked her for her kindness, but his quests to unravel such mysteries would always touch upon an event in history that a nation's forefathers had been involved with. Sentiment could not stop an explorer whatever the price.

'I know it only too well, Professor,' he said. 'Who would not have thought that a man with such strong determination to conquer would have suddenly turned to ancient relics, where the hidden secrets of the centuries were mostly speculative and had yet to be explored?'

'Had he found them though, Ralph, and if they really did possess the power of the Almighty that a lot of people believe they do, then Herr Hitler would have been invincible. World domination would have been at his fingertips.'

I sat quietly and listened to the voices of the two informative minds, hoping that one day I would have the wealth of knowledge that they both possessed. I had my own quests that I wanted to pursue.

'However great the argument, it always comes down to greed and power. Shmuel and the Hebrew scribes, the ones that wrote those ancient manuscripts did not do so for mankind to unravel the codes in the pursuit of evil and ultimate destruction.'

I liked Ralph, he was a spirited man with true values. I was fortunate that I had picked his compartment to throw my rucksack in.

'But how did he find out about the biblical code and Shmuel's book? That night of the 10th May 1933 was meant to destroy all Hebrew beliefs,' said the Professor.

'Hitler had many researchers working in various parts of the world at the start of the war. Some would call them spies. The information that they related back to the high command would result in strategy and war plans. Some of the researchers though must have had knowledge of the ancient world, the world of the Egyptians and the Romans. Through his researchers he was told about the secret of the Torah Code. If broken it would reveal perhaps the power of God. Hitler realised the foolishness of burning so many valuable other books as they may have been of similar importance. The Hebrews had recorded the secrets that he so desperately sought.'

The conversation between the Professor and Ralph raced on with them crossing all the avenues of speculation, known fact and pure fiction. The process of elimination was slow as it always has been in history. Archaeology was just an extension of that search, but without the quests of such men and women the secrets would remain undiscovered.

As I listened I tried to be peripheral with my thinking, extending my reasoning beyond the box of scientific reality, it sometimes worked and they say that sometimes the simplest route brings forth the answer to the least complex equation. My theory was that there was undoubtedly something quite significant that had been written in the text of the book that Ralph had found, but as is often the case it is the answer to the riddle which stares you directly in the face. I waited until there was a pause in their conversation and asked if I could look at the book whilst their debate deepened. Ralph handed it over to me.

The text of the book was in Hebrew, which obviously once you study becomes legible to decipher, much like reading the hieroglyphics used by the ancient Egyptians. As I read several pages I began to feel the frustration that Ralph must have felt for the past month. I read the text, then reread it just to be sure, but nothing was glaringly obvious. Then quite by chance, just like Muhammed Edh-Dhib at Qumran, I fell through the grey and into the light. The page reference and number in the Bible usually heads the direct left or right of the page, hardly ever at the bottom of the page. I took this to mean that the Almighty looked down upon his scriptures and mankind rather than up to heaven. Just my theory but hey ho you never know. I interrupted Ralph and the Professor and explained my theory. Ralph took the book back.

The three of us leant across the Professor's desk as she scribbled on her pad. We searched the book's pages for any evidence of my theory. She started to record the page number and reference, then cross-referenced the information. It was some kind of cipher, of that all three of us were sure. A cipher is a message where a letter is replaced by a different letter or symbol. A code is where a word is replaced by a different word or symbol. Patiently the Professor worked through the first few pages, changing a letter or word, or adding a symbol in Hebrew. As she worked her way down through the page more of the code began to reveal itself. I thought about the complexity of the task ahead and realised that we would not have the solution today, the search for the reason why the book had presented itself to Ralph in the German forest would remain a mystery for many days to come, perhaps weeks or months, but I'm sure like most mysteries, they eventually give up their secrets in the end. We had only just begun our quest.

As for me well I had a dissertation to write and quite a story to tell my friends back at my digs. But before I leave you I have to say that I've also had the offer to go to Germany to join Ralph on some of his quests after I leave Edinburgh University. He told me that he could certainly use an enquiring young mind like mine. I take that as a compliment and of course I said yes to his invitation. I also promised to keep my ego in check, although he is a very handsome man.

Please don't be too disappointed that the code from Shmuel's book hasn't yet been discovered or solved, that I assure you will come and it will be one day soon when all will be revealed. In the meantime keep watching the tabloids because I feel sure you'll read all about it. Professor Hinching is working tirelessly day and night for the answer.

AN UNUSUAL UNION

I suppose the tell-tale sign of a man of the cloth is his clerical collar which nestles centrally around the neck of his black shirt. My name is Robert Albright and although I am a man of faith with strong devout beliefs in my religion, I still possess that shadow from my childhood which my fellow churchmen say is distinctly rebellious. You see the dog collar as it is more commonly known is just part of my Church uniform. It has been worn by men over the centuries to denote that they belong to the Church and to belong means simply that the Church rules your life. However, I have always considered it a halo that more befits an angel than myself, so when I'm not on Church business I leave my dog collar in my beside drawer, much to the indifference of my bishop.

Having said all that the small leather-bound King James Bible that I always carry with me tells everybody who I am. You see to me it's not just the New Testament, which was written around the time of Christ and the interpretation of religious scholars down the centuries, to me it is my diary. You may well ask how or why? Well let me explain and I do hope that I have not offended you already. Very few of us actually keep a diary, recording the events, surprises and bad days of each day of our lives. Fundamentally it would be inconceivable to expect a person to do just that, but the ancient scholars without realising it did the job for me. Only you see whichever chapter or verse I may choose on any given day will act as my diary for that day. The message you see always remains the same, faith in the Lord. I guess you get the message now so I don't need to keep spouting on, suffice to say that I don't have to write any entries, other than follow those that are already written for the good of all mankind.

'Good day to you, vicar,' greeted Albert the ticket clerk. 'I presume your work takes you further afield to strange shores today!'

I smiled. 'Yes it certainly does, Albert. A return ticket to Durham please.'

'You've plenty of time, the next train won't depart for another forty minutes.'

I thanked him and took the short walk across the booking hall towards the tea room. It was a cheery refuge from the gloom of the booking hall, a room of bright colours, old photographs, books and gas-lit lanterns. I approached the tea counter and gave the waitress behind the counter my order. I have to admit that cakes are generally an indulgence I find difficult to resist. I chose the iced-topped carrot cake and a small pot of tea using the excuse of having missed lunch to good effect.

The morning rounds in the wards of the local hospital had taken much longer than I had expected. And yes, I know that I have already promoted my line of work as for the good of all mankind, but occasionally although the elderly are both interesting and responsive to my visit, they can tend to be equally tedious and demanding of my time. I feel sure that they wait all week for my visit before unloading the sins of their past misdemeanours onto me. You would be surprised at the saucy tales of daring that fall upon my ears. Is it any wonder we finish a prayer with Amen. Strict anonymity and discretion need a prayer to release some of them from their sins, I assure you.

I chose a seat nearest to the window as railway stations had always fascinated me from my boyhood days and besides I knew that the southbound train was due very soon. I had always been in awe of the locomotive engine, the power beneath its long sleek body and the sheer strength that surged through the wheels as they danced along the track.

My daydream memory was rudely interrupted by the sound of the bell above the tea-room door announcing the arrival of another customer. I watched a young Indian woman as she guardedly entered the tea room. She had in her possession a large cloth travelling bag made up of many colours and she wore the traditional sari of south Asia. What was more strikingly noticeable however was that the young woman really was very beautiful. Although the tea room was almost empty save for myself and another young couple I took the liberty of smiling in her direction, standing up to offer her a seat at my table. I accidentally scraped the legs of my chair over the wooden floor causing the waitress to look my way, so I raised a hand as an apology.

The young Indian woman walked over to the table and accepted my invitation to join me. I greeted her with a hand gesture similar to our commencement of prayer. She reciprocated the greeting.

'It's getting rather chilly outside,' I said. 'Can I offer you a drink? There is plenty in my teapot.'

She looked across at the young couple, but they were so engrossed with one another that I doubt they realised she had sat down at my table.

'That is very kind of you, sir, please, only tea, but no milk. The cow is sacred in my country and we do not drink the mother's milk. That is for the very young only.'

I caught the reflection in the mirror behind the counter of us both as we sat down. We did look an intriguing couple, an English vicar and a beautiful young Asian woman. I could only imagine what my bishop would have said had he walked into the tea room at that moment. I found the young woman incredibly engaging and delightfully conversant with her appreciation of our English language. She informed me that she was from the Haridwar district, the ancient city and municipality district of Uttarakhand in Northern India. She must have seen the look of surprise on my face, concerned that she had somehow offended me. I moved my Bible to one side as I poured the tea.

'Good heavens, no. You honour me here today with your presence. I should explain that before I settled back here in England I was a Church missionary in Chamba. You should know the village is not that far from your own at Haridwar.'

She smiled and her eyes sparkled I suspect at the thought that somebody she had only just met and on a British railway station could know of her birthplace and home.

It never ceases to amaze me how our lives can follow the paths of our souls and that destiny will take us on a journey around and across this planet, and yet by fate alone we will meet somebody who has links with that place. Our fragile life is so unpredictable and often at the mercy of God. I didn't want her to believe that I had fortunately plucked a village close to hers, so I continued with my limited knowledge of her region.

'I have also seen the Ganges, the great river whose source begins high up at Gaumukh at the edge of the Gangotri Glacier. I have chased it down the mountain and watched it rapidly grow in size as it sped towards the Indo-Gangetic plains of Northern India stretching between the banks at Haridwar for the first time.'

'You are indeed a well-travelled man, sir. You would find many Christians there. I know of them also,' she remarked.

'Yes, I did,' I agreed, 'but it was the Hindus who made me very welcome at one of their holiest of places.'

'Sapta Puri,' she said quietly, as though to have said it any louder would have offended the divine spirits.

'Indeed, a wonderful place of serene holiness.' We smiled. 'I too was fortunate to bathe with your countrymen and the women along the banks of the Ganges. They kindly invited me to join them in the ritualistic ceremony at the *footsteps of the Lord*, where he answers all of our prayers. Sapta Puri was indeed a wondrous place and great inspiration in my work today.'

We both took the chance to sip our tea as the southbound train arrived in a cloud of smoke on the platform opposite. I glanced across at the train, but there would be other times to see the locomotive so I looked back at my guest.

'I should have introduced myself,' I said. 'I am the Reverend Robert Albright from the village of Lower Ellingham. It's only a small village with just under 600 inhabitants. A lot less than Haridwar.'

The young woman suddenly reached down into her colourful travelling bag and withdrew a plastic-sleeved wallet. She selected two pictures from within and passed them across to me. One was of a proud, handsome Asian man and the other was a family photo, which I took to be her own. 'I am Avishi Kanya, which means hopes and inspiration in my language.' She pointed to the family photograph and as I suspected she pointed out her mother, father, older brother and two sisters to me. 'The man in the photograph alone is Pashwan Dumar. He is a doctor here in a town called Durham. I am travelling to Durham by train to be met by my eldest brother, who will soon preside over my marriage to the good doctor. Soon I will be Avishi Dumar.'

During my time in India I had come across many families where the arrangement of marriage had been sealed from birth. Hindus would use the *jathakam* or *janam kundali*, the astrological birthdate as a guide of a proposed union. But for Avishi to have been so forthright after having only just met me and away from her homeland rang a few alarm bells in my subliminal reasoning. Brides did not normally travel alone and show strangers photographs of their intended. It was often the case that the bride and groom did not know what the other looked like until the day of the ceremony. I picked up my Bible and held it between my fingers as I searched for the answers that I felt Avishi needed before she reached Durham.

I didn't mean the question to be as forthright as it sounded, but it was as good a place as any to start. 'Do you know Pashwan Dumar?' I asked.

'Yes.' It was almost whispered, as a reply.

At that moment I looked across at the young couple who having assembled their belongings together walked across to the counter to pay the waitress before leaving the tea room. Avishi watched also as they pulled shut the door and the waitress disappeared out of sight into the rear kitchen, the clattering of crockery reassuring us both.

'I have known Pashwan Dumar ever since I was a little girl. I have not met with him yet, but I do have his photograph, so I know of him.'

I wasn't convinced. During my travels across Northern India I had witnessed first-hand the traditional wedding ceremony of an arranged marriage. At first I admit it seemed unusual and perhaps English tradition found it hard to contemplate that a bride and groom went without a proper courtship, but I had to respect the customs of another culture. A Hindu marriage is divided into four parts and in its simplest form they are *dharma* (duty), *artha* (possessions), *kama* (physical desire), and *moska* (ultimate spiritual release).

Should you be fortunate to attend a Hindu wedding ceremony

you will find it not too dissimilar to our own Christian ceremony. It is a colourful union of celebration and dancing, joy and ancient traditions. I remember having soon returned to England speaking with my bishop on the subject of worshipping the Lord that you had to understand the beliefs of all men, irrespective of colour or creed. Only then could we truly be at one with God. The Bishop being a generation older and having never left these shores stated that the Lord had chosen him for Christendom alone, he respected other denominations' beliefs, providing they all recognised the good Lord, the Almighty. I'd soon realised when it was best not to pursue a debate with the Bishop and let sleeping dogs lie.

I looked at the photograph of the man. 'Pashwan is a handsome man,' I remarked. I looked at Avishi as I wanted to see her reaction. 'Is he a doctor of medicine or science?'

Her expression remained unchanged as she turned the photograph around so that she could see his face. 'A doctor of medicine. I understand that he studies the illnesses of children. He is sorely missed in our region where his skills would not go unnoticed.'

'And what about you, Avishi Kanya? What are your intentions when you become Mrs Dumar? Do you have a profession, or are you just going to be the wife of a children's doctor?' I studied her once again, forgetting all time or the train timetable.

As she looked at his face I thought I saw a shadow of doubt in her eyes. The polished lustre was suddenly gone.

'It is my duty to my husband to be a faithful and loyal wife. My place will be in the home to give birth to our children. I am sure that I am of a good fertile family that will give my husband sons.' She didn't look at me when she made her declaration.

I took the personal approach deeper, mentally asking the Lord for guidance. 'If such an arrangement between your families had not been made, Avishi, would you have chosen a destiny for yourself?' I asked.

For what seemed minutes, but was probably only seconds a deathly silence pervaded the tea room. The clatter of crockery out back in the kitchen had stopped too. I knew that I had pushed the young Asian woman too far. I felt ashamed of my actions and knew that I would regret causing embarrassment to Avishi. I expected her to stand and walk away, but to my surprise she remained.

Avishi Kanya looked up and directly at me. Her dark brown eyes were determined as she leant forward slightly. 'If I had been a son instead of a daughter, I would have wanted to have been a doctor for myself. But I was born a girl and so I shall not have a profession or any other destiny. My duty is to my husband-to-be. I could not dishonour or bring shame to my father whatever the price of my freedom.'

And so there it was, the answer that I'd dug so deep to find. Not the discretion that I should have used, but Avishi had said it for herself. I held my Bible to my chest as I searched my own soul for the reasons why I had been so dogmatic. I looked back at those dark brown eyes, at the kindness and softness that had made her accept my invitation to sit and join me, sharing tea. All of a sudden I felt my own vulnerability. That shadow of rebellion was attacking my very constitution. To hell with the Bishop and the others too old for this modern-day Church.

'Did your brother travel ahead of you, or does he live here?' I asked.

'No, my brother, Reyansh, which means ray of light in my village, travelled here beforehand to bring Pashwan Dumar my dowry. My father thought it best that he travelled alone as it would not attract unwanted attention from thieves or bandits, native to our region. The whole village knew of my wedding and it would have alerted them to our possessions. Had Reyansh travelled with a young village girl it was sure to have aroused suspicion. Not all men from the Haridwar district bathe in the Ganges and worship as they should at Sapta Puri,' she added. 'They are men of little belief other than in the gold that lines their pockets.'

The noise of a porter pushing a sack barrow along the platform outside made me look up at the clock behind the counter, I saw that we only had ten minutes left before our train was due to arrive. I picked up my cup not realising that the contents had gone cold, but all I wanted was something wet to moisten the inside of my mouth. Had the devil himself done a deal with my reasoning that afternoon as I sipped the cold fluid, tasting also the grains of tea that had settled to the bottom of the cup? I could only wonder at the suggestion.

'Do you have family, Reverend Albright?' Her voice interrupted my thoughts as my attention returned to the loneliness of the tea room and her.

'Yes I do. I have a brother also, he's in the army, an officer.'

I don't know why, but I suddenly wanted to tell her about my family. For whatever reason it seemed important that I did. 'We are close, although we do not see much of one another. It always seems that one or other of us is always travelling.' I chuckled. 'Only I believe my travels are somewhat more exotic than his. I wish him safe wherever he is. He'd like you, Avishi.' I didn't know why I'd said that, but it was too late to retract it, it was said. She just smiled and listened as I continued. 'And then there's my parents. My father is a shoemaker. A very good one too although his back seems to be permanently arched these days just like the sole of a boot. I suspect too many years of casting leather over a shoe last. And then there's our mother, well she's just Mother, sweet, kind and adorable. She spends her time flower arranging at the church where they live. She says it brings her closer to me and my brother, even though we live a hundred or so miles apart.'

'You have an interesting family, Reverend Albright. Do you like being a man of the Church?'

It was an interesting question and not one that I had thought about for a very long time, not unless you included this morning's session, the times at the hospital with all the elderly patients. I held my heart in check and instead I let my head reply.

'We live in such troubled times, Avishi, that my presence in the world goes unnoticed. I believe and hope that I make a difference to some people's lives, but it will not be enough to make me a saint when I die. I'm sure my bishop, that's my boss, would agree with that. He thinks I'm a loose cannon and possibly chose the wrong profession.' I realised that I hadn't directly answered the question and she probably didn't know the significance of being a loose cannon, but right at this moment in time with eight minutes left on the clock I didn't know how to give her the answer that the devil had prompted as a reply.

She suddenly surprised me with her next question. 'Are there opportunities in your country for women to become doctors, maybe even Indian women?'

'Yes. There is an ever increasing demand for females in medicine. Female patients are beginning to petition for women to treat them, especially with gender-based troubles and anatomical female problems. Some men make good, excellent doctors, but they have been historically prominent for centuries and the sphere of medical science is always spinning fast with change. Why do you ask, Avishi?' I realised that it was the first time I had referred to her by her name.

'My father once told me that Great Britain was a land of great opportunity. Queen Victoria had been on the throne when he was a young man and India had the Raj. My father had served army officers trekking upon our mountains, surveying the land. He has great respect for all British men. I was just considering that it must be nice to give your heart to something that you want so much.'

I looked up at the clock again, there were only six minutes to go. I wondered if the Lord was on my side.

'Have you ever wanted to change your destiny, Avishi, to step upon the *footsteps of the Lord* and change direction from the chosen path?'

She stared at me intently, her eyes unflinching as she pondered her answer. 'Do you refer to my journey to Durham?'

'Yes, if you like. To change the path of your destiny. Go somewhere different, where you've never been, but where you believe there will be answers to your hopes and dreams. Is that not what your name really means?'

I was clutching at straws, but I knew I could be losing the argument. This time I realised that I had gone beyond the boundary of my calling.

Avishi bowed her head and looked down at the picture of her family, then the picture of Pashwan Dumar. She reached forward gently touching the faces of her family as though their spirits were with her in the tea room. She looked up and strongly replied, 'Yes.'

To hell with the time, there was only two minutes to go and even the ticking of the clock seemed louder. Avishi was still fingering the picture of her family as I collected the cups and saucers onto the tray. Then with a minute to go and with my tongue as dry as a desert stone, I said the most ridiculous thing that had ever entered my mind. My colleagues from the parish would have thought it complete madness and as for the Bishop, well I think he would have made me the sacrificial lamb at the altar.

'Please don't go to Durham, Avishi,' I asked.

She looked up at me and I saw that there were already tears in her eyes as the years of torment of waiting and wondering came flooding out. Then as the sound of the locomotive's whistle cut through the chill air outside announcing the imminent arrival of the northbound train Avishi stood up. 'It is my duty and my father's honour.'

She walked across to the tea-room door and pulled it open. A sudden inward rush of wind swept along the platform and through the flimsy door of the tea room as the locomotive glided down the platform. It blew my Bible from the table and dropped it onto the floor. I reached down to retrieve it and picked it up at the page that it had fallen open at: Luke 12:34 'For where your treasure is, there will your heart be also.'

My interpretation of this verse has always been that man is as shallow as the gold that he seeks. Was Avishi to be the wife that she had been ordained to be since birth or was the prospect of a dowry the greater evil? I looked at her pretty young face and felt a sorrow that only she could know about. These were questions I did not have the answer to, neither did Avishi, if the truth be known. It was not my duty to interfere, but I felt it my duty to save her soul, albeit as a man or a man of the Church. I chased her out onto the platform and asked her once again not to get on the train. She looked at me imploring my mind for the right answer to her dilemma.

'But, Reverend Albright, if I do not get on the train I will be surely shamed by my brother Reyansh and Pashwan Dumar. I will bring much shame upon my father and my family back home. I could never return to Haridwar, it will be as though I am a dead woman in their eyes and those of all my village. Who will care for me then?'

It was only then that I realised why I had never worn my clerical collar. I decided there and then that it would stay forever safe in my bedroom drawer back home. Then as I discreetly dropped the King James Bible into my coat pocket, I gently placed my hand gently upon her shoulder, I said, 'I will, Avishi.' Later that day I would write to the Bishop and my brother.

THE NIGHT TRAIN

To be honest with you I was a little more than apprehensive about catching the night train from London Victoria, despite the fact that it was about to depart at 9.50 morning time. Why the reservation you may well ask, but please read on and allow me to explain my dilemma. The train itinerary detailed the journey as starting out from London, taking us south through the beauty of the Kentish countryside before joining the night ferry, where we would cross the English Channel and over into France continuing on to the Gare du Nord in Paris, arriving at 8.30 a.m. the next morning. Paris, it sounded so wonderful, that amazing, magnificent and exhilarating joyful place of romance, music, fine dining and love. No apprehension about being there it was simply the Channel that filled me with dread.

I was fine with the train, which consisted of three exuberantly furnished coaches with restaurant and overnight compartments, it was the ferry that caused the knot in my stomach. I was a dreadful traveller, both in the air and on the water, only with water it seemed to haunt me most nights leading up to a boat journey. For the past week my dreams had all the hallmarks of demons that lurked beneath the murky grey-black of the waves, waiting and ready to pounce at the right moment. Flying was also out of the question as I did not consider having a thin strip of metal between me and the ground a suitably safe option. I much preferred my feet somewhere close to terra firma but as I was left with no other alternative, it had to be the overnight train.

I collected my reserved tickets and handed over my luggage to a station porter who stated that he would escort me to the train and store my luggage for me in my intended compartment. It would allow me ample time before the train left to explore the amenities as was customary. I followed his lead along the platform stepping aside the sudden expulsions of steam from the underside of the coaches. I noticed that one or two passengers were already seated in the restaurant car and ordering breakfast. My stomach gurgled loudly reminding me that I hadn't eaten yet. I decided to get settled into my compartment then join them.

As if on cue the porter politely remarked, 'Breakfast is served until 11.30, madam.'

I thanked him.

The compartment was better than I had expected, spacious, well presented and with a small washroom provided. I removed the pin from my hat carefully laying them on the small reading table. Outside station porters rushed past my window weaving their laden trolleys in and out along the platform as they carved their way between friends and family saying goodbye to other passengers. I noticed the stationmaster look up and down the platform then blow his whistle, only to have the guard reply. I heard doors slamming shut as porters secured the train and the engineer tested the pressure in the pistons, then with a jerk forward then back, we were on our way. I waved to people I didn't know watching from the platform and they waved back. The rumblings in my stomach told me again that it was time to find the restaurant car.

Since the movement of the suffragettes after the First World War, it was not unusual to see women travelling abroad by themselves. Men would still frown at the idea, but women had been liberated and freedom of movement was now as common as a man freely signing up for a long sea voyage rather than being shanghaied. I checked that my hair was in place then locked the door and walked along the corridor eager to partake of some food and refreshment. I could think about the demons in the Channel later, my want for breakfast was long overdue.

The restaurant was as lavish in design as the rest of the coaches. I chose a table at the end near the kitchen door where I could keep a watchful eye on the comings and goings of the other passengers. I always found them to be so fascinating, how they dressed, how they would sit opposite one another and engage in whispered dialogue, keeping their secrets close and safe. I would wonder, rather surreptitiously I admit at how many of them shouldn't really have been there, other than somewhere else. I envisaged a husband or a wife, a lover or a tortured soul waiting and expecting them home that evening. It was a game that I often played and it helped pass the time mischievously.

To my delight a young couple not much older than myself appeared to fit the conditions of my game only a few tables away from my own. The waiter arrived to take my order as I watched their furtive gestures and the fluttering of her eyelids. I ordered a pot of English tea complimented by a round of toast with a side order of jam and dried fruit. The waiter disappeared just in time as I saw the young man reach across the table and hold the woman's hand. It goes to prove my point as she quickly looked around to see who had noticed, then tentatively hid her hands beneath the table.

I looked out of the window and smiled to myself, it looked like I'd won the game already and so soon. Regardless of social status, education or breeding we were all different in many ways and it was what made us so fascinating to others. I would say that any person not enchanted by something that they don't have all the answers to is a liar. We have a need to know the truth, by whatever means available to us. Discretion sometimes being the option.

I delicately poured the tea into my china cup before devouring the toast and jam, it was delicious. I ate a small portion of the dry fruit, saving the rest for later. When I saw the young couple stand to leave the restaurant I smiled at the woman encouragingly. Only then did I notice the wedding ring on her finger, perhaps it had been more a case of early matrimonial nerves, I'd never know. The young woman smiled back as she headed towards the door.

I decided to stay in the restaurant car a while longer and engaged myself with one of the many newspapers that were to hand. It was indeed a rare treat to have the time to apprise myself of the daily news. As I flicked through the numerous articles my attention was drawn to an elderly gentleman who had entered the restaurant from the end furthest from my carriage. He chose a ready-prepared table on the opposite side to my own. Settling himself down, he turned, smiled at the few diners still present then at me. I returned his smile then looked back down at the newspaper.

Although the time was almost at a quarter past eleven the gentleman ordered from the breakfast menu. The waiter took his order then returned a minute later with a small jug of water. I watched as the man popped open a small silver box, selected a tablet from within then swallowed the medication washed down by a glass of water. With the newspaper held in front of me I made out that I was reading the articles on the page, but the fascination to know more about the latecomer demanded my attention. The waiter returned with a pot of coffee and placed them before the gentleman.

As he sipped his coffee and looked out of the carriage window I got the impression that his thoughts were far off, 1,000 miles or more from the restaurant car. Outside the countryside flashed by, but I doubt he saw it as his eyes stared out into oblivion. I continued to watch when minutes later he reached inside of his jacket pocket and pulled out an envelope. The blue type that was used for international correspondence. I found myself intrigued once again.

There was something very fascinating about the man as he read. He appeared to be just an ordinary elderly gentleman, but something about him suggested otherwise. Sometimes you've only to look at a person to know instinctively that they have led an interesting life and had experiences that others could only imagine happening to them, but know they never will. He turned the pages of the letter several times absorbing every word, whatever was written had an obvious significance. He reached back into the envelope and pulled out a photograph. The gentleman stared at it for ages fingering the photograph's sides very carefully. At one point I thought he muttered a name, but I wasn't sure. What I was sure of was the tear that trickled down his cheek.

He saw me stand and walk across to his table. As I introduced myself I saw the softness that was behind his light-brown eyes.

'Is there something wrong?' I enquired. 'Something that I may help you with?'

'That is very kind of you, young lady, but I assure you that I am well.' He wiped away the tear from his cheek. 'You must excuse the emotions of a stupid old man.'

I noticed his open palm as he invited me to take the seat opposite him. I thanked him and sat down, despite now having a pang of guilt that maybe I was somewhat intruding. However, I was glad of the company.

'Paris is a wonderful place for a young lady to be visiting, especially in the springtime.' He offered me a cup of coffee, then poured.

'It is,' I agreed. 'I'm on my way to stay with an aunt and uncle there. I have a place at the Sorbonne University to read classical French and history.'

'That, my dear,' tapping lightly the top of my hand, 'is the most wonderful opportunity. We have but a few occasions in our lives that afford us such great experiences. You are young and you should hold onto them all at the envy of others.'

My eyes wandered back to the envelope and the photograph on the table. He saw me gazing down at them.

He chuckled at my embarrassment discreetly declaring that he'd seen me watching as he'd read the letter. I hadn't realised that he had, which made it worse. 'Although I know nothing of you, I deduce that you are an intelligent young lady and I see you are fascinated by my letter. If you have the time to spare and you could cope with the tedious ramblings of an old man I would offer to tell you a tale. But I warn you it's now fifty years old. It's what this letter is all about?'

I hoped as I agreed that my enthusiasm didn't appear overzealous. I replaced my cup on the saucer. 'I would not wish to impose on your personal life, but I'm very happy to listen.' The journey was turning out more interesting than I had imagined and my earlier fears had waned considerably.

The man handed me the photograph, it was an old black-and-white image probably dated from the 1920s or early 1930s. It was scarcely marked so I presumed that it had been kept somewhere very safe and hardly ever seen the light of day, it could have

164

been taken only yesterday. It was of a young woman, quite a beautiful young woman. She had the loveliest of features, strong bone structure and engaging eyes. She was sat in front of a man and a woman, I presumed it to be her mother and father. I could see why the man had held the picture so affectionately. I handed it back to him, but instead he held up his hand and refused.

'No, please, you hold onto it for a while. I want you to see her face as you read the letter. It will prove that however difficult, love will conquer all, whatever the consequences.' He handed me the pages of the letter. I took them carefully gently unfolding them again. I then began to read.

My Adorable Charles,

I begin hardly knowing where to start. Like the many migrations of the birds the years have flown past before our very eyes and time has become shorter just like the days of autumn and winter. Not my favourite time of year I add. But it's the days of spring and summer that are filled with hope that bring joy to our hearts. So many years have passed by when questions ceased to be asked and the answers eluded us. So much of life has presented itself to us in ways we could never have imagined, but you must know before we meet again how my heart never gave up hope, never stopped praying and never ceased to ask our good Lord for forgiveness.

Despite the many tears, the betrayal and all the heartache of that fated day I vowed I would take your memory to my grave. I believed with all my heart that one day, albeit if it were only our souls, we would be reunited.

My dear Alberto was taken by our Saviour just over three years ago and he now lies peacefully beside his parents at the quiet village of Camogli beside the sea. Our son Roberto and his younger sister Francesca are the product of our union and our love. I have shown them your letter, told them of the love that existed between us way back before that of their father. I have told them why you are coming to see me. They both loved their father dearly and they still do, but they understand my need to see you again. I would like you to meet them.

I cannot begin to say in such a short letter where my life began again, but as the sunshine stretched long the days again and the warmth of the sun wrapped its cloak of safety about me, I started to relive my life as best I could back in Italy. The waiting before I returned to my home town regrettably took its toll upon my parents. My father although he never showed it was broken, fractured deep inside. Those days and weeks of worry, consoling my mother turned his hair grey long before his time. He died loving me as no other father could ever love an only daughter. My mother now lives near me at Sant' Agostino. Her grandchildren have the spirit of my father and the love of my mother, especially Francesca. My mother also knows about you, Charles.

My husband ran a small, but profitable hotel business and since his death I have worked at the hotel assisting Roberto, who stepped up and into his father's shoes. I am so proud of my son, he is like his father, a true Italian, a very proud man, calm and thoughtful, especially to me. Roberto looks like his father too, but has some of me in him also. He is an adventurous young man who wants to grow the business and see the world. I am fearful of him leaving, but realise that I cannot tie my son to my apron strings forever. Do you remember, Charles, you once told me that I was a free child of the age and the world held no boundaries that could hold me back. Roberto is me, as I am my son.

I will meet you at the railway station, Charles, where we can talk about everything that happened since 15th April 1912. We will have many days to rediscover what time stole from us and where the Lord Almighty thinks we should belong.

It was signed the 'Italian maid, Ellena Michelotto' and gave her home address.

I held the letter in my hand as I looked at the photograph of the beautiful young woman and then handed back the letter again. I understood why the gentleman had asked me to keep hold of the photograph whilst I read the letter. Together they were comparable to something quite beautiful, something that had a lasting love. As I looked again at the date that Ellena had mentioned in the last paragraph I suddenly realised its significance. The date 1912 was itself legendary and for maybe the wrong reasons etched into the souls of humans globally. A night of unbelievable circumstances, dreadful tidings and hopelessness. For those of you that do not know, or cannot remember, Sunday 14th April 1912 was the night the 'unsinkable' passenger liner RMS *Titanic* collided with an iceberg and began to sink, eventually with the loss of over 1,500 passengers, men, women and children. RMS *Carpathia* the nearest ship to respond to the distress calls saved only 705 survivors.

I looked across at the gentleman who sat quietly finishing off his coffee waiting for me to say something. He must have seen the astonishment that etched my face. I folded and handed back the letter and photograph.

'I know you've probably got some questions you'd like to ask, but perhaps if you permit me to tell my tale, I will answer some of them.'

I nodded in response.

Charles began his story. He was thirty-two years old, the privileged chauffeur to a rich gentleman from Belgravia in London. In April 1912 he found himself on board the RMS *Titanic* accompanying his gentleman to New York on a business trip. It was during the journey across the Atlantic Ocean that Charles met the beautiful young Ellena, a twenty-year-old maid of Italian descent aboard the *Titanic*. Ellena was with her lady, a titled high-society lady from the Royal Borough of Kensington. Lady Sarah was en route to visit her sister in Manhattan.

On the evening of the 14th Charles had arranged to meet Ellena half an hour before midnight outside of the maids and servants' galley. However, an unexpected turn of events involving Charles's gentleman feeling unwell soon after a late supper had meant that Charles was late for the prearranged meeting with Ellena. Having put his gentleman to bed and flicking the switch of the cabin light a few moments before the bedside clock registered 11.40 p.m. a terrible grinding noise and shudder reverberated throughout the ship. At the time very few on board, other than those sailors in the crow's nest ironically on lookout, the officers and men on the bridge and the few passengers on deck realised that the hull of the ship had collided with an iceberg that had probably floated its way south from the Grand Banks of Newfoundland.

Muted screams from women still awake in the ballroom were quickly lost in the silence of the huge vessel. Many slept through the initial damage unaware of the impending disaster ahead of them. After the ship settled again only those in first class believed that something was amiss as members of the crew ran aft to stern, starboard to port inspecting any damage that might have been visible. Generally most believed it to be a problem with one of the huge turbine engines. Nobody ever imagined that the ship could be taking on water.

At the same time that Charles had been dealing with his master's needs, Ellena was already waiting outside the maids and servants' galley. She'd been there since 11.15 p.m., but Charles had failed to show up. As the hours and events of the night unfolded and panic ensued the destiny of Charles and Ellena went in different directions as the ship slowly sank and the disorganised struggle to man the lifeboats began.

For the remainder of that night and into the early hours of Monday morning the struggle went on until *Titanic* relented and with its back broken it heaved up one last time, screamed in agony and plummeted beneath the waves to the murky depths some 13,000 feet down to the darkness of the seabed. Neither Charles nor Ellena's high-society lady were seen again. However, fortune managed to smile upon Ellena and Charles's gentleman as they managed to secure places aboard one of the twenty lifeboats used, they were both picked up by RMS *Carpathia* and eventually taken to New York. In the following months Ellena caught a passage back to Italy where I presume she met her husband Alberto.

And that was it, short and sweet, not glamorised like a tabloid paper where the story developed as extra titbits made the headlines and sold more papers. Charles did not exaggerate that dreadful night. He played down any part of his being on board or the sinking of the world's greatest passenger liner. I felt my pulse race anxiously as I looked across into his lonely soft brown eyes, somewhere 375 miles south of Newfoundland Charles had lost the love of his life, his beloved Ellena. I was young and had before me my whole life, but I could not comprehend the tragedy that had befallen this kindly gentleman. My heart went out to him.

'I hope that has not bored you and perhaps answered some of your questions?' Charles enquired.

I could think of just the one that needed an answer. 'What happened to you that night?'

He laughed, not out of ridicule, but more at the thought of his own survival. 'I survived because the God Almighty willed it and I suppose it was just not my time!'

'And that's it?' I pleaded. I had expected more.

'Yes, there was I suppose more, but I've not really thought about the fortunes that kept me safe that night. I've only ever thought about Ellena.' He suddenly paused and I let him regain his composure. 'I survived because part of the wooden drinks bar from the first-class lounge broke away when the boilers finally blew. When I leapt into the darkness it became my beacon in that frozen wasteland, it served as my life raft. A man named Joseph, a steward and I shared it for the next twelve hours until the SS *Californian* picked us up. There was a huge furore about the ship that found us, but all that Joseph and I cared about was that we were alive. Apparently we were in a poor condition physically when we were found, but the captain and the crew cared for us and we survived intact. It's only our minds which bear the scars of that tragedy. Oh, and of course my heart!'

'Didn't you know that Ellena had been saved?' I asked.

'No. Aboard the *Titanic* that night all hell was let loose and with so many people trying to find a way to safety despite all my efforts to find her I failed miserably. I didn't know that Ellena had been rescued and had been taken to New York. Joseph and I, you see, ended up in Boston some 200 miles away. We were registered as missing presumed dead. Because of the worldwide news coverage of the time and the outrage against Captain Lord we were lost in the media hype of the day. By the time I managed to get back to England, Ellena was already home in Italy. I thought she'd died the night *Titanic* went down.'

'So how did you manage to find her after fifty years?'

Charles picked up Ellena's photograph again and smiled as he looked at the image staring back at him. 'Fate really. Ellena was the runner-up of the Strega Prize, an annual literary award. I read about her award in a London newspaper four weeks ago. I wrote to the organisers of the literary award and they passed my letter on to Ellena. She replied and that's the letter you've just read.'

'But how did you know it was Ellena, didn't she use her married named for the award?'

'You will do well at the Sorbonne, young lady,' he remarked. 'I only knew one Ellena from the Sant' Agostino district and that's where Ellena's family originated from. I realised that I should have gone there all those years ago, but providence serves each of us differently and for very different reasons. Had I gone I might have been too late anyway. Perhaps the Almighty meant for us to be apart until now. After surviving the *Titanic* I have never questioned the Lord's work or the way in which we live our lives.'

I wasn't quite sure precisely what Charles had meant by that last remark. It had a double meaning for sure, but it left me wondering. It seemed totally inappropriate and really bad timing when I look back, but I explained to Charles that I was concerned about our night ferry crossing as I didn't like the water. He calmly told me not to worry as he felt that everything would be just fine, I wished that I could have shared his optimism, but I still had reservations. I appreciated his support and calm manner and I felt ridiculous having revealed such a trivial concern especially knowing that Charles and Ellena had both survived the sinking of the *Titanic*.

Later that night as I lay in bed in my bunk I heard the clank of metal beneath as the train engaged the ship's track and felt the ferry gently sway as we left Dover. It wasn't until we disembarked at Calais that I realised we had made it safely across, I hadn't felt a thing. I pulled back the curtains, but the night outside still had a few hours left before the first light of dawn would signify a new day. I lay back again resting my head on my pillow and thought about Charles. I doubt he'd slept much on the crossing and the thoughts of the last fifty years must have crossed his mind. He still had a day's travel from Paris to Italy, but for Charles and Ellena the long-awaited reunion was almost over. I closed my eyes again and prayed for them both.

Charles was already in the restaurant car having breakfast when I arrived. Without being invited I sat opposite and called across the waiter for another pot of tea.

'Good morning, did you sleep well?' he enquired.

'I did, thank you and surprisingly I didn't even notice that we'd crossed the Channel.'

He smiled. 'We were never in any danger,' he exclaimed.

I wondered how he could have been so confident.

I remembered my mother always telling me to listen to people much older than me as they generally had much wiser heads on their shoulders. I don't think that I had ever put much store on the saying until today. Charles's existence, his survival and the unwavering belief that he and Ellena would meet again one day changed that.

I had to admire the man that sat opposite me. He truly believed. It wasn't until he removed his napkin that I realised just how much his belief actually meant. Wiping his lips he laid down the napkin. I sat opposite him and didn't know if I should have blessed myself or laughed. The latter seemed highly impertinent, so I did neither. Charles was wearing the vestments of a Church of England vicar, his dog collar sat proudly around his neck.

And then the penny dropped, as the saying goes, I realised there and then why the Lord Almighty had meant for Charles to survive over fifty years ago in the icy waters off Newfoundland. Why his beloved Ellena had also been rescued. Why she'd had to marry Alberto and why Roberto and his sister Francesca had to be born. Charles had explained to me only yesterday how the providence of fate and destiny was so very different for everyone. I wondered if he'd mentioned it in his letter to Ellena four weeks ago, if not she was in for one hell of a surprise.

As I poured us each a cup of tea I asked if I could have a last look at the photograph again. She really did have the most beautiful expression and I imagined that when they finally saw one another at the train station nothing would have changed, despite the ravages of time.

We talked until we parted at the Gard du Nord in Paris. I kissed him lightly on the cheek and wished them both much happiness. I doubt our paths would ever cross again as I exited the station, but for one whole day I was pleased that Charles had been with me on the night train.

THE DAY BIG BEN STOPPED

It was two years forward of the Second World War and Britain was still recovering from the drastic effects of an undisputable time when hell had seemingly dominated seventy per cent of the earth, but peace and reason prevailed with one another for harmony. Veterans however found it difficult to adjust back into a normality that wasn't a foxhole or the constant sound of bullets or shells falling all about. Those that had stayed behind and remained at home found it just as unbearable. A nation had to harmonise all over again.

Despite all the terrible hardships man had endured in that awful time I remember the latter months of 1946 and beginning of 1947 as the period when the weather almost brought our nation to a standstill. It was the whitest winter that the country had suffered. Snow fell, settled and fell again all the more with drifts of three feet and higher in the more rural areas making transportation both public and private almost impossible.

The age of technology and engineering advancement came to a grinding halt as horses were reintroduced to get supplies through, even the dead were taken to cemeteries in horse-drawn hearses. Me personally, well I thought the horse had a point to prove and for one I was glad to see them majestically trudging through our streets and lanes again. I remember my grandson getting his sledge out to help the local milkman get the bottles to the front doors of schools, hospitals and houses. It was a bleak time, but a grand time too. The nation was coming together again and nature had made it happen, not man.

You can never predict our English weather. Meteorologists

spend all the hours God sends them studying wind direction and cloud formations trying to predict today's, tomorrow's and next week's weather, but a sudden gust from Siberia or the Atlantic can wreak havoc on their hard-worked philosophies and predictions. I had a good degree of patience for them as they worked studiously through all weathers and just to keep us happy. But the winter of 1946 and 1947 had caught them on the hop. To artists however it was a pure winter wonderland.

And like the meteorologists I too had been caught on the hop. I was away from home visiting relatives over the Christmas period at the small Lincolnshire village of Ludborough and the snow was as relentless there as anywhere else. However like the many other millions nationwide I still had a job to do and do it I must. You see I was the official timekeeper at the Palace of Westminster in London. My privileged position meant that along with two other clock smiths we were responsible for the mechanics and preservation of Big Ben and the 2,000 clocks in the halls of Westminster. Yes, there really are that many.

You might consider our chosen profession extremely arduous and exactingly boring, but believe me one day is never the same as another. Time never ever hangs wearily around our necks and there's always something to attend to.

Anyhow back to Ludborough and the snow. My brother-in-law and I had checked with the station porter at Ludborough on the availability of trains going to King's Cross Station in London the next morning. It was Monday 3rd February and I was due back in London on the 5th. Reluctantly, I had one more day with my sister, her husband and my nieces before I had to go home. All too soon the festivities of Yuletide had disappeared like the sun and it would be sometime late in the next summer before I would get to see them all again.

The next morning sure enough the unpredictable happened and the weather fronts changed dramatically bringing with it a great blizzard of arctic snow. It cut scathingly across the upper regions of our northern counties, leaving many places marooned and without supplies. The skills of the Royal Air Force were brought into action once again, but only to drop food and fuel supplies to remote outlying villages and those civilians up on higher ground.

Even agricultural tractors found it difficult to cope. I stood on the desolate threshold of Ludborough Station, consisting of a station house, single ticket office and separate signal box. The wind was bitterly cold as I shuffled my feet back and forth in an effort to keep my circulation going around my body. I had only been on the platform for a few minutes, but already I could not feel my fingers through the yarn of the woollen gloves and my face felt like it belonged alongside the granite effigies that adorned a cathedral.

I watched as the train emerged from a sudden cloud of snow which had been lying aside the track forward of the engine. I enthusiastically welcomed the arrival. A minute later and I believe that the onset of hyperthermia would have claimed another victim and another name for the obituary columns, if anybody bothered to read them. I would like to cheer you up by saying that the inside of the carriage was invitingly warmer, but the formation of ice, the result of Siberian winds, had penetrated the inside of the carriage windows too.

I cheerily greeted my fellow passengers who looked as cold as I felt, promptly sitting between a well-proportioned nun and a young man who was fastidiously studying the contents of a dog-eared chemistry book, the content far beyond my comprehension, and as I was not an overly religious man the only thing that I could say that I felt comfortable with was the warm atmosphere that the three of us generated being in such close proximity. The nun who I assumed was in her late fifties was noisily chewing on a toffee, whereas the man much younger and slender of frame nervously chewed the side of his upper lip as he read. I chose the nun to be rubbing thighs with as she would generate more heat. She gave me a wistful look, but didn't budge. I assumed she was a wise old bird and knew that the physics of our physical association would benefit us both. I offered her a read of my paper, but she politely declined. Our young scholar didn't acknowledge my offer, he was too engrossed in the scientific laws of mechanical composition. I wondered if he had a secret formula in his book that could increase the heat inside our carriage.

The train's progress was excusably slow due the vast number of snowdrifts we encountered and in places I would hazard a guess that it was above five or six feet high. I noticed that only the tallest of bushes and the tops of trees in what I believed were arable fields were all that was visible above the blanket of white. It was beautiful to behold despite being a considerable nuisance as we each had destinations that we needed to reach.

We had only travelled a couple of miles when the train suddenly came to a halt. Burgh le Marsh was much further down the line, so I knew that something must have caused the unscheduled stop. Outside in the distance I could hear the sounds of excited voices, even our young scholar had place-marked his page and was wondering what all the noise was about. I forced down the carriage window avoiding the spray of ice as the metal frame slid down the window channel.

What presented itself before me was almost unbelievable, but in the aftermath of the last seven years, I found it also a very rewarding sight. Masses of German prisoners of war who I presumed were awaiting repatriation back to their own homeland were helping railway engineers clear away the huge snowdrifts from the tracks in front of our train. These men who had been the enemy of our country for five years were now peacefully battling the elements of the weather to help us on our journey. Quite ironic don't you think how peacetime can bring together such a bond of human unity that had previously disappeared from the soul of man. The nun asked that I stand aside so that she too could see what was occurring up ahead. I heard her mutter the words 'truly remarkable' as she crossed herself and gave prayer for all the men outside. I also hoped that they would be reunited with their loved ones and soon.

I would like to think that everybody aboard the train that morning waved gratefully to the men outside as the steam locomotive recommenced its journey thanks to their efforts. I wish that there was something that I could have offered in return, but I had nothing. I felt an emptiness inside that I have never forgotten. As we passed I saw small clouds of steam rise from the shoulders of their clothing and realised just how hard they had worked on our behalf. In years to come I would be fortunate to visit their beautiful Rhineland where I would visit the many clock towers and magnificent castles, conversing with clockmakers such as myself about our shared interest. Some I am proud to say are good friends.

At Lincoln we changed onto the London-bound train which would take us to King's Cross. The journey was slow and arduous because of the unrelenting weather conditions and snowdrifts lay alongside the track everywhere. I didn't envy the life of a farmer who needed to protect his cattle at this time of the year. The porter at Lincoln had warned us of delays and had said that in some parts of the country the normal three-to-four-hour train journeys were taking as much as ten hours. If that was the case I hoped that the nun would consent to join me again in the same carriage on our onward journey.

King's Cross was more chaotic than ever. Trains arriving at the platforms, especially from the more rural retreats were rapidly being relieved of snow and ice, then washed down and made ready for the outgoing journey. The nation refused to be intimidated by the weather. Units of troops lined the platforms beside large consignments of stacked crates, boxes, storage sacks and tins. As soon as a train arrived the guards van was unloaded then reloaded in perfect military fashion. The soldiers together with railway porters worked hard and effectively although at times it only seemed to add to the chaotic mood about the place.

I was glad to be free of the station and once back out in the open space of the Euston Road I decided to walk the remainder of the journey down Tottenham Court Road around Trafalgar Square, down Whitehall till I reached the corner of Westminster. I needed the freedom of London to wash away the sentiment of the last week with my sister and her family.

Snow lay about the streets everywhere and as fast as men cleared the main thoroughfares the snow fell again. It was as if the winter weather lay high above in the clouds waiting to pounce again. Arriving at work every day I had been confronted with the monumental edifice of the Elizabeth Tower, the official name of the tower that housed Big Ben and the clock face, but the sight that greeted me today was something absolutely spellbindingly beautiful. The patterned brick and gold, laced with pockets of white snow gave the tower the appearance of a decorated Christmas cake covered in a cook's icing. I crossed the junction which was inaudibly quiet without the presence of buses and taxis and headed to the north end of the palace. The magic of London had worked its spell on the walk from the railway station to the Palace of Westminster, I was pleased to be back.

Call it intuition, but as I passed the main gate I saw a man that I recognised as a commissioner of the palace and before he told me I knew something was wrong. I looked up at the clock face and realised that the time was not sequential to my own watch. This had hardly ever happened in my term as the official timekeeper.

'Something's wrong up top, Samuel,' he declared. 'The minute hand's out with the time.'

I knew what he meant as I thanked him for his help then headed straight for the tower door. I hadn't intended coming to work today as I wasn't due back until tomorrow, but the pride of the nation's heritage had only ever stopped on three previous occasions, two of them during the 1916 and 1939 conflicts. The chimes were silenced to prevent aerial attacks by the German Zeppelins and planes, then again in 1941 when a repair workman's hammer fell into the works.

This was a serious matter and as the man responsible for Big Ben I couldn't ignore it. Locating the wrought-iron key from the depths of my long coat I inserted it into the mortised lock. As I pushed open the heavy oak door, several passers-by peered in taking an opportunist view that they could tell their friends about later. I smiled and closed the door then proceeded to climb the 334 steps of the stone spiral staircase to the clock works chamber. Near the upper level I was met by my two assistants, Edward and Larry. They looked bemused to see me.

Edward piped up first. 'Thought you weren't due to return until tomorrow, Samuel?' he asked.

I told them that the commissioner had noticed a problem with the minute hand and I thought I could lend a hand to help. They seemed grateful that I was there.

Larry then explained that their investigations into the problem seemed to lie with a flock of birds which had rested all together on the minute hand. Improbable as it sounded it was the cause. 'We were just on our way up to the higher level to check the cog mechanism and rebalance wheels.'

I knew that I really should not have bothered with the climb or interfered as both Edward and Larry were proficient clock smiths with more years' service combined than I had myself, but I had always considered Big Ben as like the beat of my own heart and if it missed a beat, I wanted to know the reason why. Wouldn't you?

Gathering up a bag of large tools and time regulators we proceeded to the level where the arm of the minute hand protruded our side through the glass face. As expected it didn't take the three of us very long to reset the balance and soon the flywheels were turning as accurately as they had before. We lightly applied some engine oil to the turning mechanism and decided to check some of the other clock components especially bearing in mind the extreme weather that was ravaging the country at present. We finished the repair by taking a quick peek outside of the inspection window to ensure that both hands looked intact. It would take more than a flock of birds to cause any permanent damage to our clock. I saw a young child point up from the pavement below in awe that a man was looking out of the face of Big Ben.

As the bell struck the hour note the steam from the kettle spout whistled appropriately to announce it was time for a cuppa, it was only then that I realised that I had not had a hot drink since leaving my sister's house early that morning. It was a welcome conclusion to a job well done and as most men do when at work we sat and chatted about everything that was going on in the country at the moment. I told Edward and Larry about the tremendous help that the German prisoners of war had afforded our train on the journey back from Lincolnshire.

Larry had served in the navy during the conflict between 1939 and 1945. As I went on to describe how they had worked tirelessly to clear our line so that we could continue on our journey I noticed that Larry had his head lowered and remained very quiet. I looked across at Edward who only stared back my way not knowing what to say.

Then Larry spoke up. 'I don't hold with any malice towards

the Germans. I saw many comrades killed and injured, probably the same as they did on their side. Like us the Germans were just following orders from those up above.' He then paused for a minute, before continuing. 'I didn't know they hadn't been repatriated. That's rough.'

I detected a distinct sadness in his voice and after this morning's chance meeting I could only feel the same compassion for our fellow man. Edward and I knew also that this was one of the rare times that Larry had mentioned anything about the war. We had both served in the battlefields in the Somme as part of the Great War conflict from July to November in 1916 so we were respectful of Larry's reluctance to talk. Any man who survived either or both conflicts reserved the right to keep his own peace and only the Almighty bore witness to his nightmares.

I left the Elizabeth Tower happy that the city of London and its inhabitants could once again walk the streets regulating their journey home, turn out the office lights and listen out for the guard's whistle as the train departed from the platform. The chimes of Big Ben that echoed across the city were back on time. I thumbed up that all was well in the tower at the commissioner who was busy stamping his feet up and down on the cold step. He returned my gesture as I turned towards Victoria.

It was not that long after my return to London that I read in a copy of the *London Gazette* whilst partaking of refreshments in a tea shop near to Charing Cross corner that the repatriation of German prisoners from the war had been successfully concluded. Almost a quarter of a million men had gone back home. I almost rejoiced with delight, but it might not have been as well received by the other diners so I kept my emotions in check. I read amazingly that almost 20,000 had decided to stay in Britain. I wondered if any of them were from Lincolnshire and had been the men that had been down on the tracks that Monday morning on 4th February. Whoever they were and wherever they were I wished them well.

As I stood beside the counter and paid the waitress I felt the presence of another customer standing behind me. You feel like somebody is breathing down your neck. I collected my change then turned towards the door, where to my surprise behind me stood the same nun from the train.

'Not so cold today?' she exclaimed rather prudishly. 'Not like it was on the train.'

I nodded as I agreed refraining from answering. I was sure that the statement referred to something that I had done that day, although I couldn't say categorically exactly what it was that I was guilty of, but I stayed silent all the same as I turned away and approached the door to the Lyons' Tea Rooms, pulling together the lapels of my long coat. Only then did I smile to myself, she was a funny sight in her habit waddling across to her table to collect her coat looking like an overweight penguin. I waved goodbye to her, much to her disgust as I opened the door. Well, today was the 14th February, St Valentine's Day, and at last the snow had begun to thaw.

THE LETTER

The thing with telling a story is that the reader must themselves be imaginative enough to believe what the author writes and perhaps sometimes to have experienced circumstances similar to that of the story. The following is just a story and believe me it is true, I know I was there.

The year was 1914. It was a miserable morning in September. The Great War had been the focus of our attention now for over two months, exciting at first, but as with all events predictability bores and wanes the interest fast. Now you might think that rather impertinent considering the men who'd left home to fight a cause they probably didn't understand, but everyone hereabouts was generally laid-back about the whole affair and convinced that it should be concluded by Christmas.

The rain outside the window was considerably relentless as it fell from the heavens, in fact I cannot recall such a downpour this year, but the station at Pickering on the edge of the North Yorkshire Moors National Park was relatively open to the elements. Mercifully the station had contributed a small refreshments lounge to its amenities.

Purchasing my ticket for the short journey to Whitby I sat in the tea room as far away as I could from the draughty door. The waitress took my order for a pot of tea as I delved deep into my bag and retrieved my reading book. I checked the clock on the wall, I still had a good half an hour before the train arrived.

The refreshments manager brought over my tea tray and served me. He was a jovial man with a broad local accent. As I stirred the contents of the pot he enquired as to where I was heading, I told him Whitby. Without asking he proffered me advice about the downpour outside, informing me that if it were raining at Pickering it was more than likely raining more heavily in Whitby. It was all down to being beside the sea, he deduced. He had first-hand knowledge of this he said on account of his brother being a fisherman before the war.

Just short of ten o'clock I returned the crockery to the counter and decided it was time to brave the elements. I waited on the platform listening out for the first signs of the arrival of my train. I could never confess to being an enthusiast of train journeys, not even as a young spirited and full-of-adventure girl did the thought let alone the deed raise the palpitations of my heart. My younger brother on the other hand lived and died by the faded red-coloured dog-eared copy of Bradshaw's Guide, apparently a must for all train enthusiasts. His blazer pockets bulged unceremoniously, one bearing the railwayman's diary and the other numerous scraps of paper, bearing dates, times and train numbers recorded meticulously in his own neat handwriting, namely a scribble.

However, despite the rain, the sudden emergence of the train with long trails of steam billowing from the front of the engine was I had to admit quite magical. I could appreciate my brother's interest as the train passed beneath the latticed metal footbridge at Pickering Station. The engine arrived with an ear-piercing hissing of steam as it belched out from somewhere beneath the wheels. It was as Bradshaw had written a sight to behold that he believed to be every schoolboy's dream of pure heaven.

As normal I chose a carriage mid-train believing those in the middle were the safest, should anything untoward occur, you could never be sure in these days of doubt. The carriage had a centre aisle, but was very spacious and comfortable as I chose to sit on the far side away from the platform. At least the rain appeared to be easing now and would offer the possibility of seeing the beauty of the countryside as the train pulled away from Pickering.

Now I won't bore you with tedious irrelevant facts or oddities of our journey, save those for the avid railway enthusiast or my younger brother, but suffice to say that I wasn't one for reading on trains, the draw of the scenery outside was far in abundance and the remnants of a drizzle only added to its charm, certainly more enticing than a book could ever be.

We were just east of our first stop at Levisham when for no other reason other than to scratch an irritating itch on my ankle I was compelled to lean forward. Even now when I look back and recall the moment I still wonder why it was me on that train. Anybody could have sat at that seat, but whatever you consider as you read on, it was me and perhaps it could only have been me. Irony maybe, coincidence possibly, but definitely corny.

I agree, but maybe divine intervention puts us where we are meant to be. Didn't you ever question that time at school when you wanted to be picked for the best part in a play, you planned the precise moment, the precise place you needed to be so you maximised the teacher's attention, only to find later that you'd already been selected by her for that particular role. Divine intervention had helped with the selection.

I noticed a small fragment of paper protruding from beneath the underside of the seat opposite. My first initial reaction was that it was a discarded cigarette paper surreptitiously put there by a smoker, but it was a different colour to the normal papers my uncles used. Aware that other passengers were watching me I quickly pinched the corner and withdrew the concealed fragment until it broke free. As I righted myself I saw that it was a light-blue envelope. I ran my fingers across the seam of the seal on the back and realised that the contents were still inside.

Now here's the true bit of this story and although it may take the rest of the story to convince you, stick with it, because stranger things happen that always leave us wondering. The envelope was addressed to an unknown lady, Miss Elizabeth Higgins of Hilltop Cottage, Dales Road, Newtondale Halt, North Yorkshire. But it was the details of the correspondent on the back that made my heart miss a beat, it was from Private Benjamin Paget, Downdale Farm, Pickering. My brother was named Benjamin, our family surname was Paget and we lived at Downdale Farm. I held the letter gingerly expecting it to burst into flames at any moment. My brother was writing to a lady, a lady he'd never mentioned before. I flipped the envelope back and forth to make certain that I wasn't mistaken.

Benjamin, my older brother, was just twenty-six and as it turns out quite a dark horse. I had no idea how the letter could be under the seat or how long it had been there, but other than a few creases it looked as fresh as the day it had been written. I heard my brother talking to me, but wasn't sure whether it was in my heart or just the voice in my head. I knew I had to deliver the letter. Newtondale Halt was a station on our route and I decided I would get off, my business in Whitby would have to wait for another day. With a war on certain agendas needed to be prioritised.

I'd never had reason to stop at Newtondale Halt before, so I was not surprised to find that the station and the country lane beyond were typical of North Yorkshire, drab and rugged. The lane was unmarked, but as the wind blew the grass towards the hills over yonder I took my lead and headed off in that direction. It was not long before I came across a cottage at a turn along the lane. The occupant was an elderly lady who looked surprised that I'd gotten off the train on a day like today, but she nodded and pointed me in the direction of Hilltop Cottage. I just knew it would be the cottage at the top of the hill.

The small wooden gate led down to the front door. I reached up for the metal knocker, but the door opened before I could announce my arrival. Although I have a younger brother I was surprised to see a young boy standing before me with his arms down by his sides, a hand-made wooden sword held at the ready as if defending his castle. I decided it was best that I introduced myself, before I was marched off to the dungeons.

'Hello, I'm Victoria Paget from Pickering and who might you be, soldier?'

I took a step back as the boy raised his sword across his chest. He proudly announced, 'David Higgins.'

David reminded me of my own brothers. Father had always said that Benjamin and Samuel both had the courage to ward off any enemy, albeit man or beast. I realised it had only been a few months since I'd seen Benjamin, but his absence suddenly seemed a lot longer. It's funny how siblings hardly ever tell one another how much they love one another, but I wish I had.

'Have you got a sister called Elizabeth?'

Taking the sword from his chest and pushing back the front door he yelled out, 'Beth, there's a lady out front wanting to know if you're home?'

I smiled. The innocence of the young was so adorable. I hoped that Samuel kept it just a year or so more. I heard somebody descending the wooden staircase and moments later a pretty, but shy young lady in her early twenties, probably my age, appeared in the doorway. I introduced myself and briefly explained the purpose of my visit. David stood aside as I was invited in and like a true knight he kept his sword at the ready just in case he had to defend his big sister.

I sat in the parlour chair as Beth silently read the letter. I watched as she read. I could see the words had a profound effect and as she finally looked back up I saw the tears that were welling along the eyelids.

I leant forward and placed my hand above hers. 'I hope I have not brought you bad tidings?'

'No. Please excuse my tears,' as a handkerchief wiped dry her eyes, 'the news is so welcome, yet a little worrying at the same time.'

David had decided that I was not a threat and as this looked like girls' stuff he departed noisily up to the battlements of his bedroom. I raised my eyes skyward.

'I've a younger brother just like him!'

It helped diffuse the tension of the moment. 'This really is so good of you to come all this way to deliver the letter.'

I proceeded to explain to Beth how my journey had been to Whitby, but having by accident found the letter from Benjamin I had felt compelled to deliver it. Although I didn't know the contents I'd guessed that if Benjamin had taken the time to pen a letter, then it must have been important.

'Do you or your family know where Benjamin is?' asked Beth.

'No, not really,' I replied. 'He wrote to Mother and Father at the end of May to say that he was training with his regiment somewhere not too far from the Dales. Benjamin was a keen marksman so he had been assigned specialist training besides the basics of warfare. I explained that he and Father would pitch out at night to bag a fox that was sheep-worrying, so Benjamin was quite proficient in the art of handling a rifle.' I didn't say it, but I wasn't surprised that he was doing something special. It was in his nature. 'Are you and Benjamin walking out so to speak?' Damn, I hadn't meant to be so impolite.

Beth lowered her eyes as I regretted asking. 'Yes. I thought Benjamin had told you and your family the last time he was home. He promised me he would.'

I chuckled, more to myself than at her reply and realised that I had to save my brother here. I gave Beth an insight into Benjamin, perhaps there was a side to him she had yet to discover. I explained, that I expected that by the time Benjamin had left her and returned back home he'd almost certainly have lost some of the courage he'd have needed to tell us that he was seeing a young lady. Benjamin would rather face an angry warthog than Samuel and myself. I recalled the last time we'd all been together over the festive season and my teasing him that he was getting on in years and still not married. I'm sure that it made Beth feel easier. I knew my brother and if he was writing to a girl then his intentions must have been serious. I'd hoped that Beth knew it too.

'Would you like to read the letter?' Her suggestion caught me quite by surprise and before I could refuse she'd thrust the envelope into my hand. 'Please, Victoria, it would please me if you did. It might help too if you knew where Benjamin was.'

I realised that Benjamin must have written of his whereabouts and that her earlier question was not for her satisfaction, but mine. I took the envelope and removed the pages from within. The petals of a flower started to fall, but I quickly caught them in the palm of my free hand. I put them back in the envelope then started to read. It was the first time that I'd read a letter written by my brother. Benjamin had nice writing. Beth sat opposite me watching and waiting.

My Dearest Beth,
    Here I am again only this time writing to you, although I truly wish that I was with you, but that unmentionable time has approached us quicker than was anticipated.

I'm sorry that I have not put pen to paper before now, but I've been on a special training programme. I assure you that it is nothing to worry about, just an extra bit of marksmanship out on the range and only because I know how to handle a rifle.

It was a bit like the days and nights spent with my father when we'd shoot for rabbits and hares as they scurried about the Dales. At least he'd say that all his efforts in teaching me to get it right paid off for something. I'm probably receiving the extra training to help bolster the cooks back at the canteen with additional supplies.

The mood in the camp is mixed at the moment and changes daily. When another group of officers from headquarters visit an air of intrigue spreads throughout the camp, but we're rarely told the truth about what's being planned. I pray each day to the Lord Almighty that he sees fit to give me the courage to fight alongside my comrades when the time arrives.

I miss you terribly, Beth. I know that I have your love and feel you beside me wherever I go and the promise that we will have a better life together when this conflict is over.

You might hear the rumours that the unrest on the other side of the Channel is becoming extremely fragile and more unstable with each passing day. I believe that this is where my feet will land very soon. I will need your love all the more, Beth, to bring me back home again. Be strong for us both, my love.

I did not find the opportunity when I was last home with my family to tell them about you. Please forgive me. There is no man prouder than I to have you, but I never found the right moment to explain. I promise that when I next see them they will know and so will the Reverend Ramhock. Yes, my darling, I meant what I said the last time we met. It seems funny now although not at the time, but my younger sister Victoria was only teasing me shortly after Christmas about being too old to marry, but didn't the tortoise win the race. If she knew about us, Beth, she'd laugh I feel sure. I wish I could tell her how much I think of her and our younger brother, Samuel.

A vision of my brother appeared in my mind and how happy we had all been that last Christmas. I sniffed and raised my forefinger to my nostrils. Beth knew to which part of the letter I had just read. I smiled reassuringly at her then continued.

Please do not fret, my love, Mother and Father will adore you, just as I do. The days are long and the nights longer without you, Beth. God only knows how long this conflict will last. Some mention that we'll be back home by Christmas and that we will have the Hun scurrying east again when they see us. As for me I'm not sure, but I pray that the optimists are right and the pessimists wrong.

Do you remember our day together in the national park? When the sun made the sky that brilliant blue, when the birds never stopped singing and we touched the new buds of spring that brought forth flowers onto the shrubs and trees. I remember us as we lay in the tall grass watching as the world went by, the ravages of the unsettled world were that day as far away as we could have wished for them to be. We were the masters of our destiny, Beth. That was a very good day. Well, one day soon we will go back again and relive that day. And when we have children of our own they too will experience what we had and more. Have hope and pray for that day to come soon, Beth. I do.

My darling Beth, I wish I could go on, but word has just been received that we are to muster soon, kit and man, as we're finally going over the sea. I know it's a place somewhere in France. I cannot remember the exact name other than it's the Loire river estuary and where it meets the Atlantic Ocean. If it were not for the cause that we go there to fight I would look forward to it, but instead I look forward to the day that I return to this land of green and hope, this land of richness and peace. Most of all I look forward to the day that I return to you my dearest, and my dear family. I will write again whenever I get the chance.

Yours always with affectionate love,
Benjamin

I folded the letter carefully as though it were made of the finest silk, replaced it in the envelope and handed it back to Beth. I took a deep breath. My eldest brother was not a sly old fox, but the bravest man I had ever known. I realised just how much love a sister has for a brother. I wish I could have told him so once more.

I looked at Beth as the tears ran freely down her cheeks then reached across so that we could be close. Upstairs David stopped bouncing about as he heard us crying, it was the first time he'd ever heard Beth cry and it frightened him. Quietly he shut his bedroom door. He wanted to shut it out, I didn't blame him.

A short time later Beth and I went for a long walk that morning. We ignored the rough gradient of the hill as our conversation helped to ease the thoughts that troubled us both. We talked as though we'd known each other for years, not hours. About ourselves, our families, our lives, but more than anything else we talked about Benjamin. It was good for both of us, therapeutic that he was the main topic of conversation, it brought Benjamin closer to us both.

It was a little past lunchtime when we returned to Hilltop Cottage that afternoon. There was a note on the kitchen table from Beth's parents to say that David was with them over in butterfly meadow. Beth walked with me back to the station. Strangely I felt it difficult to say goodbye to her as I felt that part of Benjamin was saying goodbye too. However, we arranged to meet up again. It made us both feel as though we could embrace each day with extra hope.

As the train pulled away in the opposite direction to which I had travelled earlier I leant out of the carriage window and waved. I liked Beth, she was the right woman for my brother Benjamin. I hoped there and then that they too had lots of children.

Christmas came and went as did three more and the days have got longer, the weeks have become months and the months have become years, even the skies seemed to grow bigger and occasionally greyer. Beth and I were true to our word, we saw one another as often as we could. It made the uncertainty of it all, that dreadful waiting easier if we were together.

Beth only received just one other letter from Benjamin. It was a short letter with very little detail, no mention of his previous letter, the one that I'd found on the train and not a detail about the war or the conditions, but more about his friends in his regiment. I guessed it mentioned how much he missed Beth and longed for the day that he would return home. I never saw the letter. Beth had decided to keep the letter tucked away somewhere safe. She said it was her salvation. I understood.

It's difficult to imagine unless you've experienced it, just how much resolve we need to suppress the unknown and keep going, but whatever that certain element is inside of us that keeps us going, it does somehow and we find the courage to overcome the most difficult of situations, circumstances and dread. We experience emotions that we never knew could be part of our make-up, our chemistry and life. But without all of them we would not survive. I could not begin to imagine what experiences my brother and all the thousands of men like him saw and witnessed, but I know that when he did finally return home, he did as a man and some of that boyish charm had disappeared. I felt sorry for Benjamin because he'd lost something that was very precious that most of us keep deep inside forever.

Armistice Day was a day of great celebration and a considerable lot of tears. I would say more tears than celebration especially from all the mothers in the world. For me personally, well, as you guessed I took that short train ride to Newtondale Halt to be with Beth. Understandably you could question why I did not stay with my family to celebrate, but even they would not have understood. For almost five years Beth and I had seen this war through together and at the end we needed each other to realise that the end had really arrived. We felt sure that being together would also bring Benjamin home safe and sound. It was a long wait till 2nd December 1918, but the day those size-ten boots crunched the gravel outside of the kitchen door was the best day of my life.

The family stood for a long time that day in the farm kitchen simply huddled together once again as a family unit. None of us wanted to be the first to let go, but I could feel the restlessness energy surging through Benjamin's arms. I knew that he wanted and needed to be somewhere else. I was the one that broke free.

And Mother being Mother said, 'Have you had a good brew lately, lad?'

Father coughed. 'Let him be, Mother, thou knows where he wants to be!'

Benjamin looked firstly at Mother and Father, then Samuel and finally me. He had a look of both confusion and relief in his eyes. How do they know and how did they find out? Had he and Beth been seen together before he left five years ago?

I walked across and slipped my arm through my brother's. 'It's OK, Benjamin, we know all about Beth!'

I then proceeded to tell him how I'd found his letter hidden under the train carriage seat. How I'd met Beth and how that day we had walked and talked. How Beth had become part of our family now. How Beth had become my best friend. Benjamin sat at the kitchen table his face a picture of amazement as he sipped his tea and listened.

'You found my letter, Victoria, you of all people, thank the Lord you did. I had to quickly conceal it somewhere, anywhere as the non-commissioned officers were searching us and our kit for any last letters. We could not reveal anything that might compromise us or our going overseas. It might have resulted in my appearing before a court martial. You found my hiding place. It must have been there all of two months before you found it. I had hoped that one day, somebody, anybody other than the army would find it. I thought a railway cleaner might find it. It's unbelievable that my own sister would find it though.' He looked at all of us with a sigh. 'It's made my introducing Beth to you all the easier!'

Mother hugged her eldest son. The war might have returned him back home a man, but to her he would always be a boy. A boy with a secret. Soon after Benjamin walked out of the kitchen door once again promising to be back soon, and as good as his word several hours later, introductions made at the Higgins household, he returned. He proudly walked back into the kitchen with Beth on his arm.

'This 'ere is Elizabeth Higgins and I'm pleased to announce that very soon she's going to be my wife.'

Monday 11th November 1918 was indeed a great day for celebration and a good many tears, but nothing compared to Saturday 11th January 1919. That was the day Elizabeth Higgins said 'I do' before a packed church and a true man born and bred in North Yorkshire who took this lady to be his lawful wedded wife and Mrs Benjamin Paget. The sky was a magnificent blue, filled with birds singing as they swooped and the crocuses outside the church added to the beauty of the day.

Beth and I are still the best of friends, but it's much better now as sisters-in-law. We rarely talk about the years between 1914 and 1918, remembering instead the awful wait, but you don't need to reminisce about a time when you find love and friendship, a time when hope and belief counted for everything. We do sometimes talk about the day I found the letter under the train carriage seat, the day I was confronted by a brave soldier armed with a wooden sword and ponder why it was me who found the letter. We once asked the vicar after his Sunday sermon to see if he could offer an explanation, but all he said was that the Lord worked in mysterious ways. Amen.

Now as I told you at the start of this story, it is true, however, I understand your scepticism even after reading it, but you had to be there, you had to feel the experience and you have to believe in the power of the unknown. Why am I so certain that you might yourself now have a tinge of doubt about yourself and maybe actually begin to believe? Well, go ahead and ask yourself, if you found yourselves in similar circumstances where you'd just found a letter concealed somewhere on a train, wouldn't you be tempted to scratch an itchy ankle?

Oh, and so I can prove this story to be true, I have three nieces and a nephew, and my nephew is just like his father.

THE TRAIN TO NOWHERE

I remember saying goodbye to my Aunt Emma at Paddington Station on platform three as I looked out from the carriage window of the 5.10 p.m. train to Stockton Ferris via York, waving frantically trying her catch her attention as a soot-laden cloud of white smoke from the steam locomotive continued to belch back along the platform. Having lost sight of her I sat back moodily on the seat of my empty carriage, I didn't want to go home. Lying beside me was a small brown paper parcel, no doubt neatly prepared jam sandwiches courtesy of Aunt Emma.

I had begun to detest this journey home much preferring the journey down into London where I was fondly among familiar surroundings. As normal there was very little to see on the walls of the compartment other than the usual route planner that was always pasted beside the small mirror that the railway provided and below the baggage rack. I wondered if this just was a ploy to promote rail travel as you attended to your hair.

I had been travelling alone undertaking this journey since turning twelve, but annoyingly and I cannot explain why I found myself counting the regular station stops between Paddington and Stockton Ferris, eight – nine – ten. The usual number, that was correct and my pocket timetable stated that this train was due to arrive at 8.47 p.m.

Since lying in bed last night I found myself going over the same arguments mentally again today, annoyingly finding no new answers or with little difference. The fact of the matter was that I simply could not stay with Aunt Emma any longer and it just wasn't fair on my mother, father and younger brother. I felt angry and cheated as London had always been our home, whereas County Durham held little or no appeal whatsoever to me. I wanted so much for us to move back to London and approvingly, as unusual as it was for his age, seven to be precise, I know my brother felt the same.

I tried to disengage myself from the reality of the situation and channel my thoughts on the journey home. I watched as the countryside flashed by my window outside, the downdraught of the train causing the last crispy rustic stragglers clinging to the branches of nearby trees to shake violently making some lose their grip and fall to the ground below. I gazed on innocently imagining the leaves to be waving hello as we hurtled past. The period twelve to thirteen, the age of lost innocence to many young girls, the signature of our teens and maturity, is hard enough, but there were some things that I wanted to cling on to and refused to release. An image of autumn leaves dancing gracefully downward was one of them. I closed my eyes momentarily, no wonder these years can cause so much confusion.

Beyond the trees in the meadows beneath the skyline cattle happily grazed and I saw small pockets of children run excitedly up to the end of their garden as the steam train thundered past. The driver sounding the steam whistle just for them. I envied the children as they waved at him. It really was the age of innocence and I wished we could all stay there forever, never growing old.

Instinctively I found myself waving at them from the carriage window, not knowing if it was me that they were waving back at or another passenger in another carriage, however the significance of their actions was soon lost as they disappeared from sight and instead I let the warmth of the late evening sun cascade across my face as its hue dazzled a splash of fiery red against the bodywork of the train as we swept around a curve on the track. And as the miles clattered on by with thoughts of London fading I felt a sudden mood change sweeping through me as if a spirit had nestled beside me. I watched as the huge ball of fire hid behind a copse of trees.

At York Station I busied myself by watching the multitude of

195

passengers disembark from the train taking note of the few that replaced them for the onward journey north. I spied on a pair of chambermaids leaning out of a guest's bedroom window in the grand Railway Hotel next to the station. They innocently went about their duty dusting down a large chamber mat from the third-floor level oblivious of their folly as the whole train bore witness. As I watched on I wondered how many feet had trodden across that mat and what interesting tales it could tell. Like Aladdin, I expect its secrets were probably woven deep into the pattern of the mat and it would take a magician to unravel them.

I read the advertising posters on the station walls and they reminded me of my week with Aunt Emma in London, our visits to Regent's Park Zoo, Buckingham Palace, watching the Changing of the Guard and the boat trip down the River Thames. Precious memories that would stay with me forever.

My attention was abruptly drawn to a man as he entered from the ticket office hall and who walked purposefully across to the newspaper stand. There was nothing odd about his manner and I think the only reason I paid him any attention at all was the big, black, wide-brimmed hat that sat majestically upon his head. With his long-tailed black coat he looked every inch the archetypical sorcerer. He fascinated me and I imagined his image being used in some Disney feature-length cartoon one day.

He pondered his choice at the news stand seemingly having no concern for the timetable even when the station porter blew his whistle to announce the imminent departure of our train. I watched as he calmly selected a newspaper, paid the stall attendant then turned and stepped across the platform into the open door of a carriage two coaches down from my own, which had been held open by another railway employee. I had never seen York Station this interesting and especially in the early evening.

I thought nothing further of the sorcerer, his presence at the station was only that of just another passenger, but it had seemed an interesting interlude at the time that was until the door of my carriage suddenly opened and the man stepped in. Why he'd picked my carriage I could only wonder, when undoubtedly there were plenty of others and in all probability empty compartments judging by the number of travellers that had got off at York Station? His presence mystified me, but I didn't dwell on it as I had little reason to complain, for I had been fortunate enough to have an empty carriage all to myself for the last part of the journey to York.

The man in the black hat and long coat politely asked if he could join me and of course I agreed. He thanked me as he chose the seat opposite, resting his hat beside him before creasing back the page of the newspaper, making it easier for him to read. Below the floor of the carriage I could feel the large wheels gripping the track as they spun faster and faster gathering speed as the train engaged the long decline as we dropped down amongst the hillsides. I watched as the last rays of the sun chased us all the way down side by side like a shadow in a race. It was fascinating to watch the landscape contours change then suddenly disappear altogether.

We sat in silence as he continued to read his paper, I picked up the girls' magazine that Aunt Emma had bought for me at Paddington Station, but I couldn't engage my mind upon any of the contents as I peeped over the top of the pages at the man opposite. He had long legs and even though he was sitting down I envisaged that he was a tall man. His white hair was beginning to thin on top and his face was gently creased around the silver-rimmed glasses that hid the softness of his eyes. I noticed too that he was an elegant gentleman that apparently took a pride in what he wore. Perhaps he was not a sorcerer after all.

He quietly read his newspaper flicking through the pages and I couldn't be certain, but I'm sure that at one point he realised that I was observing him. He caught me looking at one time, but smiled before returning to his paper. It wasn't until he craned his neck right and looked out of the carriage window beyond the door to the darkness outside that I saw the mark on his neck, just below the ear lobe. It was definitely a mole about the same size and same place as my own. At first I dismissed the notion as sheer coincidence, but I did find it strange all the same and although I knew that it was rude to stare I couldn't help myself.

My thoughts were interrupted as the compartment door suddenly opened and in walked the ticket collector. He requested that we show him our tickets, I delved into my pocket and produced mine in readiness. I watched as the man produced something different from his pocket, it wasn't the same as my own it was much bigger, almost raffle-ticket-sized, but I guessed that they had issued something entirely appropriate for the journey from York Station. The ticket collector then clipped the corner of mine and thanked me.

To my surprise the gentleman then asked a question of the railway official. 'Can you please tell me what time we are due to arrive at Wrenhoe Station?'

The ticket collector pulled upon a long chain and produced a pocket watch from his waistcoat. 'In about fifteen minutes' time, sir,' he proclaimed.

The carriage door clicked shut as he left and I heard him enter the next compartment asking the passengers for their tickets.

I was still wondering about the man's ticket, when it suddenly dawned on me that the name of the station that he had enquired about with the ticket collector was one that I had never heard of and as far as I was concerned was certainly not on this rail route. I had undertaken this journey many times before and not once had we stopped at a place called Wrenhoe. Neither had I seen it recorded on the route planner either at Paddington Station or on the compartment wall.

I stood up to check with the planner above my head, however to my utter amazement I saw it was there in big bold black letters – Wrenhoe Station, first stop after York and before Middleton Down. I checked again in case it had been a trick of the light, but it had been daylight, natural light when I had checked at Paddington, and at that time nothing had changed on the planner. I could have sworn that it had not been there earlier and just to prove that I was sane I even recounted the stations again eight – nine – ten – eleven. I was right, there was one more so it had definitely not been there before. I tried to stifle the gasp of surprise that escaped from my open mouth.

The man opposite folded his newspaper and placed it

beside him. He looked across to where I was still standing. He suggested that I should sit down, so I did.

'The place, Wrenhoe Station does exist, Susan, believe me as I know some people who have been there before me.'

I told him that I had checked the route planner at Paddington and it most definitely had not been on the route then.

He smiled and told me, 'I know, I saw you get on the train. It's always the same with Wrenhoe, it never fails to take young travellers by surprise. Please don't be alarmed, the train only ever stops at the station for somebody special and today it's stopping for you and me.'

What did he mean, he had watched me get on the train at Paddington? I saw him get on at York after purchasing a newspaper, hadn't I and how did he know my name was Susan?

I protested, 'But I'm going home to Stockton Ferris, where I live with my mum, dad and little brother.' I don't mind admitting to being a little frightened by now and the concern must have registered across my face.

He continued with his strange introduction. 'You will meet your family at Stockton Ferris tonight, Susan, I promise. Please do not be afraid as I will not harm you. My name is Thomas Alfred Wyle and I am your late great-grandfather.

The revelations about my home, my family and me personally were already stifling me, but the fact that he had just announced himself as a late, dead and deceased relative, a ghost, was almost too much. If I hadn't remembered my mum telling me about her grandfather and his father, Thomas Alfred Wyle, I think I would have screamed at this point. Instead I closed my mouth and tried to appear normal, or as normal as anybody would in front of a ghost.

Just then the engine driver must have applied the brake as we started to slow down on the approach to a station stop. I looked out of the carriage window for some clarity of where we were stopping, but the station looked unfamiliar to me and then I saw it. A freshly painted station name board with white background and large black letters – *Wrenhoe Station*. I turned back in my seat to see the gentleman standing beside me.

'This is where we get off for a little while, Susan, but

regrettably our visit is only a short one, so we best make the most of it.' His voice was calm and gentle as he turned the handle of the carriage door and stepped down onto the platform waiting for me to join him. 'Please do not be afraid, I promise that you will soon understand and that this stop will be special to both of us.' I looked into his eyes as I got up from my seat and stepped down onto the platform, I wasn't sure what I expected to see. As we walked side by side along the platform heading towards the station building I couldn't think of anything to say although I was sure that there were a number of questions that I could have asked.

'I have watched you make this journey back and forth from your Aunt Emma's many times, Susan, and I have known the reason why you visit London so often. Wrenhoe Station is a very special place and we all need special permission to visit here. This is the only place where we are allowed to stop and speak with our loved ones. We will not have long here before you have to rejoin the train. I promise that you will still get to Stockton Ferris in time to meet and be with your family.'

The feeling of trust and calmness passed through my body as the chill of the night air caused the faintest cloud of spent breath as I exhaled. I turned to see if Thomas Alfred Wyle did the same, surprisingly he did. Ghosts breathed just like us.

'Do I have to do anything?' I asked.

The spirit of my great-grandfather laughed and I noticed the similarity to when my mum laughed, it was quite remarkable and if I'd closed my eyes, I could have sworn that she was here right now beside me. As we continued to walk I noticed that the shape of his nose was similar to mine and my brother Thomas's. There was a distinct family connection.

He suddenly sniffed and rubbed his nose. I wondered if he could read my mind as well, that could be dangerous. 'It's a bit fresh tonight.' He commented.

Ghosts could also feel the cold, you'd have thought that it would not affect them.

'In this life, Susan, you need not do anything that you don't want to and at Wrenhoe you don't have to do anything, except join me in the tea room.'

We arrived at the tea-room door which was kindly opened by the stationmaster who greeted him as I just knew he would. 'Welcome to Wrenhoe, Susan,' he said.

I was not shocked, there was something magical about this place. I was about to step inside when I noticed that two other children, similarly around my age were making their way towards the tea room each accompanied by an adult.

Inside I noticed that three tables had been laid specifically for today's guests and each table had a reserved name card beside a laden cake stand. My name and that of my great-grandfather was written on one of the cards. As the other boy and girl entered the tearoom I took my seat with Thomas Alfred Wyle choosing a chair opposite. A waitress immediately appeared armed with a pad and pencil to take our order.

'I would like a cup of tea, please, and I'm sure that Susan would appreciate a tall glass of lemonade.'

I nodded my approval.

The waitress scribbled down the order and turned away muttering to herself, 'Always the same order.' I wondered to who else she was referring, but let the thought vanish from my mind.

My great-grandfather picked up the cake stand and passed it across to my side of the table. 'Please choose a cake, Susan, it's your special day and you should have a cake to suit it.'

I thanked him and selected a chocolate slice with cream and cherries. 'Could I please take one for my brother Thomas?' I asked.

He smiled and said that it was a nice gesture. He suggested a strawberry-jam-and-cream doughnut. I agreed with his choice, knowing it was one of Thomas's favourite cakes. I wrapped it carefully in a large napkin leaving it on the table for when we left.

The waitress returned with our order and seeing my napkin said that she'd get a bag for it to go in as it would prevent the contents from spoiling the lining of my pocket. I thanked her as she pushed the trolley across the tea-room floor and gave the other tables their orders too. My great-grandfather poured himself a cup of tea from the teapot as I sipped at my lemonade.

I watched as he took a mouthful of tea, looking down at the floor to see if he leaked or his shoes filled up, but again amazingly nothing happened. Ghosts were not as I had expected. Thomas Alfred Wyle replaced his cup upon the saucer, then took a cake for himself, I wasn't surprised.

'The reason that we were able to stop at Wrenhoe Station today, Susan, is that I could meet with you in the flesh, only you see I am not just your great-grandfather, but I am also your guardian angel.'

I stopped drinking the lemonade, this was something that I had not expected.

He continued, 'Everybody has a guardian angel and I am yours, but not anybody else's. This means that your brother Thomas has his own angel, as does your mother and father, not forgetting your Aunt Emma.'

I asked why he hadn't introduced himself on the train where we could have talked before arriving at this station. He explained that it was not permitted as the train did not possess the magical spirit that was found at Wrenhoe Station. It was a place where guardian angels could meet with their loved ones even if only for a short time and let them know that angels really did exist. Today was the day that had been set for us to meet. I thought about asking who had arranged the meeting, but maybe it was best left as a mystery. I looked across at the other tables and wondered if the boy and the girl were having a similar conversation.

'I know that you have been very unhappy at your new school since you moved to County Durham, Susan, but although you don't realise it, you and your family had to move away from London because of your father's work and it's why you now spend so much time with your Aunt Emma back in London. It was however important that your father took this position to secure a future for you and your family. But I assure you that you are not the only one that is unhappy living in County Durham, your mother, father and your younger brother Thomas are also as unhappy as you. They miss you terribly when you spend time away from them.'

I didn't realise how selfish I had been until I heard this and I felt quite ashamed.

He saw my distress and tried to lighten the tension that I was feeling. 'When you see them again soon you can tell your mother and father how pleased I am that they chose Thomas for my great-grandson's name. It's a great name.'

I smiled again.

He must have read my thoughts as I finished off my cake. 'You know, Susan, we all do things that we don't always realise we are doing, so don't feel too ashamed. Life can take many twists and turns and sometimes mistakes need to be made before life turns out good. Don't be in too much of hurry either to have your young years pass you by, the older ones are not always as good as they appear.'

I didn't understand everything that he had said, but I would in later years.

He looked up at the clock ticking on the wall in the tea room. 'I'm afraid that our time together is almost over and the train must arrive on time,' he exclaimed.

I looked up at the clock and couldn't believe that we had been in the tea room for the past twenty minutes. There was no way that the train would reach Stockton Ferris at 8.47 p.m. I finished off my lemonade as my great-grandfather emptied the remnants of his cup.

As we tidied the table and got ready to depart he put his hand upon my arm, it was the first human contact that we'd had. I expected his hand to pass through my arm, but of course it didn't. It was no different and felt like my mother touching me. 'There are some big changes ahead as you will see when you get home, Susan, but our time is almost at an end so we'd best head back to the train.'

I couldn't leave without asking at least one question that was suddenly gnawing at my insides. 'Have you made something happen that will help us all be happy?' I asked.

He wiped his lips with the serviette then neatly folded it before replacing it beside his cup and saucer.

'Remember what I told you, Susan. There are many guardian angels and each one for a particular special person, not even I know who watches over your mother, your father, brother, aunt and other members of the family or friends, that information remains a secret even in our world, so to answer your question I cannot tell or give you the answer because that is the unknown element of our work. We all live in the spirit world as protectors of love, life and happiness.' He picked up his hat from the chair beside him. 'Don't forget your brother's cake,' he reminded me.

As we stood up ready to leave I looked across at the other tables and saw that they too were getting ready to return to the train. Our time at Wrenhoe had been so short-lived that I wondered if it would ever happen again. I caught the eye of the young girl and was curious to know if she'd had any startling revelations made known to her this night. As we passed through the door of the tea room and out onto the platform I waved at the waitress who smiled back and said goodbye. The stationmaster saw us reappear then gave a short, sharp, high-pitched whistle to the driver to get ready the train. I wanted to ignore the signal, but my destiny lay elsewhere with my family.

The stationmaster enquired of me, asking if I had enjoyed my visit to his station. I told him that I had and thanked him, although I wanted to stay a while longer.

As Thomas Alfred Wyle and I walked across to our carriage I noticed that none of the other passengers who had remained on the train engaged us as we walked by, it was as if we weren't really there.

I opened the carriage door and stepped inside expecting my great-grandfather to follow, but unexpectedly he closed the door. I felt a mixture of both hurt and surprise as I leant through the compartment window.

'Why are you not getting on board, are you not coming with me?' I asked.

He held my hand in his. 'This unfortunately is as far as I am allowed to go with you, Susan, our time together today was as it should have been and I have been most fortunate to spend it with you, but here the magic stops, remember it only happens at Wrenhoe Station.'

I felt the tears crease the corners of my eyes, then trickle down my cheeks as lost thoughts challenged the reasoning of his words. 'This just isn't fair, I have so much that I want to ask you.'

The stationmaster blew his whistle again and the driver released the brake, I felt the train move away very slowly. I tried to reach out again for my great-grandfather, but the train suddenly gained momentum. He stood and waved. 'Remember, Susan, I am always there for you, always. Ask the questions when you are alone.' He kept waving. 'Night-time is best for me.'

The blurred vision from my tears frustrated me as I tried to look back and see him clearly, but all too soon he and Wrenhoe Station disappeared as a column of smoke from the engine filled the platform, it would have seemed all too ghostly if I hadn't known different.

I remained at the window until the train entered the tunnel and it wasn't until then that I felt very lonely. I saw my reflection in the glass as I touched the mole on the side of my neck just beneath my earlobe. I could have sworn that a hand gently brushed my cheek, but there was nobody in the compartment only me.

I looked out into the gloom outside and whispered, 'Goodbye, Great-Granddad, I love you.'

Minutes later the train emerged from the other side of the tunnel into familiar surroundings, next stop Stockton Ferris. I reached up and retrieved my luggage from the storage rack.

The train slowed and rolled into the station as the platform lights flashed by like campers' torches. I checked my watch and saw that it was exactly 8.47 p.m. How could that be? I wondered. We'd spent at least twenty minutes at Wrenhoe Station. It certainly had a magic that was indescribable. I leant out of the carriage window and saw my mother, father and brother waiting on the platform, I waved at them and Thomas waved back. I was so pleased to see them all there waiting for me.

As the train stopped almost opposite to where they were standing I threw open the carriage door and threw myself into my mother's arms.

She hugged me tight, kissing my forehead. 'We've missed you, little lady,' she said, 'and once you've greeted your father and brother, he has some wonderful news to tell you!'

I hugged my father, then to the surprise of my parents I did the same to Thomas. I reached inside my coat pocket and gave him the bag that contained the serviette and the cake. 'Here, Thomas,' I said, 'a little present from Wrenhoe Station.'

He thanked me and took the cake a little bemused as to what I meant. I saw my mother look my way and smile.

'I've been given my old job back, Susan,' my father suddenly declared. 'We're moving back to London, somewhere close to your Aunt Emma.'

I almost leapt skyward with joy, but instead I hugged my father as tight as my arms would allow me. I couldn't believe it, the news was better than I had imagined. This time I did feel the hand as it gently brushed my cheek.

'That's wonderful, Daddy,' I cried. 'Absolutely brilliant!' I shrieked, but then don't all twelve-year-old girls when they are excited. Even Thomas smiled as Mum put an encouraging hand around his shoulder and hugged him close to her. Things had definitely changed just as Thomas Alfred Wyle said that they would.

It was my mother who asked, 'So you stopped at Wrenhoe Station then, Susan?'

'Yes,' I replied, a little coyly, 'it's still hard to imagine though that it really did exist,' but Thomas clutched the evidence in his hand, so there was no denying it.

She winked at me then suggested that we all get out of the night air.

My father collected my luggage from the carriage then closed the door, just as the guard signalled for the train to leave. We walked towards the ticket collector.

'Oh, it's there alright and always will be I expect.'

I looked up at her in surprise.

'Only, you see, I once stopped there and met somebody very special to me.'

'But, I met with my great-grandfather, Thomas Alfred Wyle, he told me that he was my guardian angel.' It sounded like I was trying to convince myself, but I wasn't. 'And I've never heard of Wrenhoe Station before today,' I said.

It was my father that looked across at Thomas and me and

said, 'Trust me, you two, it does exist, I too have been there, when I was a young boy.'

I gave my ticket to the porter who smiled and asked if I had enjoyed my journey, I'm sure that I saw the twinkle in his eye. I thanked him and told him that the journey had been a good one before walking out towards the car park. Out of the corner of my eye I saw my father wink at the ticket collector. It proved that the magic of Wrenhoe Station spread far and wide, beyond the platform or the tea room. I felt sure that my acceptance of that special place would have pleased Thomas Alfred Wyle.

Later that night as I sat beside my bedroom window and stared out at the night sky I felt a light gust of wind flick aside the curtain tails as I suddenly realised that by rearranging the letters Wrenhoe it became Nowhere. I had been on the train to Nowhere. It really was a magical station where it seemed only young children go before they reach their teens. A place where they meet somebody very special, their guardian angel.

I looked up at the moon and blew a kiss across the palm of my hand. 'Goodnight, Thomas Alfred Wyle, and thank you,' I whispered.

THE CLOTHES WITH NO BODY

Have you ever had that feeling, the same one as I was experiencing today? You know the one I mean where from the minute you open your eyes the day doesn't have the same feel as it did yesterday, or the day before. When everything seemed to fall into place and that place felt just right.

Today though, felt distinctly as if it was a day that I should not be going about my normal business and instead generating my energies elsewhere. However, as usual and because most of us are institutionalised individuals we do habitually drag ourselves from the slumbers of our bed, we do consume some form of breakfast that most of us don't really want and then a vast majority of us go to work.

It is an inexplicable, strange phenomenon the mind. It plays tricks on you sometimes and as I'm no mystic or clairvoyant I still can't fathom out or offer any form of explanation as to what exactly this feeling of apprehension was that had me concerned. You wake up and instantly you have a foreboding that something is going to happen and in all probability something bad. I believe the ancient seers used to say it was due to the path of our fate and destiny.

But duty beckoned as I arrived at the railway station. The usual throng of commuters hurrying to work caused the concourse to hum as engines revved into life and newspaper stalls announced today's latest drama. I clocked in, then proceeded through to the locker room nodding at several other railway employees as they watched my arrival. I proudly donned my guard's tunic and cap, checked myself in the mirror, adjusted my tie then left the confines of the locker room to report to Bert Kelsey, the stationmaster. He was a jovial man with family ties going back three generations on the railways and he once told me that during the 18th to 19th century his family had links with the stagecoach service in Kent.

'Morning, Harry. You're as punctual as ever,' Bert said as I approached. He checked the running order of the trains for the day 'I've picked you a nice journey today, down to the coast at Brighton. There's also a two-hour turn-around so you've got time to stroll along the pier.'

London Victoria Railway Station was as busy a place as any of the other London terminal stations, but from experience I knew that Brighton was almost on a par with any of them. The gem on the south coast always seemed full of tourists whatever time of the year. I found them distractingly annoying sometimes especially after a long journey. As soon as they arrived they wanted the answers to so many questions. Where is the best place to stay? How far away is the Brighton Pavilion? And where is the best place to eat? Sometimes, instead of being a train guard I felt more like a tourist guide. Despite my apprehension about today I saw no reason why I should pass it on to Bert.

I thanked him for picking out the coast run for me. 'It'll be nice to see the pier again and take in some of that fresh sea air.' I smiled then headed off across to my train.

The guard's carriage was nearest the platform barrier and moments later I was on board and settling myself ready for the journey. There was a lot to do before we departed from Victoria so I quickly engaged myself with checking off the many trunks, parcels and oddities that were stowed beyond the mesh net hold. Now as you can imagine some funny things travel on the railways and believe me I've had my fair share in my time. I once had a snake sent up north on an express overnight in a length of plastic drainpipe. I don't know if the owner was just ignorant or whether they thought it was more comfortable for the snake to be stretched out to its entire length. I wasn't happy with that pipe as I never did determine which end of the pipe had the head or the tail. Some of the parcels are wrapped quite peculiarly too and you wonder from the shape what precisely is inside. I check the delivery address and the sender's details, it can be quite interesting especially if you have a vivid imagination. But there you have it, some of the freight can be as queer as the folk we get in the carriages. It wasn't my place to question any of it, just ensure it all arrived in one piece. I ticked off the checklist and put it safely away in the dispatch pouch.

The Brighton train patiently waited as its passengers started to arrive, some wandering aimlessly about the platform inhaling a last cigarette, others running up to the barrier because they thought they were late and others already seated anxiously feeling the tension of the train engine, eager to break free of the platform. You probably feel the same, I know I do even after all these years, but when the red flag waves, the station whistles blow and the steam escapes the exhaust valve of the locomotive engine up front, I can feel the surge of adrenalin invigorate my whole body with excitement. Starting out on a journey is as exhilarating as the day I had joined as an apprentice wheelwright.

'Here we go then, Harry boy,' I muttered to myself. 'I wonder what this journey has in store!'

From the guard's carriage I watched the train weave along the track out of Victoria as the engine driver pushed forward the throttle handle and the huge metal wheels crossed the jump-over sections before gathering more speed as we headed towards London Bridge and over the river.

At Clapham Junction we picked up more passengers, but were soon on our way again. I checked the route master schedule to see if there had been any last-minute additions or changes, even though I knew the journey back to front. Croydon East – Redhill Junction – Haywards Heath – Burgess Hill – Hassocks – Preston Park – then down into Brighton. The managers at Victoria had left it as a straight run so by my reckoning we should make the south coast in just under two hours. I checked my pocket watch against the clock on the wall, twelve minutes past the hour we were making good time.

There were a few more pickups at Croydon as expected, holidaymakers armed with suitcases, children, buckets and spades and the odd smartly dressed gentleman travelling down to a business meeting. Croydon had grown in stature in the past few years and was now seen as an up-and-coming town, at least that's what the new editor of the *Croydon Guardian* had reckoned in his opening story to the townspeople.

We had not been long out of Croydon when it happened as I

knew it would when I'd first opened my eyes that morning. Marge, the wife, said it was in my tea leaves at breakfast. 'Load of old twaddle,' I'd scoffed, but happen it did.

The first thing I knew that something was wrong was when the alarm rang in my carriage indicating that the emergency stop, to halt the train had been pulled and secondly was when I was thrown from my stool across the carriage floor as the train screeched and lurched to a sudden stop.

Rubbing a sore knee, I muttered angrily to myself, 'What bloody idiot's stopped the train?'

I immediately started walking through the train carriages checking the red-coloured emergency stops until I came across the activated chain. The carriage was completely silent as the passengers all looked at me expectantly, waiting for me to do something magical and get the train moving again. I checked the tension on the chain, which had reset as expected. Then looked around at all the eyes watching me.

'Who pulled the emergency cord?' I asked, scanning from seat to seat.

Midway down the carriage a young girl of about twelve stood up and sidestepped out into the aisle. Sometimes you immediately know just from somebody's appearance that they are going to cause you trouble. Gut instinct or sixth sense, you choose which. She was fresh and freckle-faced, had dark blue bows in her ponytails that seemed to peep out from beneath a straw boater and her hands were bunched against her hips in a manner depicting an air of authority. Brighton-bound I assumed.

I asked 'Did you pull it, Miss?'

'Indeed I did,' the girl proudly accepted, obviously of good breeding and without a shadow of remorse.

'Do you know it's in contravention of the Railways Act and company policy to pull the emergency stop unless the circumstances are exceptional.'

'Of course.' She added, 'That's precisely why I did it. It is not in my nature to do things unless they are absolutely necessary!'

I sighed. I could see that I was right in my assumption, I had a right one here. The young lady was quite emphatic that her reason for stopping the train, ejecting many of the passengers from their seats and tossing about my freight in the guard's carriage was made in good judgement. But before I could say anything to the contrary, the girl raised her hand as if commanding me to be silent, then she politely asked me to follow her. I looked around and to the amusement of some of the passengers nearest me I shrugged my shoulders then proceeded to follow.

Passing by a family of holidaymakers near to where the girl had been sitting, I quickly enquired of them, 'Is she on the train with anyone, an adult maybe?'

The mother told me that the girl had been alone when she had got on at Croydon East.

Pulling aside the adjoining carriage door I passed through to where the young girl was standing outside of the carriage passenger toilet. She was waiting patiently for me to arrive. She then pushed open the toilet door and pointed directly at a pile of men's clothes which had been neatly folded and positioned in one corner.

'There is the reason I stopped the train,' she declared, pointing to the clothes. 'And I am quite used to travelling alone on trains, my aunt is expecting me at Brighton just before luncheon.'

Well, that was me admonished. Now I was closer I looked at her again, just to see that she was only a teenager, or only twelve.

I was about to ask her name when the train driver and engineer joined us in the carriage lobby and I could see from their expressions that neither was happy. I knew precisely why they had joined us so before either of them asked I pre-empted them with an explanation concerning the pile of clothes. I could see however that it had not quelled the temptation to throttle our young sleuth and throw her from the train, so I suggested that they both return to the engine and travel on to the next station where I would speak with the stationmaster. In the meantime I would check the clothes with the young girl as my witness to see if there was anything within or thereabouts to determine their owner.

I wasn't sure that my plan of action entirely convinced young Jack the engineer as he still had murder in his eyes. I could see the bruise that was slowly developing on his forehead and guessed it might have been attributed to our young lady's actions, so I stepped between him and her and pointed at the adjoining door.

'I've got it from here, Jack, and I'm sure her intentions were good. Best we get under way again, we've a lot of people on board keen to get to Brighton.'

Henry, the driver, tugged Jack's arm and they left. Crisis over, I sighed as I eyed the girl.

'I suppose that I'd better check the train for a naked man,' I said and before I knew it, although I could have guessed she would, the girl followed me through to the next carriage as the wheels spun on the track below as we headed off again.

I didn't see the point in arguing with her, she had a determined look that told me it would be futile. I would deal with the situation, should we find a naked man, as and when it happened.

'So what's your name, young lady?' I asked as we passed through the carriages, 'only I need it for my report.'

'Janine Holmes of Watermount Lodge, All Saints, Sanderstead.'

Now why wasn't I surprised? However, I resisted the temptation to ask if she was by the remotest chance related to the famous Sherlock Holmes. She had a look about her that was far in advance of her young years.

'My uncle, on my mother's side is a police officer, a detective with the Surrey Constabulary.'

I smiled hesitantly. 'I don't suppose his name is Watson by any chance?' I asked flippantly.

She ignored the question and instead asked what I intended to do about the clothing, as nobody had been found travelling on the train naked. I instinctively knew that my answer had to be both good and convincing otherwise she would not be satisfied. And then I thought of Holmes.

'What would you do with it?' I enquired. Pure genius, I was quite proud of myself, now the young sleuth would have to solve the mystery.

'Well, I suggest that we leave the clothes where they are and you should lock the door restricting anybody from using the toilet. You should then place an 'Out of Order' sign on the door, which won't give anybody reason to be nosey and lastly we should involve the police as the clothes have no body, which might suggest a sinister reason.'

See, I told you it was best I let her decide. I agreed wholeheartedly with everything she suggested and as expected she watched as I locked the door and waited until I returned with an 'Out of Order' sign.

To the annoyance of the driver, Jack and the passengers, I reported the mystery of the clothes and the missing owner to the stationmaster at Redhill. He promptly called upon the constable patrolling outside of the station and together with Janine Holmes we all stepped back on the train and inspected the pile of clothes in the passenger toilet. The constable decided to the delight of Miss Holmes that they were best left in situ in case they were involved in something that would result in an investigation. I replaced the 'Out of Order' sign as the constable and the stationmaster got off the train. I signalled to the driver and we headed off again. The constable meanwhile telephoned through to Brighton Central and spoke to the duty sergeant, who in turn called CID. The stationmaster telephoned back along the stations that we had passed to see if a naked man had got off the train or anything untoward had been reported to the railway authorities. I'm sure a naked man running along a railway line was sure to catch somebody's attention.

Thankfully the remainder of the journey was uneventful much to my relief, until we arrived at Brighton. As is often the case I suppose in such circumstances somehow, somebody had leaked the story to the press at the *Brighton Gazette*. As the train pulled into platform one I saw a gathering of two smartly dressed men hounded by at least four others and a photographer. I suspected that somebody had overheard the policeman or the stationmaster at Preston Park calling about the unusual circumstances and they themselves had called the press. Clothes without a body was sure to be a decent scoop for the evening edition of the south-coast papers and could possibly notch up the career of an investigative reporter.

As I waited patiently in the wings the two smartly dressed detectives spoke with Janine Holmes, and she clearly outlined the sequence of events and her response. I wondered what she was conveying to them of my involvement. I saw her point my way several times. I felt like the condemned man.

Conveniently her aunt appeared and joined her niece and the detectives. A few minutes later they left the station. Miss Holmes turned and waved just once before she was lost in the never-ending crowd. I watched as the detectives headed across to where I was sitting.

My version of events was very similar to that of Miss Holmes, which both the officers found tiresome so after giving my name and address they told me that other officers would be in touch if they needed any other information. As they turned and walked away I was left feeling a little deflated, as though the matter warranted a greater degree of investigation and consideration on their behalf, but I was also relieved that the matter did not involve me any more. I noticed that the reporters and photographer had also left, no career step up there then.

I managed to find the time to stroll along the pier taking in the hustle and bustle upon which Brighton seemed to thrive, the town never seemed to rest. I wondered if anybody old retired to Brighton or was it just too busy? The air was refreshingly welcoming and after the events of the journey down it was just what I needed, even the disparaging feeling of apprehension that had hung around me all morning had gone. Destiny had run its course and if I had not gone to work then some other guard would have had to deal with this morning's events and Janine Holmes.

I made sure that I arrived back at the Queens Road Station in time for the 2.20 p.m. return to London, I would be glad to be back in London later. I watched the passengers board from my carriage and wondered if any of the men on the platform had come back to look for his clothes, not that I would have known, nor them for that matter as they were now wrapped in lost and found. The journey back was dull in comparison to the one down. I even have to admit that as I walked through the carriages clipping tickets I was disappointed not to see Janine Holmes on the return trip back to Croydon East. I rather liked that young lady, she was intelligent, forthright and would make a damn fine detective one day. I never would find out what she said to the detectives at Brighton Station.

Just after five I took off my cap and replaced my tunic back in the locker. As I engaged the keep on the padlock one of my colleagues entered the changing room.

'Hello, Harry. Was it you who was the guard on the 9.40 a.m. to Brighton this morning?' he enquired.

'Yes I was. Why do you ask?' I replied.

He handed over a late midday edition of a London newspaper. 'Turn to page five and read the article bottom right.'

I opened the paper to the page as instructed and started to read the article. I looked back up in amazement.

'He was on board my train!'

'I know,' replied my colleague, 'but not long enough for you to check his ticket.' He laughed, then as he left the locker room he told me to keep the paper as he had a train to catch.

I sat down to read the article in full.

An unconscious man described as a white European is currently in St Thomas's Hospital lying in the intensive care ward due to the extensive injuries that he sustained whilst jumping naked from London Bridge. The man believed to have been a passenger aboard the 9.40 a.m. London Victoria to Brighton train was seen to climb over the parapet barrier then plunge feet first down into the River Thames fifty feet below. Had the man waited a few minutes more he would have missed the cargo barge that at the same time emerged from the underside of the bridge. The captain and crew were treated for shock at Westminster Pier, but did not require any further treatment. The man's fall caused slight damaged to the cargo being transported aboard the barge.

Identification of the man is still not known or the reason why he was naked. Speculation surrounds his circumstances as to why he chose to jump from London Bridge into the River Thames. He is described as five feet eight inches in height, possibly taller, but the fall resulted in compressed compound fractures of both lower limbs. Dark shoulder-length hair, with possible wavy texture, but the barge was carrying used oil. Brown eyes and a small shaped moustache. He has a tanned tone to his skin which might suggest that he has been abroad recently. The only other discernible features are a three-inch appendix scar and two tattoos on the upper limbs, one on each arm. They are described as images of exotic ladies. The Thames River Police and New Scotland Yard would like anybody who recognises the description of the man or knows of his whereabouts before today's events to contact them on Whitehall 1212.

I sat with the paper open at the page and stared at it for longer than I realised. Why was the man on board my train and why did he undress then jump into the Thames? I was just plain old Harry Robbins, a married man with a quiet unassuming nature, a train guard of twenty-eight years' service. I didn't have the answers to another man's frailty of mind or the reason why he should jump naked off London Bridge, but I knew a young lady from Watermount Lodge, All Saints, Sanderstead, who would probably have some damn good theories. That young lady bore the same surname as the great Mr Sherlock Holmes and for all I knew she could very well have been related. I walked out of the locker room with the newspaper secreted safely in my coat pocket. I walked towards the newsagents as I needed to buy a large envelope and a stamp on the way home, I had a very important newspaper to send to a very important young lady.

So why is it that some mornings we wake up and immediately a foreboding feeling sweeps through our body? I suppose nobody really knows, no more than when a man leaves home, travels to work and is involved in a collision with another car or a woman wakes up and washes her hair, spending longer than normal before the mirror having a bad hair day. No one day is ever the same as the last, today or tomorrow. Fate and destiny have been around since time began and however our lives are predetermined maybe the jumper from the bridge can give an answer to that equation, when he eventually wakes.

As for me I will still go to work tomorrow regardless of how I feel when I wake up. After thirty years of marriage it takes more than a foreboding feeling to keep me at home and just as a word of advice keep a lookout for the name of Janine Holmes, only I feel sure that one day she will be a known household name.

THE MAIDEN JOURNEY

Some folk would say that something occurs like an event in time that passes us by, or is it briefly just the presence of a person whereby certain circumstances happen and we remember how we ourselves were part of that experience? A simple occurrence will rest easy with us for the rest of our life as a good memory. This is a story about such a journey taken on a train in the year of 1854 and the amazing outcome that changed my complete perspective of life and quite possibly has affected the lives of all of us, even you.

My own journey began in the parlour of my grandparents' cottage and even now I can still envisage that room, small with abandoned dark corners, meagre furniture and a large burnt stone fireplace that never ceased to engage my thoughts. I would spend hours sitting beside it as the fiery embers of spent coal spat out angrily at me from the cast-iron fire basket. My grandfather, Ewan Amlodd Bryn, a deeply religious Welshman of eighty-eight years, would draw me into his conversation that would stretch my imagination and send me dreamily believing that beyond the green hills and mountains of the valleys there was a whole world to explore and capture. However, today as he gently tapped the side of his unlit pipe and lifted the cloth cap from his forehead, he told a tale that I shall never forget.

'Do you know, my boy, that I once met the famous engineer Isambard Kingdom Brunel?'

He looked up from the embers to see that I was paying attention. And that was it, the beginning of another of his stories, only this tale was different, this was about a man that I had only heard about, a man that himself changed history. I sat looking into his smiling eyes totally absorbed already as the fire continued to spit about my feet ignoring the interruption. He relaxed back into the cushion of the chair and reminisced.

'It's the truth, young Gawain, and it's a day that I could never forget.' I watched as he relived the event in his mind, fondly remembering each moment as it transcribed the changes of his fortune. Then returning from the shadow of time he licked his lips, puffed at the dry pipe and continued.

'Aye, it was a day like no other that I knew and one that I have never experienced since and a day that a man at peace will take to his grave, but you need to know about it, my boy!' And so the story gathered pace just like a steam train of the era.

'That February morning started like many others for the month, cold and frosty as I walked to work, lifting the collar of my jacket to keep the chill air at bay. As a trainee furnace worker at the Crawshay Family Ironworks my shift started early, long before many of the lights in the cottages illuminated the cobbled street down to the foundry. I rubbed my hands together exhaling a long breath of spent carbon dioxide into the atmosphere, just as a cockerel three houses back from the gate announced the arrival of a new day. I was one of the lucky ones as conditions at the foundry were ultimately better than descending the rock seams to the coal mines where my uncles laboured.

'I passed through the imposing wrought-iron gates acknowledging the arrival of other men from the village noticing that like me they too carried a small brown paper parcel, the contents of which were the scraps from the previous evening's meal which would serve as lunch, portions barely sufficient to sustain us through an arduous twelve-hour shift. But I'd never heard a man complain, not around here anyway because that was life and we'd been resigned to the hardship of work long before we left school. It was the way of the Valleys and as common as Holy Communion on the day of the Lord when the Almighty called for all men to rest, pray, sing his hymns and enjoy time with the family, the only person permitted to work was naturally the preacher himself and he had a damn good excuse because he was doing the Almighty's work.

'I remember that morning quite vividly as Samuel Phillips the foundry foreman a tall brusque native approached me and informed me that Mr Crawshay senior himself wanted to see me in the yard office and without any hesitation. Of course I obliged pulling my collar smartly together as I stood before the wooden opening and hesitantly knocked twice moments later hearing the reply from within. I entered and found the ironworks owner sitting astride a wooden table reading some papers that were pinned to the wall. Mr Crawshay welcomed me into his office whereupon there followed a brief conversation where I learnt that Mr Crawshay wanted me to go to Merthyr High Street Railway where I was to take the train to Cwmaman Colliery and deliver a very important machine part for the colliery turn-wheel which had broken down Thursday last.'

Grandfather sucked relentlessly on his pipe as he recalled the developing events of that day. He told me that he'd found it hard to contain the excitement that had built like a raging cyclone in his empty stomach. Realising that it was an important assignment that Mr Crawshay had given him. The owner of the foundry must have been confident about his ability to deliver, only at the time he was still only a young man and he'd expected the task to have been given to one of the older men. He said he remembered buffing the toecaps of his boots against the rear of his baggy trousers as he had listened intently to the instructions regarding the journey and the delivery. Women probably ask why all men polish their boots in this fashion, but I can honestly say that I have done the same, only you see it's taking a pride in one's appearance regardless of dress and more importantly a mark of respect for the man who pays your wages. It's been a practice down the centuries by men even as far back as William the Conqueror. I've noticed my father still does it before he enters our local church, not that I am saying that the Lord pays his wages, goodness no he paid for the sins of all mankind.

Grandfather rubbed the ache that ravaged his knees, telling some more of his story. 'As is customary hereabouts and especially in the early mornings a mist had descended from the hills and engulfed the valley below, but despite the dismal weather I arrived at Merthyr High Street in good time and paid for my train ticket enquiring of David Roberts the stationmaster what time I should expect the train to arrive. 'Oh, anytime in the next quarter of an hour' was his reply.

'Life in the Welsh Valleys was ordinarily relaxed and nobody hardly ever gave you an exact answer, not even the preacher who would say to my mother that he would visit Tuesday, only you never really knew exactly what Tuesday he actually referred too. I often thought it was his way of keeping control of his flock, keeping them on their toes and his office in a mixed emotion of holy suspense.

'Standing on the platform watching the mist dance above the rooftops I listened intently for the rattle on the rails and the telltale hiss of the steam as it escaped from the train engine. A younger boy might have thought that a dragon lived in the black chasm and you could be forgiven for imagining that one did as the locomotive would suddenly emerge from the tunnel mouth in a blaze of white cloud, thunder and energy. Embarrassingly I heard my stomach rumble to the amusement of the middle-aged couple that waited patiently not too far away from where I was standing and then as if by magic, just as David Roberts had predicted, the rails on the track began to rattle almost instantly followed by the chugging puffing hiss of the steam as it emerged from the tunnel cascading about the grassy banks on either side. As you can imagine, Gawain, I'd never travelled by train before as I stood transfixed in a mixture of awe and amazement as the monster approached me, coming at speed. I remember thinking back then as the entire length of the train emerged from the tunnel including the passenger carriages that I didn't see how it was possible to bring the whole train to a complete halt.

'In resolute fascination I watched as David Roberts acknowledged the greeting given by the engine driver and his engineer as the locomotive passed us by gradually losing speed and stopping short of the sloped descent that graced all station platforms. I watched as the middle-aged couple stepped into the next carriage holding open the door for me. I thanked them and placed the machine part on the floor beneath my seat before closing the door, hearing David Roberts blow his whistle to the sound of the locomotive's brakes being released as the train juddered forward heading for Aberdare Station.

'There was as you would imagine just so much to take in on my maiden journey, the gripping power of the locomotive that pulled our carriages, the familiarity of our countryside, although never seen it before through the window of a train carriage and the untroubled ease with which the other passengers accepted our mode of travel. I felt as if I had been thrust into an unknown adventure for which I was totally unprepared. As I looked around at the other passengers in the carriage my attention was drawn to a man who sat at the far end of the seat, reading a newspaper. A rarity itself hereabouts as folk could not afford such luxuries. He saw me watching so put aside his paper.

'Good morning,' he said. 'I hope that I do not intrude upon your intended task, but I noticed that the object you placed beneath your seat appeared quite heavy and I heard the telltale clank of metal from within the sacking that protects it.'

'I hoisted the sack-wrapped machine part onto the carriage seat, carefully opening it so that the gentleman could see. 'It's a piston cylinder for the Cwmaman Colliery wheel,' I explained.

'He smiled. 'A young engineer,' he announced enthusiastically, 'a man after my own heart.'

'His assumption of my profession although very worthy and gracious of my presence was inaccurate and quite far-reaching of my own expectations. He however was a gentleman of that there was no mistake, but I needed to address his mistake.

'I am no engineer, sir, only a trainee furnace worker,' I explained.

'But the gentleman was having none of my professional ineptitude. He told me that any man who understood the mechanics of a colliery wheel was indeed capable of being an engineer. He put out his hand to shake mine which I duly accepted. 'I am pleased to make your acquaintance, young sir. I am Isambard Kingdom Brunel, mechanical and civil engineer, at your service.'

'I couldn't believe what I was hearing only I'd heard of Mr Brunel at the foundry from the older men who said that he was a great man of engineering inventions, science and learning.

Here I was sitting opposite the very same man. I introduced myself. 'I'm pleased to meet you too, sir. My name is Ewan Amlodd Bryn from Merthyr Tydfil.' The truth of the matter was that I was very pleased to meet such an eminent man, but I couldn't let him go on believing that I was an engineer, whatever the cost to my ego. "I am as I introduced, sir, only a trainee furnace man.'

'He laughed. 'As you wish.'

'I've heard of you, sir,' I confessed, 'from the men who work at the foundry.' He asked me which foundry I referred to and so I told him, 'The Crawshay Family Ironworks.'

'Just then a rider on horseback jumped a fence in the field beyond our window interrupting our conversation. I admired the rider's horsemanship and the majestic grace of the beautiful animal.

'Fascinating, is it not? The countryside I mean,' said Mr Brunel. 'Here we are on a magical machine travelling faster than that horse can gallop and yet the hills over yonder seem to sit there hardly moving at all as they watch us go by, but instead we are the ones moving all the time.'

'Yes, indeed,' I answered back, not really seeing the perception of what he meant. "This is my first time on a train.'

'Then you should be congratulated, Mr Bryn, because you bear witness to one of the wonders of our modern times. The age of invention travels as fast as this locomotive that pulls us along the track.'

'I had to agree as the train really was magnificent.

'This is one of many, but more will come,' he added, 'and I expect that the country will see many, many more great marvels of science in the future years to come.'

'Beneath the carriage I could feel the wheels rhythmically beating like a horse on a treadmill as they glided over the track. What a story I would have to tell my family when I saw them again that evening. We watched the rider turn his steer towards the early morning sun feeling the warmth through the carriage windows as it burnt away the last of the mountain mist.

'You know, Mr Bryn, if it were not for men such as yourself, I would almost certainly have no present or future aspirations myself, you are the men who cast my iron and forge my designs that help bring my creative ideas to life. Without you, young sir, I would be but a penniless civil engineer and no doubt the laughing stock of the nation's pessimists. Despite what you say or consider about yourself your work bears an importance that many others do not recognise. You might be just a trainee at present, but do you not think that I myself held such a title when I studied engineering? We all have to start somewhere, but your skills will become honed and you will one day help mould our world of tomorrow and you might forge the years of your life as a professional foundry man, although I see in your eyes the look of a man hungering for knowledge and other adventures!'

As I sat riveted to the stool beside the fire my grandfather looked at me. He told me that he struggled that day to comprehend everything that the great man was saying to him. He was in awe of the man and his reputed achievements. Mr Brunel was indeed a kind man as well with his respect of his fellow man. Grandfather said that he had never imagined his work at the foundry works as being so important and neither did he realise how their meeting that day would bring about changes to his destiny.

'Thank you, Mr Brunel, that is very kind of you to say so,' I said.

'Isambard Kingdom Brunel then reached up to the rack above his head and pulled down a long cardboard tube from which he withdrew a couple of large sheets of paper. He handed them across to me and politely asked, 'These are some drawings that I have been working on for the past few months, Mr Bryn, and I would be most grateful if you could spare a few minutes of our journey to see what you think and should you have any ideas, I would indeed be only too pleased to hear them. Ignore me, sir, as if I were not here. It helps sometimes.' He smiled encouragingly and I knew that he was indeed sincere.

'I couldn't believe that this great engineer had actually believed that I could have any ideas that he would not already have considered for his drawings and plans. I was both a little embarrassed, but at the same time immensely pleased to accept his challenge. I carefully laid the sheets of paper out on my seat and studied the contents. They were the drawings of a new suspension bridge across a very large gorge. They were neatly, but elaborately drawn and were accompanied by detailed scaled measurements and dimensions with nothing left to chance. I could but admit that Mr Brunel was a man of genius and his design should it work would greatly benefit the people of that area.

'I studied and looked over the drawings without saying anything for at least ten minutes, the massive brick towers on either side of the gorge were notably magnificent in design as were the elaborate fixings that bedded themselves into the cliff face and the span dimensions and weight calculations of which there were many, were truly the work of a skilled civil engineer. In reality, and I knew it, there were far too many engineering details for me to absorb or readily understand, I felt extremely humbled that he should have asked for my opinion.

'This is truly wonderful, Mr Brunel,' I replied and I meant it. 'The bridge will look magnificent when it has been built.'

'He looked very pleased that I had not just given his drawings a cursory viewing, but had actually spent time to look at the minutest detail.

'I did as you requested and have studied your drawings, but to be honest I could not really say that I saw anything that needed changing or adding to, the complexity of the design and the architecture is without doubt beyond the comprehension of a furnace worker, but the work of a skilled man.'

'He seemed to ignore the inference of my professional status again, but instead went on to explain about the design. 'Thank you for taking the time to look, Mr Bryn. A second pair of eyes and your opinion is always valuable, especially as we engineers do sometimes get carried away with our own ideas, thus the word grandeur sometimes springs to mind.' I saw the spark of genius in his eyes, they seemed to have a life of their very own as he continued to relate to me about his next project. 'This bridge is intended to be made of wrought iron and will span the gorge at Bristol across the River Avon. There was a set of previous plans and construction had commenced, but regrettably been thwarted in the year 1831 by the disturbances of the Bristol uprisings, a truly great shame that it was interrupted, only a great deal of employment meant the area became prosperous and many local businesses had never thrived so well as during that time. It was inexcusably as I said a great shame.'

'I could only nod approvingly.

'Fortunately for me the gentlemen of that area and some in higher authority had never lost sight of my design. It had been their wish that one day work would recommence on the bridge. I therefore find myself here now going over my previous and latest drawings once again. It is why I appreciate so much you looking at them and with an untrained eye. You see, Mr Bryn, a man that deals with the fundamental raw materials of such a design would have the most rewarding of views and opinions, irrespective of their experience.'

'There he went again disbelieving my inexperience of such matters, although I tried hard to not let him down.

'It certainly is a lot of iron, Mr Brunel,' I said.

'It was all that I could think of to say at that precise moment, but little did I realise that in that one sentence, my destiny was about to change.

'Indeed it is, Mr Bryn, and would almost certainly need supplying locally by a very well-established and most reputable foundry. It would require the best-grade iron and not from a commercially minded entrepreneur who only had riches at the forefront of his venture. This project would require their support as well.' He then caught me unawares with a question that I would least have expected him to ask: 'What do you consider of the Crawshay Ironworks, Mr Bryn?'

'I didn't want to seem to fumble, but here I was a lowly trainee foundry man with a given task to deliver an important piston cylinder to a local colliery, on a train for the first time in my life and with a man of renowned civil-engineering fame. I was now being asked to comment on my honest opinion of the abilities and integrity of the family-run business belonging to Mr Crawshay.

'I took my time and thought hard for a few minutes, realising that my answer could dramatically affect the fate of my colleagues and the Crawshay family itself, not to say that of my own life and future prospects. I think Mr Brunel realised that he had presented me with quite a conundrum, however I looked directly at him and gave the most honest answer that I could think of praying to the Almighty that he saw fit to stand at my side as I delivered it. I needed his guidance.

'Well, Mr Brunel, for me the Crawshay Family Ironworks is a good place to work. There are long hours as expected at the foundry, but nevertheless it is a very good place to be employed and the Crawshay family are fair and just people who know their workers. They have good contracts with the local coal pits and importantly with the Cwmaman Colliery, which is more commonly known locally and hereabouts as Shepherd's Pit because it's owned by a Mr Thomas Shepherd himself a good, honest and religious man. I doubt very much that Mr Crawshay senior would have little if any dealings with Mr Thomas if it were not the case. As for my own position, well, to be truthful I was very fortunate to get employment at the ironworks as a trainee. I still have another year and a bit left of my training before I become proficient enough to deal with some of the more involved work on my own and I will probably undertake a few more years of learning after that, but I owe the Crawshay family a debt of gratitude for my good fortune so I cannot speak ill of them or their works. I am sure that any man looking to use their services would not be disappointed, sir.'

'I had delivered my speech and I watched his reaction wondering if I had said too much, but Mr Brunel sat back on the cushion of his seat then placed his thumbs in the pockets of his waistcoat. He pondered himself for several moments and I could see the wisdom furrowed across his brow as he looked at me with a smile.

'Do you know, I have not known you long, Mr Bryn, but it is without question my good fortune that I have because in that short time I have found you a very welcome companion to travel with, you are an incredibly sensible young man with the most pleasing disposition and outlook on life. You speak highly of your employers and their foundry works; and I am in no doubt that you will prosper well in years to come whatever position you choose for your career. I will indeed visit the Crawshay Family Ironworks and speak with your Mr Crawshay; and with your permission I will request that you too be at our meeting.'

My grandfather looked across at me engagingly as he stoked the fire sending a shower of sparks up the chimney.

'And that, young Gawain, was the making of my adult life for you see as true as his word a week later Mr Brunel arrived by pony and trap at the foundry ironworks. Again Samuel the foreman told me to get across to the yard office as quick as I like where I was wanted for an important meeting with a very special visitor. I remember that moment as if it were only yesterday, despite the general noise of the ironworks you could have heard a pin drop in the yard as I knocked on the wooden door for the second time in as many weeks. I looked around to see the faces of my colleagues staring in wonder at what fate awaited me and possibly them on the other side of the door and who the stranger was to see Mr Crawshay senior.

'Inside the yard office I found Mr Crawshay senior and Mr Brunel enthusiastically poring over plans and drawings some of which I had seen that day on the train to Aberdare. For my part I found my involvement at the meeting was more supportive than as an actual participant and one could say that the shadows in the corner of the office served me well as I just wanted to remain silent and observe as their deliberations were way over my head in complexity of commercial dealings. However, as the discussions came to a close it was Mr Brunel who turned to me and placed a hand upon my shoulder.

'Young Mr Bryn, you have done this foundry a great service and I am very pleased that we met that day on the train. Good fortune will smile favourably upon all because of this meeting with Mr Crawshay today.'

I added another log to the fire as my grandfather told me that later that morning he was recalled to the office of Mr Crawshay senior where he was congratulated on bringing a large contract of valuable work to the family ironworks. It would mean that the foundry men of the Merthyr Valley would all prosper from the order for many years to come. And not least ignoring you the reader, you might ask what happened on that February morning as the steam train approached the railway station in Aberdare. Well, I will tell you. The famous civil engineer Isambard Kingdom Brunel and the young trainee furnace man Ewan Bryn had talked also of their home towns, their respective families and their aspirations, or do we rather call them dreams because that is what many men have, dreams of ambition. The roads of destiny had crossed in the most unusual of circumstances and although they both had a common link albeit neither knew it at the time, it bound them together all the same. Destiny has a knack of doing just that.

'So you see, Gawain,' said my grandfather, 'going around with your head in the clouds, wondering what fate lies before you, like your mother does when she waits for the preacher to visit, you have to keep your feet on the ground and think about your future. My destiny changed the day that I got on that train to Aberdare and I met with Isambard Kingdom Brunel. The suspension bridge across the Avon Gorge was built and I eventually became the foundry manager, working with the Crawshay family and Mr Brunel on some of his other projects. I expect you will meet somebody one day as well in unusual circumstances and it may well change your life by means that you least expect.'

As I watched Grandfather suck on his unlit pipe I laughed to myself, young Gawain indeed. Here I was twenty-three years of age, not that he'd noticed lately, but then I could forgive him as he was a few weeks shy of his eighty-ninth birthday. I'd long since travelled my maiden journey many years ago down to London, but I had never mentioned it for he was a true Welshman and was not an avid fan of the people from the fast city, as he called it. My own journey of destiny had indeed begun in my grandparents' parlour many years ago for it was where I had sat beside their fire, dodging the cinders and adding more logs or coal, listening to my grandfather's stories and it was because of that parlour that I had acquired an avid interest in fire as a whole.

When I was eighteen years of age I applied to the South Wales Fire Brigade where I work now as a fireman at Monmouth Fire Station working alongside a great bunch of men, but that's not why I came to their cottage today and heard this amazing story, I came to tell my grandparents that I was getting married soon to a beautiful French girl from the Loire Valley and one day I will tell my grandfather about how I met my future wife on a train journey which coincidentally turned out to be her maiden journey.

And finally should you need to know, yes I have been across the suspension bridge that spans the Avon Gorge many times, you know the one that Isambard Kingdom Brunel designed and the ironwork of which was supplied by the foundry in Merthyr Tydfil where my grandfather Ewan Amlodd Bryn worked.

HOW I MET MY HUSBAND ON A TRAIN

We all take time for granted never really noticing it, unless it actually means something to us in a particular given moment or a day in the history of our lives. For me in particular tomorrow was going to be one of those days. I had already started today and I had just under twenty-four hours to make the next day as momentous as fate and destiny would allow.

I departed from the coffee lounge at Waterloo Station and headed towards platform two for the nine fifty train to Weymouth via Basingstoke. In my right hand I balanced an armful of books on anatomy, infectious diseases and biology. However much I turned the spine titles away the titles still managed to raise an eyebrow or two in the coffee shop as they sat beside me.

I should really explain for the concerned among you that I am a medical student in the final year of my postgraduate course and tomorrow was my finals. My head was crammed full of facts and figures, anatomical figures that is, so much so that lately I'd seen skeletal figures dancing through my dreams. Even people on the station concourse appeared before me taking on a skeletal form as I mentally attached bones to ligaments and so forth.

I had spent the last few days with my family in Bayswater. It was good to have them around me and grab wholeheartedly the faith that they all had in me. It encouraged me to study all the harder. I suppose this is a good juncture in the story to tell you that my father was an eminent surgeon at St Thomas's Hospital in London. A very well-respected man and widely known throughout many areas of the medical world. So as you can imagine there was absolutely no pressure on me to pass my finals.

I remember when I was a young boy visiting my father at his hospital office, playing on the floor as other doctors would come to ask for his advice. He always had time for them and me. I would patiently sit and listen as they discussed the progress or imminent demise of a patient. The world of medicine had fascinated me for as long as I could remember, but of all the things that I heard the one statement that I remember above all else, was that all doctors male or female, young or old have one belief throughout their profession and that is they never discuss the failure of a patient. Doctors as a universal body all have an unwavering faith that medical science advances with every examination, diagnosis and procedure.

For the past few days using the facilities of my father's study at our family home I'd managed to bury my head in the medical books that sat before me now away from the noise of the doctors' quarters. The prospect of failure was daunting and haunted me as I'd studied the many certificates that had adorned the study wall, I wondered if I would ever sit among my father's colleagues and he too as a peer keeping their belief alive.

Showing my ticket at the barrier, I passed through proceeding down the platform to the train coaches at the end of the platform. I always found the front coaches to be quieter as many passengers seemed to select the carriages at the rear, being the closest once through the barrier.

I took a quick look at Waterloo Station as I opened the door of the carriage and hoped that the next time I saw the end of the platform would be as Dr Stanley Winchester. The carriage was empty, which was perfect for my journey and I could use the quiet effectively to revise. Being at home with Mum and Dad had been great, but Ben our family dog was a springer and as nature had intended rarely sat still and needed my attention when all I could really have wished for was peace and solitude. The only time he'd actually been of any use was when I'd asked him to lie down so I could check his vitals.

I settled myself into the bench seat, laying my head back momentarily to listen to the sound of the engine beyond my carriage. There was something very soothing, boyishly romantic and genuinely splendid about being aboard a steam train. I still loved these old engines. They were marvels of an era when men have been brave as they'd stepped beyond the boundaries of engineering and science and threw themselves to the sceptical wolves of society.

Often gambling with everything they owned, they would spend every hour God spared them to design and manufacture a product so magnificent that it would transform our lives, taking us places, seeing different cultures and going beyond their own wildest of dreams. I admired their tenacity and courage to have seen into the future.

I could feel the throb of the engine as the engineer applied more coal to the furnace, the heart of the dragon, our train was preparing itself. I would dare and defy any young boy and maybe the odd girl to say that it was not a dream of theirs to step onto the engineer's footplate and marvel at the array of brass levers and gauges that made up the driver's cab.

I heard carriage doors being closed further back along the train. We would be leaving Waterloo very soon. I decided to open the window a fraction and place my holdall in the overhead mesh netting. Settling back down into the patterned fabric of the seat I placed my books to the side of me. I closed my eyes again as several whistles echoed around the station, followed by shouts from guards and porters. The sounds that you only ever hear so fascinatingly at a railway station. By the way if you ever do it yourself it's an excellent audiology check. Goodness I was beginning to sound like my father's ear, nose and throat colleagues already. I heard a child shout out 'Hurry up' as the engineer tested the whistle of our train. Moments later as the last carriage door shut tight a loud expulsion of escaping steam billowed across the platform and we were off, on our way to Weymouth. The nine fifty was on time as always.

Outside of London the train gathered speed and the countryside seemed to flash by. It's ironic but when you need to concentrate on something specific you feel yourself tempted to look about you and become mesmerised by something totally unrelated. It's something we find hard to control and my mother would often say to me, 'Stanley Winchester, you're such a daydreamer, I wonder if one day you'll actually catch yourself up?' Me personally, I'd never worried about my daydreams, they were my moments of escapism when I could transport the chaos of my mind to another plane, where I could lose touch with reality and become a boy again. Admit it, we all go there sometime, it helps keep us sane!

However, back to reality. I had an important exam tomorrow with the Dean and other consultants at the South Shore Hospital. I picked up my first book on infectious diseases. As I read the contents I wondered why some travellers ever went abroad. I read the causes and complications of malaria, thyroid and the lesser stomach complaints. I wrote on my revision pad the diagnosis and treatment. It all looked so easy in front of me, but books were not an added prompt in the Dean's interview.

It was all going quite well, absorbing what I needed to remember when the train stopped at Dorchester South. I was so thoroughly engrossed with my studies that I didn't even hear the carriage door open. It wasn't until the latch clicked shut that I turned to face a young man and a woman. They looked at me quite bemused and it took a few moments before I realised why. My hands had been systematically wandering over the anatomy of my body picking out specific parts. They hadn't noticed the open page of the book on the seat in front of me. I quickly sat down so that they could pass by and choose their own seat. I picked up my book again avoiding any eye contact with them.

As the train pulled away the couple engaged in small talk, keeping their voices lowered, not to interfere with my reading, I appreciated their consideration. Once again the countryside flashed by and I resisted the urge to look, but I found myself tempted elsewhere as my eyes wandered across to the young couple opposite. A human trait we all suffer, inquisitiveness. I was surprised and embarrassed to see the woman looking directly back at me. She had the most amazing brown eyes, they were very dark and full of mystique. She smiled. I was used to meeting strangers, I'd met many being a medical student at the South Shore Hospital, but this woman was different. Fortunately her companion had been staring out of the other window so he'd missed our visual exchange. I smiled at her then quickly buried my nose back into the page of my book.

'That looks like heavy reading?' she suddenly exclaimed.

Albeit that I was reading the book's contents, I turned over the cover and read the title, *Grant's Atlas of Anatomy* by John Charles Boileau Grant (1960 version).

'I'm looking at the pictures more than reading it.'

It was my opening introduction and must have made me sound like a fool. I was annoyed at myself, I was never like this, especially with members of the opposite gender, but I found myself floundering for words. I felt the draw of her eyes looking across at me as I looked up from the book. I couldn't help it, she was just so mesmerising. Just then I noticed too that the young man sitting beside her had turned around and he was also looking my way.

'That was dumb of me,' uttering a lame excuse. What I should have said was that I was studying the contents for an exam!

The man chuckled. 'Better you than me, mate, it looks like heavy stuff.'

'What kind of exam?' Brown Eyes asked.

'I'm a medical student at Weybourne Hospital. We have our finals tomorrow.'

'Pleased to meet you, Doc,' said the young man, proffering his hand.

I placed my palm in his and returned the greeting.

'I'm not actually a doctor yet. I won't know that until later tomorrow afternoon.'

The woman grinned warmly. 'So that was why you were all over yourself when we entered the carriage!'

I wish she hadn't brought that up again, but I noticed that certain spark of mischief in her eyes.

'Yes, I am sorry about that, I was checking I still had all my bones in the right places.'

She laughed. 'Michael thought that you were a practising mime artiste.' She'd saved my blushes.

'Right at the moment, that's probably a better choice of profession than a doctor. It would certainly be easier than going before the Dean and his colleagues. Come tomorrow I'll probably forget all the answers and resort to miming instead!'

I stood and opened my holdall removing a brown paper parcel from within. 'My mother made some sandwiches for the journey, would you like to share them with me? I'm afraid it's all I've got to offer.'

Michael declined, which surprised me as he looked like he could do with a good hearty meal, then more to my surprise he announced that he was getting off at Bournemouth. Brown Eyes immediately piped in that she was staying on till Weymouth. I found myself secretly pleased.

Michael nudged his companion's arm. 'You take one, Sophie, you're always ravenous.'

I held out the brown parcel, offering the contents. Sophie took a half-sandwich with a smile.

And there it was, that moment when we become distracted from what we should really be doing. For the moment my revision was on hold as I watched Sophie munch her way delicately through her sandwich.

We all talked about London and the sweeping changes from rock 'n' roll to the Beatles and Rolling Stones, and the flower power revolution that was sweeping through our land and beyond to America. They were fascinated that I lived in Bayswater. Sophie told me that she'd always wanted to visit the boutiques in Carnaby Street, but other distractions had always got in the way. I wondered what, but she never elaborated and left me guessing instead.

Our conversation and time seemed to pass quickly as the train suddenly slowed and halted at Bournemouth. Michael got up, shook my hand as he left and wished me success for tomorrow, then surprisingly Sophie stood up and hugged Michael goodbye. She kissed him lightly on the cheek before closing the door again. We waved as the train pulled away from the platform and continued on its way to Brockenhurst.

We sat opposite one another slowly devouring the remainder of the sandwiches. I was pondering how to take the conversation forward when without thinking I blurted it out.

'I thought Michael was your boyfriend?'

Sophie laughed. 'No, he's a friend of my brother. He only joined me because I was going home today. What's your name?'

'Stanley, Stanley Winchester,' I declared.

'Dr Winchester. I like that!' she exclaimed.

'I agree it does have a nice ring to it, but I've still got my finals to pass!'

'Well, Stanley, as I've eaten your mother's sandwiches, I think it's only fitting that I help you with your revision. Do we have a deal?'

I think at that precise moment I would have agreed to anything that Sophie wanted as part of her deal. I graciously handed across to her my copy of *Grant's Atlas*. With a natural aptitude for questioning Sophie flicked through the pages of the book, quick-fire questioning asking where was the left suprarenal gland, the inferior limit of pleura, the left kidney, the ascending colon, the iliac crest, the small intestine and the sigmoid colon, to name but a few.

With her help I found myself absorbing all that she said and prompted, the information seemed to be sinking in. Sophie had a relaxed manner that made everything seem to fall into place. I admit that I wanted to ask her about herself, who she was, where she was from and where she was going, but as selfish as it was I needed the road of my destiny to be straight for once. I resisted the urge to ask the questions, perhaps I'd find the answers later. As she flicked over the pages I watched her, fascinated by her natural beauty. Fate and destiny sometimes deals an ace card, as long as you know how to play it.

We went over the aspects of biology, physiology and human reaction to medicine. My confidence grew as the wheels of the train got closer and closer to Weybourne, shortening the miles as I wanted to extend them. Like the wheels of the train that turn and turn, so do our lives. Sometimes something quite unexpected occurs that puts all the aspects of our life into a calm order albeit we may not realise it for many years ahead. We look back over our life and we question why that happened that day, what if we'd been somewhere else, what if we'd never met that person, had that conversation or even looked that way. Our life is made up of *what if*s, but then maybe it's only our subconscious that has all the answers. Who knows? The only certain thing that I knew when I woke up this morning and when I boarded the Weymouth-bound train was that I had a date with destiny tomorrow morning starting at nine o'clock, only now I had two things on my mind.

Too soon the release of steam and the sound of brakes engaging announced the arrival at Weymouth. I gathered my books together and retrieved my holdall. I sat back down as the train slowed to a halt alongside the platform. A strange thing to do as we were getting off in a minute or so. Sophie straightened her jacket and reached inside for her rail ticket.

It was now or never.

'Could I see you later this evening?' I asked impetuously.

'No. I think you should get an early night as you've a big day tomorrow!'

My face must have reached out and grabbed the mask of disappointment, but I couldn't hide it. Then to my astonishment Sophie stepped forward and kissed me on the cheek.

'Go knock them dead tomorrow, Stanley Winchester, and when it's all over you can give me a call.' Sophie slipped a telephone number into my palm.

I looked at her beautiful brown eyes and smiled. 'Deal.'

With that Sophie was gone, making her way through the throng of passengers disembarking from the train. I realised that I didn't even know her surname. That night I left my books to one side, I had done enough revision and I didn't want a bad case of information overload. I was tempted to walk to the hall telephone just the once, but when I did I admit that I replaced the receiver without even dialling the number. It must have been one in the morning before I fell asleep. I assumed wildly that somewhere in Weymouth Sophie had been asleep hours. The passing hours before sleep came still hadn't offered any answers about her.

Dean Clarke, Mr Thompson and Dr Anderson, the examining board, started promptly on the stroke of nine. The Dean prodded his finger into my skeleton and asked what part of my anatomy I was fortunate to have as my own, then he progressed to what other ligaments, organs and arteries lay around and about his extended digit. He finished our session with one more question.

'How many bones are there in the human body, Winchester?'

'A thousand, Dean,' I replied.

The Dean was non-committal as I was directed to the next booth. There I encountered Mr Thompson, senior surgeon of South Shore Hospital. He commenced the examination announcing that he'd had the pleasure of talking with my father at St Thomas's earlier in the week, again no pressure on me.

Pointing out the major organs and arteries of the body that I would encounter in surgery we scythed our way through the various questions. I could feel the beads of perspiration trickle down my spine as I pulled together his booth curtain and walked across to the last booth containing Dr William Anderson.

Willie Anderson as he was more affectionately known to the medical students was a kind, understanding man, but extremely passionate about his subject, general medicine. We touched on tropical diseases, infectious diseases, the left suprarenal gland, the sigmoid colon and the small intestine. Well done, Sophie. Like Dean Clarke, Willie said nothing when he'd finished his line of questioning, he just shook my hand and told me to wait in the common room.

Two hours later and I suspect after a well-earned afternoon tea followed by a long deliberation, the three senior members of the medical board walked into the common room. I have to admit that the time in that room blurred into insignificance as I only heard five words late that afternoon. 'Dr Stanley Winchester – passed. Congratulations.'

Eagerly congratulating those around me that had also been successful I quickly excused myself and ran through the hospital and across the gardens to the doctors' hall of residence. I felt it was my duty to call my parents first with my news. My mother was as expected absolutely thrilled and wouldn't stop whooping about the hallway. When Father came on the phone he appeared to already know, I'd hoped it was from Mother's reaction, but I suspected that Mr Thompson had given him the nod. Next I took the scrap of paper from my trouser back pocket. I dialled the number, the sweat was still trickling down my back as I anxiously waited for somebody to pick up the receiver at the other end.

To my relief Sophie answered. I didn't know if she lived alone, at home or with anyone else, there was so much to know.

I wasn't sure whether it was the exhilaration of passing my finals or hearing her voice, both I guess, but I introduced myself as 'Dr Winchester calling'. Sophie reacted like my mother. I guessed it must have been a female thing.

Hello there, reader, My name is Sophie. The surname was Paige, but it's now Winchester. You guessed it, I accepted Stanley's proposal of marriage the same day that he passed his finals. Oh, I can hear you say it was all too quick and it was too big a decision to have made on the spur of the moment as we'd only met twenty-four hours before, but aren't all proposals of marriage supposed to take us by surprise and be unexpected. Besides I'm a true believer in fate and destiny.

I had to write the last paragraphs of this story as Stanley was so excited when I agreed to meet with him on that wonderful day when he passed his medical finals and I suppose what with all the excitement, the proposal of marriage, having to call back his mum and dad, and the evening that we spent together it completely sent his vocal cords into submission. Now don't get me wrong as I'm very happy to write the conclusion of this story as it's a story that I've told our two lovely daughters many times.

And so to the final chapter. You never know just who you will meet on a train or just how that meeting can change the course of your life. I met a man who had the most kind and loving eyes that I had ever seen. I met a man who is a wonderful doctor and respected amongst his peers. I met a man who is both generous and more loving than I could ever have wished for. I met a man who adores our beautiful daughters. But that day on the journey back to Weymouth I met my husband on a train.